2

THE ASSOCIATION FOR SCOTTISH LITERARY STUDIES
NUMBER SIXTEEN

THE ASSOCIATION FOR SCOTTISH LITERARY STUDIES

ANNUAL VOLUMES PUBLISHED BY SCOTTISH ACADEMIC PRESS

1971   James Hogg, *The Three Perils of Man*, ed. Douglas Gifford.

1972   *The Poems of John Davidson*, vol. I, ed. Andrew Turnbull.

1973   *The Poems of John Davidson*, vol. II, ed. Andrew Turnbull.

1974   Allan Ramsay and Robert Fergusson, *Poems*, ed. Alexander M. Kinghorn and Alexander Law.

1975   John Galt, *The Member*, ed. Ian A. Gordon.

1976   William Drummond of Hawthornden, *Poems and Prose*, ed. Robert H. MacDonald.

1977   John G. Lockhart, *Peter's Letters to his Kinsfolk*, ed. William Ruddick.

1978   John Galt, *Selected Short Stories*, ed. Ian A. Gordon.

1979   Andrew Fletcher of Saltoun, *Selected Political Writings and Speeches*, ed. David Daiches.

1980   *Scott on Himself*, ed. David Hewitt.

1981   *The Party-Coloured Mind*, ed. David Reid.

1982   James Hogg, *Selected Stories and Sketches*, ed. Douglas S. Mack.

1983   Sir Thomas Urquhart of Cromarty, *The Jewel*, ed. R. D. S. Jack and R. J. Lyall.

1984   John Galt, *Ringan Gilhaize*, ed. Patricia J. Wilson.

1985   Margaret Oliphant, *Selected Short Stories of the Supernatural*, ed. Margaret K. Gray.

1986   James Hogg, *Selected Poems and Songs*, ed. David Groves.

THE ASSOCIATION FOR SCOTTISH LITERARY STUDIES

GENERAL EDITOR—DOUGLAS S. MACK

James Hogg

SELECTED POEMS AND SONGS

Edited by
DAVID GROVES

SCOTTISH ACADEMIC PRESS
EDINBURGH
1986

First published in Great Britain, 1986
by Scottish Academic Press Limited,
33 Montgomery Street, Edinburgh EH7 5JX,
for
The Association for Scottish Literary Studies.

ISBN 0 7073 0471 7

Introduction and Notes
© 1986, David Groves

The Association for Scottish Literary Studies
acknowledges subsidy from the Scottish Arts Council
towards the publication of this volume.

British Library Cataloguing in Publication Data

Hogg, James, *1770–1835*
Selected poems and songs.
I. Title   II. Groves, David
821'.7   PR4791.A4

ISBN 0-7073-0471-7

Printed in Great Britain by
Billing & Sons, Worcester
Typeset at Oxford University Computing Service
from a machine-readable text
prepared by Wilma S. Mack, Dollar

CONTENTS

vi

ACKNOWLEDGEMENTS

I AM deeply indebted to Dr Douglas S. Mack of Stirling University, who first suggested the need for a new selection of Hogg's poetry, and subsequently read the work at several stages of completion and offered useful suggestions for improvement. Any errors or omissions are of course my own responsibility. Special thanks are also due to David Johnson for his numerous suggestions about the music and the relation of words to music, and for his work in preparing adaptations of the traditional airs specified by Hogg.

In locating the Beethoven scores I was aided by Dr Barbara Bloedé of France, and by Roger Duce and Miss Ruzena Wood of the Music Room at the National Library of Scotland in Edinburgh. I would also like to record my gratitude to the James Hogg Society, and in particular to Elaine Petrie, Gillian Hughes, Emma Letley, Judy Steel, and Robin MacLachlan. Four of Hogg's descendants in New Zealand—Mrs Norah Parr, Robert Gilkison, David Parr and Miss Diana Parr—deserve thanks for their continued interest and their generosity in making unpublished letters and poems available to the public. Mrs Wilma Mack was exceedingly helpful and patient in preparing this text in machine-readable form.

Permission to quote and reproduce material in their possession has been kindly granted by the Alexander Turnbull Library of Wellington New Zealand, the Trustees of the National Library of Scotland, the British Library, Yale University Library, the Bodleian Library, and Stirling University Library. I would also like to thank the courteous staffs at those institutions, as well as at Edinburgh University Library, Edinburgh Public Library, the Mitchell Library in Glasgow, the Ewart Library in Dumfries, St Andrews University Library, Aberdeen University Library, Sheffield Public Library, and York University Library in Toronto.

A fellowship from the Social Sciences and Humanities Research Council of Canada made it possible for me to live in Scotland while preparing this edition.

THE ASSOCIATION
FOR
SCOTTISH LITERARY STUDIES

THE Association for Scottish Literary Studies aims to promote the study, teaching and writing of Scottish literature, and to further the study of the languages of Scotland.

To these ends, the ASLS publishes neglected works of Scottish literature (of which this volume is an example), literary criticism in *Scottish Literary Journal*, scholarly studies of language in *Scottish Language*, and in-depth reviews of Scottish books in *SLJ Supplements*. And it publishes *New Writing Scotland*, an annual anthology of new poetry, drama and short fiction, in Scots, English and Gaelic, by Scottish writers.

All these publications are available as a single 'package', in return for an annual subscription. Enquiries should be sent to:

ASLS
c/o Department of English
University of Aberdeen
ABERDEEN
AB9 2UB

INTRODUCTION

IN 1786 a fifteen-year-old shepherd in the Borders of Scotland bought a violin for five shillings. For many years after this, James Hogg 'generally spent an hour or two every night in sawing over my favourite old Scottish tunes; and my bed being always in stables and cow-houses, I disturbed nobody but myself and my associated quadrupeds'. He had not been to school since the age of seven, but his love of songs soon led him to teach himself to read and write.

By the early 1790s James Hogg was writing 'songs and ballads ... for the lasses to sing in chorus'. 'Whenever a leisure minute or two offered', the young shepherd could sit on a rock, take out his bottle of ink and a few sheets of paper he had sewn together, and write down 'four or six lines at a sitting',[1] while his dog Sirrah kept an eye on the sheep. There were also 'singing matches almost every night' with the other servants, and whenever the cows or ewes were milked the

> young men ... joined the girls in their melting lays. We had again our kirns at the end of harvest, and our lint-swinglings in almost every farm-house and cottage, which proved as a weekly bout for the greater part of the winter. And then, with the exception of *Wads*, and a little kissing and toying in conse-quence, song, song alone, was the sole amusement. I never heard any music that thrilled my heart half so much as when these nymphs joined their voices, all in one key, and sung a slow Scottish melody.

As a fiddler James Hogg held a high position in Ettrick Forest and the Borders, where he lived until his late thirties. He played at fairs, dances, and weddings, and on special occasions like 'the sheep-shearing', 'the end of harvest', 'the end of the year', and 'the end of seed time'. 'On all these occasions', he recalls, 'the neigh-bours were summoned, and the night spent in dancing and singing'.[2]

During his twenties Hogg worked for a well-educated and kindly farmer named Laidlaw. 'He was not long', writes Laidlaw's son,

> in going through all the books belonging to my father; and learning from me that Mr Elder, bookseller, Peebles, had a large collection of books which he used as a circulating lib-rary, he forthwith became a subscriber, and by that means read Smollett's and Fielding's novels, and those voyages and travels which were published at the time, including those of Cook, Carteret, and others.[3]

In this decade and shortly after, James Hogg was also reading Shakespeare, Spenser, Ramsay, Burns, Pope, and Dryden's translation of Virgil. Another strong influence was Thomas Burnet's *Sacred Theory of the Earth*, which, he says, 'nearly overturned my brain altogether'.[4] Burnet's book, although published a century earlier, was greatly admired by Wordsworth, Coleridge, and other Romantic poets for its sublime descriptions of the Alps and other natural scenes. The 'great Concave of the Heavens, and those boundless Regions where the Stars inhabit', as well as 'the wide Sea and the Mountains of the Earth', have, according to Burnet, an 'august and stately' quality 'that inspires the mind with great thoughts and passions', filling us with admiration until we grasp 'the shadow and appearance of INFINITE'.[5] James Hogg describes comets, stars, and celestial journeys so often in his poetry, that an 1825 critic suggested that Burnet's *Sacred Theory*, 'one of the sublimest works of imagination ever produced', had 'left a deep though vague impression upon [Hogg's] mind, which has never since been eradicated'.[6]

In his early thirties the shepherd was living alone in a hillside 'bothy', a cave-like dwelling which could only be entered 'on all-fours'. It was here that Hogg, with his 'bare feet and ragged coat', first entertained the poets Allan and James Cunningham. Leaving the dog Hector to guard the sheep, the three men crawled inside the dark bothy, drank sweet milk and 'brandy or rum',[7] and recited their poems.

James Hogg moved to Edinburgh when he was thirty-nine. His collection of ballads called *The Queen's Wake* was widely acclaimed, and he gained the respect of other writers like Wordsworth, Byron, Scott, Southey, and Washington Irving. Soon the former shepherd was 'a source of wonder' in the capital, arranging 'music-parties after his own fancy' at the homes of his friends, where he sang, played the violin, and 'tried again and again the notes for his "Border Garland" '.[8] 'The effect of the champagne on the Ettrick Shepherd', records one guest at these parties, 'was quite delightful';

> Before the ladies left the dining-room, he insisted upon having a violin put into his hands, and really produced a measure of sweet sounds, quite beyond what I should have expected from the workmanship of such horny fingers. It seems, however, he had long been accustomed to minister in this way at the fairs and penny-weddings in Ettrick.[9]

Also present on these Edinburgh evenings was Hogg's good friend Margaret Phillips, whom he married after a long courtship in 1820. James and Margaret then settled as tenant-farmers in Ettrick, where their five children were born. For his last fifteen years James Hogg led a spirited life of fishing, hunting, archery, farming, and writing. A hired shepherd on their farm recalls one evening when some literary folk arrived from Edinburgh. After dark James took the men outside to fish for salmon, then to the pub for whisky toddy, and finally home again for a dinner of salmon 'boiled and served up hot with potatoes', followed by more toddy. The Ettrick Shepherd was 'not a hard, much less a solitary, drinker',[10] however, and most reports agree that he drank appreciatively but in moderation.

The year 1832 began with the arrival of James Hogg in London for a three-month visit. The sixty-one-year-old poet sang, recited, and found himself a celebrity. After a dinner party where he persuaded the upper-class guests 'to abandon the claret and stick to the whiskey-toddy, which he brewed ... and ladled out with beaming good-will',[11] Hogg proceeded to the home of Mrs Anna Hall, a respected author, editor, and temperance crusader. The Halls had invited about sixty guests, including Maria Edgeworth, Allan Cunningham, and David Wilkie. 'I can recall James Hogg sitting on the sofa', writes Mrs Hall,

> his countenance flushed with the excitement and the 'toddy' ... — expressing wild earnestness, not, I thought, unmixed with irascibility. He was then, certainly, more like a buoyant Irishman ... as he shouted forth, in an untunable voice, songs that were his own especial favourites, giving us some account of the origin of each at its conclusion. One I particularly remember—'The Women Folk.' 'Ha, ha!' he exclaimed, echoing our applause with his own broad hands—'that song, which I am often forced to sing to the *leddies*, sometimes against my will, that song never will be sung so well again by any one after I be done wi' it.' I remember Cunningham's comment 'That's because you have the *nature* in you!'[12]

Back in Ettrick in the same year, Hogg agreed to play the fiddle at a dance at Tibbie Shiel's Inn, after a day's fishing. 'Half the inhabitants of the district' were present when 'Mr Hogg ... made his appearance, rod in hand, and in the folds of his inseparable plaid a fiddle'. 'The shepherd was in his glory', playing 'with spirit and a supple wrist', and giving 'limbs of speed and faces of joy' to the dancers, until finally, having 'induced ... an extraordinary degree of thirst',[13] he consented to stay the night.

It would be wrong to conclude that James Hogg was not a serious writer, merely because he led an exuberant life. On the contrary, his poetry complements his life in trying to lead the way to a recovery of man's natural, primitive, and creative potential. Hogg's dislike of refinement partly accounts for his imitation of the Psalms in one section of 'Pilgrims of the Sun', and his use of medieval Scots in 'The Witch of Fife'. The 'ruder times of a nation', he claimed, were the 'period for invention, for the bold creations of an unbridled fancy'. A creative poet, if he happened to live in an age of excessive civilisation, could only

> step back to an early age; and if the original stamina of genius is yours, the fame you covet is secure. Take the simplicity of Moses, the splendour of Job, David, and Isaiah. Take Homer, and, if you like, Hesiod, Pindar, and Ossian; and by all means William Shakespeare. In short, borrow the fire and vigour of an early period of society, when a nation is verging from barbarism into civilisation; and then you will imbibe the force of genius from its original source. Nourish the inspiration, and despise the cold rules of criticism.[14]

Always distrustful of urban, modern, or English sophistication, James Hogg hoped to achieve 'vigour' and 'genius' by learning from early poets, and by writing mainly in Scots, a language he undoubtedly found more emotive, powerful, and onomatopoeic, than English.

Hogg was echoing a common desire of Romantic poets in his search for a more primitive and energetic style of poetry. 'The earliest poets of all nations generally wrote ... naturally, and as men', declared Wordsworth; 'feeling powerfully as they did, their language was daring, and figurative'.[15] A popular book by an Edinburgh professor suggested that 'in its ancient original condition' poetry had been

> more vigorous than it is in its modern state. It included then the whole burst of the human mind. ... It spoke then the language of passion, and no other. ... [The primitive poet] sung indeed in wild and disorderly strains; but they were ... the ardent conceptions of admiration or resentment, of sorrow or friendship, which he poured forth. It is no wonder, therefore, that in the rude and artless strain of the first poetry of all nations, we should often find somewhat that captivates and transports the mind. In after-ages, when poetry became a regular art, studied for reputation and for gain, authors began to affect what they did not feel.[16]

Another way in which James Hogg hoped to regain the creativity and originality of early poets was by composing in a fairly spontaneous manner. 'I sat down and wrote out my thoughts as I found them', he tells us; 'I cannot make out one sentence by study, without the pen in my hand to catch the ideas as they arise, and I never write two copies of the same thing'. This is not quite the same as automatic writing, since it involved forethought, choice, and a prior knowledge of the shape and extent of each poem: 'Let the piece be of what length it will, I compose and correct it wholly in my mind, or on a slate, ere ever I put pen to paper; and then I write it down as fast as the A, B, C'.[17] After thinking of a subject for a poem, Hogg would use a piece of chalk and a slate to work through the 'sad torment' of choosing between his '*rowth*' of ideas and images, before finally setting the words rapidly on paper.

His method of writing saved him from the deadly refinement, polish, moralism, or intellectualism that makes most of the poetry of his time virtually unreadable. By insisting on rapid, unrevised, and relatively spontaneous creativity, he invented a demanding self-discipline which must have helped to focus his mind by clearing away inessentials. It must also have made James Hogg acutely aware of writing as an *act*, something begun and finished within a certain length of time, requiring intense concentration, and bringing self-revelation. Not all his attempts were successful, but Hogg's better poems have a freshness, energy, and simplicity, as a consequence of the way they were composed. There is directness and genuine vitality when he describes an Edinburgh gypsy in 'A Common Lot':

> The tatter'd coat, the old straw hat,
> The breeches pepper'd at the knees;

—or when he pictures the future of a self-enamoured young maiden in 'Lines for the Eye of the Beautiful Miss E.B.':

> With face of languor sipping tea!
> Wi' hoffats rather bleached an' thin,
> An' cheekbanes blue out through the skin.
> 'Tis really waesome like to look at
> The very toast she's like to puke at;

—or when he satirises money-mad stock-market investors in his 1824 'New Christmas Carol':

> Then fy let us a' to subscribing,
>   And build up a tower to the moon;
> And get fou on the tap, and, in daffing,
>   Dad out the wee stars wi' our shoon;—
> Then, hey fal de ray, fal de rady,
>   Let's see a' how proud we can be,
> And build ower a brig to Kirkaldy,
>   And drown a' the French in the sea!

Several conversations recorded by Hogg's Edinburgh friend Robert Gillies help us to understand his poetics better. Each individual mind, Hogg told Gillies, 'is like a magic well, that yields all things, if only ye hae discretion and patience, and work deep eneuch'. The poet's role, then, is to explore his own mind, and by expressing his self-knowledge to help readers in understanding *their* own minds. In Hogg's view, an ideal poet would find books and formal education largely irrelevant: 'Every sensible man', he declared, 'has a book in his ain *heart and mind*', worth all the libraries in the world, 'if he could but understand it, and make the best of it.' 'The book of one's own mind and heart', said the Ettrick Shepherd, 'is inexhaustible, if it be properly studied'.[18]

By descending into the 'magic well' of his own mind, the poet would be attempting a similar task in each of his poems. As a result, Hogg's verse takes on a continuity, a gradual development and growth which can be charted through his changing themes, symbols, and images. Most of his poems are based on the idea of a journey, which may be either explicit or implicit, literal or symbolic. His first published work, 'The Mistakes of a Night', depicts a 'wise' young man who sets out one evening to visit his sweetheart:

> Awa' gaed Geordie hip and thigh,
>   Out-o'er the muir to Maggy.

But unfortunately on this foggy night Geordie fails to notice that the woman he meets is actually his girlfriend's mother:

> He kiss't her o'er and o'er again,
>   O'erjoy'd she was sae willin';
> An' vow'd if she'd reject his flame,
>   The very thought was killin'.
> Then aff into the barn they hye,
>   To spend the night in courtin';
> The widow's heart did sing for joy,
>   To think o' her good fortune,
>   That Friday's night.

As well as a physical journey across the moor, Geordie goes on a spiritual journey from initial confidence down to a realm of confusion and error. The hero's descent into confusion should be seen as a parallel to the poet's descending journey within his own consciousness, as he struggles to write the poem; appropriately, then, the forced marriage at the end resolves both the author's dilemma, and Geordie's dilemma. In poem after poem Hogg re-enacts this fundamental, metaphorical voyage, in which the poet and/or his protagonist move from proud self-confidence down to a more realistic or mature acceptance of the limitations, imperfections, and relativity of the self. In 'The First Sermon' a novice clergyman tries to preach spontaneously, and undergoes a similar psychological journey when his confidence evaporates to leave him facing his own

> loss of reccollection. All within
> Became a blank, a chaos of confusion
> Producing naht but agony of soul.

The comic poem 'Connel of Dee' presents the same general movement from initial self-confidence down to a realm of utter chaos where the terrified Connel must flee from his bloodthirsty wife:

> Thro' gallwood and bramble he floundered amain
>   No bar his advancement could stay
> Tho' heels-o'er-head whirled again and again
>   Still faster he gained on his way
> This moment on swinging bough powerless he lay
>   The next he was rolling along
> So lightly he scarce made the green leaf to quake
> Impetous he splashed thro the bog and the lake
> He rainbowed the hawthorn he needled the brake
>   With power supernaturally strong.

Here the chaotic rhythms and the symbol of Connel's hectic flight provide fitting correlatives to the mental journey or mental process that takes place simultaneously within the poet's imagination. It is quite appropriate then that Connel becomes a poet himself, and he ends his days, much like Coleridge's Ancient Mariner, trying to share with his audience the wisdom gained during his descent:

> And oft on the shelve of the rock he reclined
>   Light carolling humoursome rhyme
> Of his midsummer dream, of his feelings refined,
>   Or some song of the good olden time.

Other poems by James Hogg present more implicit, internal, or subtle versions of his characteristic journey. In 'The Summer Midnight' the movement is entirely within the poet's own mind, as he suddenly pauses to reflect on his loss of inspiration, his isolation as a writer, and his approaching death:

> O for some sadly dying note
> Upon this silent hour to float,
> Where, from the headlong world remote,
>   The lyre might wake its melody:
> One feeble strain is all can swell
> From mine almost deserted shell,
> In mournful accents yet to tell
>   That slumbers not its minstrelsy.

This poem becomes interesting as soon as the poet admits that what he has written in the first four stanzas is only a 'feeble strain'; the process or movement within his mind is similar to Hogg's more explicit journeys, since its meaning is to demonstrate again the frailty of the individual consciousness.

Many of Hogg's best poems try to shake the reader out of pride and self-sufficiency by showing the need to accept time, process, and involvement. 'Time wears unchancy mortals doun', he admits in 'The Cutting o' my Hair'. With 'A True Story of a Glasgow Tailor' he warns his countrymen against living in the historical past, just as he warns the vain 'Miss E. B.' against living in a personal past by trying to prolong her youth. A reader should learn that

> The best thing in life is to mak
> The maist o't that we can,

like that infinitely wise philosopher, the 'Lass o' Carlisle', who joins in the journey or process of life by giving up pride in favour of relationship and love:

> This lassie had routh o' wooers,
>   As beauty an' wealth should hae:
> This lassie she took her a man,
>   An' then she could get nae mae.
> This lassie had bairns galore,
>   That keepit her han's astir,
> An' then she dee'd an' was buried,
>   An' there was an end o' her.

The theme of these various journeys is the weakness, hollowness, or essential confusion of the human self. Throughout his life as a writer, James Hogg wanted to warn his audience against more successful, more respectable authors, whose work depicted 'men all pure, and maidens all divine'.[19] His allegorical poem 'Halbert of Lyne' urges the reader to reject the dangerous illusion of perfection, both in regard to people and to works of art:

> Now, dear Horatio, when thou makest choice
> Of book, of friend, companion, or of wife,
> Think of the sage advice of John of Manor;
> CHUSE EVER THAT WHICH HAS THE FEWEST FAULTS.

As readers, then, we should forget about looking for aesthetic or moral perfection, and remember that all have 'their foibles and their faults'.

Even the ballad 'Kilmeny', so highly praised in its day for the purity of its heroine, enforces Hogg's conviction that perfection is not applicable to adult life on earth. A 'sinless virgin, free of stain / In mind and body', young Kilmeny is taken away from 'the snares of men' to heaven, so that 'sin or death she never may ken'. In heaven Kilmeny sees a panorama of human suffering, past and future, that includes Mary Queen of Scots, John Knox ('a gruff untoward bedeman'), the French Revolution, and Napoleon (symbolised by an eagle). Kilmeny comes back to earth, tries to share her spiritual purity and vision, but finds that all the people regard her with suspicion:

> It wasna her hame, and she couldna remain;
> She left this world of sorrow and pain,
> And returned to the land of thought again.

As Douglas Mack suggests, the ballad 'Kilmeny' expresses 'the beauty and peace of that ultimate [Christian] joy, seen against a background of the sadness of the contrast between the glory of heaven and our present situation'.[20]

Hogg's way of writing poetry coincides with his rejection of perfection or purity as models of human life. His theory of relatively spontaneous composition assumes that the mind discovers itself through motion, transition, and process, rather than through any static or idealised image of itself. By disallowing revision and by transcribing his thoughts as they occurred in succession, he resisted the temptation of trying to sound more refined, proper, intelligent, rational, or inventive, than in reality he was. And rather than simply looking within his own mind and trying to report passively the thoughts that he finds there, Hogg attempts to delve and confront the inner chaos or the void, so that most of his better poems become momentary acts of self-definition, with a structure that embodies the journey of a creative mind from its initial sense of freedom and power to its inevitable sense of weakness, and finally towards some kind of resolution.

This simple, profound honesty allows James Hogg to unleash his great comic potential by exposing contradictions and frailties within the minds of his characters. Jock Linton of 'The Great Muckle Village of Balmaquhapple', for instance, gives himself away when he prays for the salvation of his townsfolk, but with certain notable exceptions:

> If these gang to heaven, we'll a' be sae shockit,
> Your garrat o' blue will but thinly be stockit.

Another of Hogg's delightfully confused heroes is Jock M'Pherson, an ebullient young man who has never quite mastered the letters of the alphabet:

> Of course, Jock's advancement in learning was slow;
> He got with perplexity as far as O;
> But the p and the q, that sister and brother,
> He wish'd at the deil, and he never wan further.

Yet after a marvellous life on the high seas, Jock returns to triumph over his smug detractors, and even enjoys a victory over the p and q:

> "And blast my two eyes!" Jack would swear and would say,
> "If I do not believe to this here blessed day,
> That the trimmers were nothing for all the kick-up just,
> Than a b and a d with their bottoms turn'd upmost!"

Hogg's songs are of course too brief to enact his full metaphorical journey. Instead, they generally explore one segment of the journey—often by showing a human mind admitting or actively confronting its own confused nature. The hero is 'all driven heels-o'er-head' in 'Doctor Monro', while in 'Love's Like a Dizziness' he laments,

> Ye little ken what pains I prove!
>   Or how severe my plisky, O!
> I swear I'm sairer drunk wi' love
>   Than e'er I was wi' whisky, O!
> For love has rak'd me for an' aft,
>   I scarce can lift a leggy, O:

I first grew dizzy, then gaed daft,
An' now I'll dee for Peggy, O.

In 'Love Came to the Door o' my Heart' (which is possibly the
Shepherd's best song) the singer is filled with 'wild dismay' after
opening his door to Cupid; he cries 'Gae away, gae away, thou
wicked wean', until fortunately he learns to accept love and to leave
the door of his heart ajar. A few songs celebrate the end of the
journey by giving a sense of togetherness symbolised by marriage,
friendship, or dancing, as in 'My Emma my Darling', where the
young man invites his sweetheart to 'mix with the world and enjoy
humankind' by going with him to the city,

Where the dance is so light, and the hall is so bright
And life whirls onward one round of delight.

'If E'er I Am Thine' gives a different version of the end of the
journey, with the singer predicting that the birds, beasts, and fish

Shall in our love and happiness share,
Within their elements fair and free,
And rejoice because I am thine, love.

Energy, motion, process, and journey, are the main features of
Hogg's poetry. When he makes fun of other authors, it is usually by
showing that they are incapable of genuine freedom or movement.
His parody 'James Rigg' makes an analogy between William
Wordsworth writing poetry, and someone boring a hole in a rock.
Equally 'boring' is the figure of Wordsworth in Hogg's 'Andrew the
Packman', a sad, pompous versifier who lugubriously defends
religion by comparing it to a hat-stand. Christianity, intones this
long-winded pseudo-Wordsworth, is like a piece of furniture

Of pyramidal form, which I had seen
Within the lobby of that noble peer,
The Earl of Lonsdale. On the right hand side,
As entering from the door, there doth it stand
For hanging hats upon. Not unapplausive
Have I beheld it cover'd o'er with hats.
Apt simile in dissimilitude
Of that most noble fabric, which I have
In majesty of matter and of voice
Aroused me to defend. "Sir, hear me speak,"
(Now at that time my cheek was gently lean'd
On palm of my left hand; my right one moving

Backwards and forwards with decisive motion,)—
"Sir, hear me speak. Will you unblushingly
Stretch your weak hand to sap the mighty fabric,
On which hang millions all proleptical
Of everlasting life? That glorious structure,
Rear'd at the fount of Mercy ..."

According to this portrait, Wordsworth is slow-witted, blustery, essentially static, and self-absorbed almost to the point of solipsism. Hogg makes a similar attack on the Poet Laureate Robert Southey in his witty parody 'Peter of Barnet'. Like Southey, the hero Peter of Barnet warmly admires the work of Robert Burns, but fears

That Burns, of whom you spake, was a bad man,
A man of a most vicious, tainted mind,
Fit to corrupt an age.—Was it not so?

However, when the narrator replies that Burns was the victim of a puritanical society, Peter (i.e., Southey) instantly steps back into his rather unconvincing pretence of emulating Robert Burns:

D—n them! said Peter,—he thrust back his chair,
Dashed one knee o'er the other furiously,
Took snuff a double portion,— swallowed down
His glass at once,—looked all around the room
With wrathful eye, and then took snuff again.

Hogg implies that despite their desire to appear energetic, Wordsworth and Southey remain trapped by their verboseness, puritanism, politeness, book-learning, and other qualities which are inimical to primitive genius.

It is quite possible to enjoy the parodies in Hogg's two *Poetic Mirrors*, without being very familiar with the poets that are mimicked in them. 'Peter of Barnet' comes to life if we simply know that Southey was stuffy, a tee-totaller, ultra-conservative, and notorious for experimenting with metre. A prominent and fairly typical review (which Hogg had read) found the Laureate's muse 'remarkably childish', with 'a general air of heaviness and labour', and criticised Southey for the 'great irregularity' of 'mix[ing] up all sorts of measures in every canto'.[21] In 'Peter of Barnet' Hogg repeats these charges by comparing Southey to a fatuously sentimental, ponderous but well-intentioned man, who has adopted a lame child. With 'his foot on edge', he

walked across the field and back
With awkward limp, to show me how the boy
Walked out the way,—the fancy pleased him much,
For ever and anon he laughed at it,
And yet the tear was pacing down his cheek.
'Twas just this way he walked, poor soul, said Peter;
And then, with turned-up foot, and gait oblique,
Again he halted lamely o'er the ridge,
Laughing with shrilly voice, and all the while
Wiping his eyes.

Southey's extreme Toryism is ridiculed in 'Peter of Barnet',
while in 'A Common Lot' James Hogg takes aim at the Radical
Whig politics of James Montgomery. Montgomery was an Angli-
cised Scot who lived in Sheffield, where he became one of the most
highly-paid poets of the age. Through the metaphor of a gipsy or
tinkler, Hogg caricatures Montgomery's wandering youth, his
former imprisonment for libel and his dislike of authority, his
melancholy, and his utilitarian outlook and prosaic, mundanely
realistic poetry. He also seems to hint that Montgomery stole from
other poets (but 'Oblivion hid the bones'), and that in later years he
was deserted by his muse:

He loved—but her he loved, a scamp
  One evening bore from his embrace;
Oh! she was fair, but prone to tramp
  With every taking face.

At one time the Ettrick Shepherd had thought highly of the
Sheffield poet, but he is not likely to have enjoyed Montgomery's
loudly-reported outburst against 'the writers of Scottish verse',
who employ a 'lawless ... dialect' and 'are so limited in their range
of subjects, and the compass of their song, that their pieces must of
necessity be brief'.[22]
There is one supreme paradox in the poetic theory and practice
of James Hogg. His characteristic starting-point is a high confidence in the free, creative powers of the individual, but then
immediately he almost always moves on to confront and explore the
dependence, weakness, hollowness, or relativity inherent in each
human self. The two opposite attitudes might be called innocence
and experience, each one having its own validity. In his autobiographical poem 'The Minstrel Boy', Hogg fondly recalls the naive
'conceit' and 'high resolve' of his youth, and insists that without
such

> resolve that mocks controul,
> A conscious energy of soul
> That views no height to human skill,
> Man never excelled and never will.

Although it must inevitably give way to a more realistic view, then, the initial stage of self-confident elation is a necessary starting-point for a successful journey, whether in life or in writing a poem.

The journey may be one of descent and disillusionment, as in 'Connel of Dee' and most of Hogg's work, or one of joyous ascent into spiritual awareness, as in 'Kilmeny' or 'The Pilgrims of the Sun', where

> all were in progression—moving on
> Still to perfection. In conformity
> The human soul is modelled—hoping still
> In something onward!

Just as Connel of Dee disintegrates in a physical sense—

> The minnow, with gushet se gouden and braw,
> The siller-ribbed perch, and the indolent craw,
> And the ravenous ged with his teeth like a saw,
>   Came all on poor Connel to feed!

—so the two heroes of 'Pilgrims of the Sun' experience disintegration or loss of self in a spiritual sense, with their visionary powers being 'subtilised' to allow them to fly 'So swift and so untroubled' through the universe. Many of James Hogg's poems depict only one section of the journey, but the full passage leads through relativism, despair, or confusion to a renewed personal dignity based on community values and social vision. Thus, Connel of Dee becomes socially-concerned and responsible, while in 'Pilgrims of the Sun' Mary Lee marries and becomes once again a helpful member of society.

Some of Hogg's ideas about creativity are echoed in Shelley's *Defence of Poetry*. Much like Hogg, Shelley imagined that poetry has 'no necessary connection with the consciousness or will', cannot be 'produced by labour and study', and represents 'the visitations of the divinity in man'. And Shelley, too, implies that the act of creation is a process of loss, descent, or disintegration, since when he sits down to write the poet can never quite recapture in words that original, exhilarating spark of inspiration. '[T]he mind in creation', wrote Shelley in 1821, is as a fading coal, which some invisible influence, like an inconstant wind, awakens to transitory brightness. ... Could this influence be durable in its original purity and force, it is impossible to predict the greatness of the results; but when composition begins, inspiration is already on the decline, and the most glorious poetry ... is probably a feeble shadow of the original conception of the Poet.[23]

This passage by Shelley might almost be describing both the method of composing verse developed by James Hogg, and the distinctive journey which he enacts in so many of his best poems. A poem, for Hogg, has its own intrinsic, organic shape, a shape that embodies the contrast between the primitive and exciting nature of inspiration, and the author's inevitable difficulty and confusion when he tries to convey that original vision in words. In Hogg's song 'The Lark' (which was quite possibly a source for Shelley's 'Skylark'), the poet begins by identifying with the bird through his graceful, swooping lines—

> Bird of the wilderness,
> Blithsome an' cumberless,
> Sweet be thy matin o'er moorland an' lea

—but by the end of the song his yearning, 'O to abide in the desert with thee', indicates the distance or difference between the poet and the lark, and conveys the artist's inevitable failure. One of Hogg's very best works is 'To Miss M. A. C.', in which the poet describes himself as 'Nature's error', a meteor or a lark 'lost in the heavens blue' and impelled by 'elemental energies' which are both natural and divine. As a 'meteor of the wild' coursing across a 'boundless' sky, the poet's role is simply 'To gleam, to tremble, and to die'.

The Ettrick Shepherd's most ambitious poem is his 'Pilgrims of the Sun', composed in 1815 shortly after 'Connel of Dee'. At first he had intended these as complementary pieces, to be published in a single volume, but unfortunately a friend convinced him 'to give up my design of the Midsummer Night Dreams, ... and to publish ['Pilgrims'] as an entire work by itself'.[24] Hogg later regretted this decision, and a close look at the two pieces reveals that they were carefully designed to make a single whole. In 'Pilgrims of the Sun' the protagonist is a young woman, led by a male angel named Cela, who flies upward through the sky on a voyage of spiritual and imaginative discovery; in 'Connel of Dee' the protagonist is a young man, chased by an angry wife, who flees downward on an all-too-worldly and physical journey before drowning in the Dee. At the end of 'Pilgrims' Mary Lee is thought to be dead, but she comes back to life when a greedy monk tries to cut the rings off her fingers; similarly in 'Connel' the hero assumes that he has drowned, but at the sound of his persistent wife's voice he 'started upright in horror and fear', only to find that he has been dreaming. The two poems together form a circle or ring, representing the downward parabola of Connel's flight and the upward one of Mary's.

As with most of Hogg's poems, 'Pilgrims of the Sun' is best appreciated as a whole, for its shape, theme, and sense of movement or freedom, rather than for specific images or passages. It is crucial to notice the parallels between Mary's journey, the ideas expressed by the poet, and the poet's changes of style. The first few stanzas are in Hogg's own conversational voice, which then quickly modulates to a slightly more formal strain representing the style of Border ballads. Once Mary leaves Scotland the poet lays aside his 'hill-harp' for the older 'Harp of Jerusalem', an instrument of 'sacred string' more suitable to this part of Mary's and the poet's journeys:

> Soft let it be,
> And simple as its own primeval airs;
> And, Minstrel, when on angel wing thou soar'st,
> Then will the harp of David rise with thee.

This style in turn modulates into a fine imitation of Milton, which inspires the poet to speculate on the nature of life, the universe, — and comets:

> Down amain
> Into the void the outcast world descended,
> Wheeling and thundering on! Its troubled seas
> Were churned into a spray, and, whizzing, flurred
> Around it like a dew.

> Away into the sunless starless void
> Rushed the abandoned world; and thro' its caves,
> And rifted channels, airs of chaos sung.

> When meteor-like,
> Bursting away upon an arching track,
> Wide as the universe, again it scaled
> The dusky regions.

In Part Third the poet borrows the harp of Augustan English verse, to write in heroic couplets that recall 'Dryden's twang, and Pope's malicious knell'. Less 'sublime' and more analytical, this style corresponds to the social and moral concerns of this section of

'Pilgrims'. The poet now sings 'of the globes our travellers viewed', as Mary and Cela fly through worlds of lovers ('a land so fair'), soldiers (a 'gloomy sphere'), lawyers ('a world accursed / Of all the globes the dreariest and the worst'), narrowminded churchmen ('Their frames their God'), reviewers ('bent with aspect sour'), politicians ('Raving aloud'), and courtiers ('a land effeminate'). As the poem nears its close, and as Mary Lee returns to the Borders, the poet returns to his 'ancient harp again', writing in a manner that recalls Walter Scott's longer narrative poems.

The imitations of Milton, Dryden, and Pope are all slightly distorted, so that Hogg can convey his reservations about those poets by introducing subtle changes in their respective planets. Milton's heaven now includes 'men of all creeds, / Features, and hues', while the eternal lovers in Alexander Pope's world are now, thanks to James Hogg, 'free of jealousy, their mortal bane':

> In love's delights they bask without alloy;
> The night their transport, and the day their joy.

In other words James Hogg shows us how to appreciate the poetry of the past, while rejecting the narrower values of the past. He repudiates militarism, defends the dignity of animals ('generous comrades'), and insists on equality between the sexes: 'Let human reason equal judgment frame'.

The more Mary travels from her Border home, the more she accepts these universal, humanitarian values. At first shocked to see Cela bowing with reverence to the sun, she soon decides that much of what clergymen have said 'was neither true nor ever could be'. She gradually accepts Cela's sun-worship and comes to share the Romantic Christian pantheism that underlies the whole poem.

Mary's and Cela's trip to the sun is clearly not meant to be taken literally. The worlds they visit represent ideas rather than realities, and their flight takes them 'Along, along, thro' mind's unwearied range'. The two pilgrims can be seen as *readers*, because they travel through literary worlds based on well-known poems. At each stage of their voyage Hogg's verse imitates whichever poet Mary and Cela are, in effect, reading. It is highly appropriate that Mary Lee should be a reader, since in the other main poem of *Midsummer Night Dreams*, the protagonist Connel of Dee is a poet.

Apparently the metaphor of flying in 'Pilgrims of the Sun' indicates how James Hogg wanted us to read his poetry. In our reading it seems we should imitate Cela and Mary, who glide 'swift as fleets the stayless mind', with an attitude of openness and joy, 'On the yielding winds so light and boon':

> And away, and away they journeyed on,
> Faster than wild bird ever flew.

Their broad, universal values allow them to read critically, and at the same time passively, receptively, so that they are free of aggressive intellect and can let their minds expand under the influence of poetry. Soaring lightly 'on the liquid air, / Like twin-born eagles', they learn to trust the moving power of imagination:

> So swift and so untroubled was their flight,
> 'Twas like the journey of a dream by night.

A literal-minded reader would be like 'the earthly pilgrim', stumbling over anything unusual and 'Fainting with hunger, thirst, and burning feet', but a good reader will travel freely 'thro' regions of delight', finding symbolic meanings and enjoying the sense of a journey.

The Ettrick Shepherd offers us similar advice in his book of *Lay Sermons*. A reader should ignore the critics and 'judge of the work solely by the effect it produces on yourself'. This means that we should try to sympathise with the poet, to notice the general direction and shape of each piece, and finally to bear in mind that reading (like writing) is a kind of journey:

> If the author carries you into the regions of fancy, and amuses you with a creation of new and beautiful images, why not approve of them, though of a different political creed? If he goes along the beaten road of nature, and introduces you to characters having manners and attitudes such as you meet with in the world, why not converse with him as you do with a friend? You ought to give yourself no trouble ... provided he takes you along with him, and makes an agreeable companion on the road. Never say in your heart, "He is mine enemy who thus delighteth me;" nor ever stoop to be told by [a critic] what you are to be pleased with. Your taste and imagination are exclusively your own.[25]

Some of Hogg's favourite symbols would include mist, water, mirrors, the journey, and the ring or circle. The circle first becomes prominent in his *Queen's Wake*, with its repeated allusions to 'circling years', a 'magic ring', and a 'courtly circle'. Hogg's next long poem, *Mador of the Moor* (not included in the present selection), develops the symbolism of the 'ryng' uniting two parabolic paths representing the hero's (and the sun's) upward journey, and the heroine's (and the river's) downward course to the sea. Through the symbol of a ring Hogg suggests the possibility of reconciling opposites like male and female, Highland and Lowland, natural and spiritual, and reason and imagination. In his *Midsummer Night Dreams* the imaginary circle is formed by the two complementary journeys of 'Pilgrims of the Sun' and 'Connel of Dee'. The poet tries to draw the full circle of human experience by symbolically uniting aesthetic or spiritual wisdom with physical realities, and by pairing the experience of a reader (represented by Mary Lee) with that of a poet (represented by Connel). James Hogg begins to lose interest in his rings and circles after 1818, but still his later poems usually contain remnants of the two contrasting journeys, with narrators and protagonists who begin as isolated individuals, and then either descend into chaos or ascend in flights of imagination. The open-ended journeys of 'A Boy's Song' and 'To Miss M. A. C.' are a pointed contrast to Hogg's earlier ideal of a closed circle.[26]

Often in Hogg's poems the poet speaks through a mask or *persona* which represents either an actual person or a common character-type of the present or past. He pretends to be a new-fangled businessman in his 'New Christmas Carol', and pretends to be a forlorn lover in songs like 'Doctor Monro', 'Love's Like a Dizziness', or 'The Drinkin', O'. In 'The Lament of Flora Macdonald' the poet speaks as a Jacobite, while in 'The Poor Man' he becomes a persecuted Covenanter or extreme Presbyterian. Although a sincere Christian in real life, James Hogg speaks as a religious hyprocite in his satirical 'Great Muckle Village of Balmaquhapple', and as a smug, snobbish church-goer in 'The First Sermon'.

Literal-minded critics often had difficulty understanding Hogg's technique of speaking through a mask. Unlike the open-minded Mary and Cela, most reviewers of the time were simply content to judge poetry according to preconceived theories mainly derived from politics or religion. At times the Shepherd was accused of siding with Whigs and Cameronians, at other times of 'blow[ing] the pipe of rebellion'[27] in the Tory or Jacobite cause. Critics delighted in flatly declaring that Hogg was either pro-aristocratic or anti-aristocratic, or that he was 'a violent Jacobite' who, had he 'lived in the year 1745 ... would have been killed at Culloden, or hanged afterwards'.[28] But in fact the Shepherd's approach to these various shades of human experience is always the same: he assumes that by delving within his own mind, he will discover an inner truth which will be essentially identical to the inner experience of any other honest and self-reflective person. Since all people are basically the same, then, the poet is free to pretend to be a Tory, Whig, or Radical, a misogynist or a lover, a drunkard or a tee-totaller, a Highlander, Lowlander, or Englishman, an ancient balladeer, or a more recent poet like Milton, Pope, Wordsworth, or Southey. Most of these types or individuals would be unlikely to appreciate Hogg's concept of a metaphorical journey, and so most of them enact partial voyages that end in despair, tragedy, or bathos (like the husband in 'The Witch of Fife'), or satire (like the forlorn poets of the two *Poetic Mirrors*). The full passage, however, leads to new-found purpose based on community,[29] as we may see from the two main poems of *Midsummer Night Dreams*, or even from the raucous comic ballad 'The p and the q'. For James Hogg this awareness of a meaningful journey leads both author and reader towards a more natural, essential, or universal self:

> Most men will relish what is natural and simple, if they are permitted to judge for themselves. If you take the most ad-mired passages from the best authors, you will find them to be the natural expressions of men of good sense; and you will admire them, because you feel that they are precisely what you would have thought and said yourself on the same occa-sion; that they are, in fact, the things which have always been thought, but never so well expressed.

The 'lash of criticism', according to Hogg, 'is an adder in the path, and has marred the mental journey of many an ardent and promising genius'.[30] His later poems often try for a more balanced effect as a way of preventing misunderstanding by the critics. The satire against modern life in 'Disagreeables', for example, becomes more restrained, more pointed, and more precisely defined when the poet looks back to his own youth in Ettrick to give an *exemplum* or brief portrait of the virtuous person:

> A thousand times I've dined upon the waste,
> On dry-pease bannock, by the silver spring.
> O, it was sweet—was healthful—had a zest;
> Which at the paste, my palate ne'er enjoyed!
> My bonnet laid aside, I turned mine eyes
> With reverence and humility to heaven,
> Craving a blessing from the bounteous Giver;
> Then grateful thanks returned. There was a joy
> In these lone meals, shared by my faithful dog,
> Which I remind with pleasure, and has given
> A verdure to my spirit's age. Then think
> Of such a man, beside a guzzler set;
> And how his stomach nauseates the repast.

A similar short interlude in 'Halbert of Lyne' describes a better society in the past, in order to stress the folly of modern genteel refinement and the gross inequalities of the present:

> There was a time, Horatio—but 'tis gone,
> Would that we saw't again—when every hind
> Of Scotland's southern dales tilled his own field;
> When master, dame, and maid, servant and son,
> At the same board eat of the same plain meal.
> The health and happiness of that repast
> Made every meal a feast.

Yet generally Hogg avoids the *exemplum*, often preferring to show a highly imperfect world where everyone, including the speaker or poet, has characteristic personal weaknesses. Superb examples of this would include his 'Anti-Burgher in Love', 'Village of Balmaquhapple', 'First Sermon', and the amazingly naughty 'Chickens in the Corn'. 'The First Sermon', like Hogg's *Confessions of a Justified Sinner*, begins by ridiculing extreme religion, but gradually implies equal and analogous limitations underlying the extreme rationalism of the narrator; both the poem and the novel achieve balance through the mirroring of opposite personality types, and through Hogg's favourite theme of fellowship, community, and common human nature. These various satires provoke us to work out the ironic implications on our own, and at the same time they set a kind of trap for proud, intolerant, or literal-minded readers, who are likely to be misled into accepting at face value the narrator's opening statements.

It is frequently wrong, therefore, to assume that the author is expressing his personal opinions directly through his verse. Yet paradoxically it is still James Hogg, and not some entirely fictitious, invented narrator, who speaks to us in his poems. Even the distortions, the masks, and caricatures are part of his personal repertoire, and beneath them we can usually recognise the real personality of the author. 'I draw only from myself', he writes in 'Halbert of Lyne'; 'he who draws otherwise / Than from his feelings never shall draw true'. His poems will survive, he predicts, because they reflect

> The feelings that congenial minds will love;
> And to each other genial minds will cling
> Long as this world has being, and the shades
> Of nature hold their endless variation.

James Hogg speaks directly and unironically in some poems (like his 'Address to his Youngest Daughter', 'Minstrel Boy', 'Summer Midnight', and 'Monitors'), but quite often his main speaker is a fictional character who corresponds to only one side of Hogg's personality. By deeply exploring his own mind, and by imagining fictional minds, he tries to rescue us from our superficial, refined, and modern attitudes, so that we may each find within ourselves a more honest, vital, primitive, and universal consciousness. A reader 'must toil' for the 'Treasures of the deep', says the poet with ironic solemnity in 'Halbert of Lyne', 'else he cannot win':

> Wilt thou never
> Learn for thyself to judge, and turn thine eye
> Into that page of life, the human soul,
> With all its rays, shades, and dependencies,
> For ever varied, and for ever new?

Like Mary Lee, the reader who takes up this challenge will soon be travelling towards a brilliant sun ('With all its rays, shades, and dependencies') through the poems and songs of James Hogg.

In his last years the Ettrick Shepherd warned that critical dogmas are harmful to a poet, since the only valid criteria 'ought to be in every man's breast', and true genius can only flow from 'original powers of ... mind'.[31] He never became trapped within his own theories. Although his ideal of spontaneous writing undoubtedly helped him to avoid artificiality, he nevertheless often *did* revise his own work, either to please himself or to make it more saleable. A love for primitive ballads did not prevent him from composing an anti-heroic satire called 'A True Story of a Glasgow Tailor', which laughs at ballad conventions and even seems to be mocking some aspects of *The Queen's Wake*. And although he clearly regarded the Scots language as more poetic, he still felt free to use English whenever he wanted, and even to shift between Scots and English within a single poem. James Hogg was not a purist in any sense, he allowed himself the freedom of contradiction and growth, and he always gave priority to life, energy, and imagination, as opposed to intellectual theories.

'There is no one who has contributed more to the literature of the present age than James Hogg', announced an English poet in 1825; the Shepherd's verses 'must fill every person with astonishment at the versatility of his genius'.[32] Despite the snobbish, partisan reactions of many critics, a small number of reviewers were sensitive to Hogg's 'great, original, and truly poetic mind',[33] and his 'energy of intellect, and vigour of imagination'. [34]

Hogg himself draws our attention to one influential review which seemed to him to contain 'the highest commendation ... ever ... bestowed on a work of genius'.[35] This London critic defended Hogg's poetry by denouncing what he called 'a sort of literary *materialism*, which holds ... that language, the mere vehicle and medium of Thought, is itself the measure of the mind, and the ultimate object of attention'. Instead, poetry should 'please for its own sake', for its 'intellectual essence' and its 'pure, imaginative cast'. A poem has a 'soul', and requires to be read for its symbols, metaphors, and nuances, its half-hidden 'intrinsic qualities', its appeal to 'genuine pleasures of imagination'. According to this reviewer 'The Pilgrims of the Sun' is 'delightfully adapted to the wildest rovings of our untamed fancy', with 'a liveliness of conception' and above all a 'free scope for ... imagination' that raised Hogg to the level 'of Southey and of Wordsworth, of Byron and of Campbell, of Montgomery and of Scott'.[36] These remarks also impressed an American writer, Washington Irving, who happened to be travelling in Britain at the time; Irving promptly arranged for both the article and Hogg's 'Pilgrims of the Sun' to be reprinted in America, where the poem proved much more popular than it did in Scotland or England.

James Hogg wanted his poems to be read, sung, danced to, and enjoyed. In his own time his verses were regularly reprinted in newspapers and magazines in places as diverse as Aberdeen, Glasgow, Edinburgh, Newcastle, Sheffield, Leeds, Liverpool, London, Philadelphia, New York and Connecticut. Even Beethoven, who had a fondness for Scottish poetry, was enthusiastic about writing the music for some of Hogg's lyrics. Yet after his death Hogg's popularity plummeted, thanks largely to supposedly 'complete' Victorian editions which altered or omitted so many of his liveliest or best poems. Most twentieth-century assessments have unfortunately been based, not on James Hogg himself, but on the false image of him engendered by bowdlerised posthumous editions of his work. Beginning with the appearance of Douglas Mack's *James Hogg: Selected Poems* in 1970, however, there has been a strong movement towards reclaiming Hogg's texts in the form in which they were written by him or published during his lifetime.

The present selection tries to reflect the discoveries and scholarship of recent years. More than two-thirds of its songs and poems are now reprinted for the first time in their original form, either from manuscripts or from first editions. Musical accompaniments have also been added wherever Hogg has indicated the relevant tune. Although first editions of his poems have been preferred, Hogg's own revisions of six pieces have been accepted, on the grounds that they seem more approachable or enjoyable to a modern audience. Obvious printing errors have been corrected, and all changes are noted in the Commentary. No attempt has been made to alter Hogg's idiosyncratic spelling or his freedom from punctuation except in a few places where it seemed necessary in order to help readers travel freely.

Regrettably some readers outside Scotland will probably allow Hogg's language to become a barrier to their enjoyment of his poems. As a North American, I feel that this excuse is not only groundless and lazy, but also very self-limiting. It takes about twenty minutes for the average English-speaking person to become reasonably familiar with Scots. None of us will ever equal Mary Lee in her smooth, rapid gliding 'thro' regions of delight', but we can all emulate her openness of mind, her freedom, and her desire for self-expansion. Indeed, an acquaintance with the Scottish language might help unilingual readers to gain a feeling for words as organic, historical, living entities with connections, depths, and shades of meaning.

NOTES

1   James Hogg, 'Memoir of the Author's Life', in Hogg, *Memoir of the Author's Life* and *Familiar Anecdotes of Sir Walter Scott*, edited by Douglas S. Mack (Edinburgh, 1972), pp. 7, 10.

2   James Hogg, 'On the Changes in the Habits, Amusements, and Condition of the Scottish Peasantry', *Quarterly Journal of Agriculture*, Sept. 1832, pp. 257, 261.

3   William Laidlaw, cited in Charles Rogers's *The Modern Scottish Minstrel*, 2 vols (London, 1855), II, 5.

4   Hogg, 'Memoir of the Author's Life', p. 10.

5   Thomas Burnet, *The Sacred Theory of the Earth* (1684; rpt. London 1965), ed. Basil Willey, p. 109.

6   Anonymous review of Hogg's *Queen Hynde, a Poem*, *Philomathic Journal*, Spring 1825, p. 175.

7   Hogg, 'Memoir of the Author's Life', pp. 72, 73.

8   R. P. Gillies, *Memoirs of a Literary Veteran*, 3 vols (London, 1851), II, 242.

9   [John Gibson Lockhart], *Peter's Letters to his Kinsfolk*, 3 vols (Edinburgh, 1819), III, 133.

10 Anonymous, 'A Living Link with Scott, Hogg, and Wilson', *Chambers's Journal*, May 1897, pp. 281, 282.

11 *An Autobiography of William Jerdan*, 4 vols (London, 1853), IV, 298.

12 Anna Maria Hall, cited in Samuel Carter Hall's *A Book of Memories of Great Men and Women of the Age* (London, 1871), p. 390.

13 Thomas Tod Stoddart, *An Angler's Rambles, and Angling Songs* (Edinburgh, 1866), p. 211.

14 James Hogg, *A Series of Lay Sermons on Good Principles and Good Breeding* (London, 1834), pp. 280, 281-82.

15 Wordsworth, Appendix to the Preface to *Lyrical Ballads*, reprinted in *The Poetical Works of Wordsworth*, ed. E. de Selincourt, 5 vols (Oxford, 1940-49), II, 405.

16 Hugh Blair, *Lectures on Rhetoric and Belles Lettres* (1783; rev., 2 vols, Edinburgh, 1814), II, 228.

17 Hogg, 'Memoir of the Author's Life', p. 11.

18 [Robert Gillies], 'Some Recollections of James Hogg', *Fraser's Magazine*, Oct. 1839, p. 421.

19 Hogg, *Mador of the Moor* (Edinburgh, 1816), p. 9.

20 Mack, Introduction to *James Hogg: Selected Poems* (Oxford, 1970), p. xxiv.

21 Anon. rev. of Southey's *Curse of Kehama* , *Edinburgh Review*, February 1811, pp. 433, 435, 452.

22 James Montgomery, *Lectures on Poetry and General Literature, delivered at the Royal Institution in 1830 and 1831* (London, 1833), p. 158.

23 Shelley, 'A Defence of Poetry', reprinted in *The Complete Works of Percy Bysshe Shelley*, ed. Roger Ingpen and Walter Peck, 10 vols (London and New York, 1926-30), VII, 135.

24 Hogg, 'Memoir of the Author's Life', p. 32.

25 Hogg, *A Series of Lay Sermons*, pp. 271, 271-72.

26 These image-patterns are discussed at length in my book, *James Hogg and his Art: 'The Mind Set Free'* (forthcoming).

27 Anon. rev. of Hogg's *Jacobite Relics of Scotland*, *Caledonian*, June 1820, p. 22. This critic from Dundee accuses the poet of treasonable sentiments, and adds, 'Think of that, Mr. James Hogg, and tremble! ... Down upon thy knees, Mr. James Hogg!' (p. 22). Yet despite its title, Hogg's collection of *Jacobite Relics* contains almost equal numbers of Whig and Tory songs, and is balanced in its discussion of the Jacobite Rebellions.

28 Anon. rev. of Hogg's novel *The Three Perils of Woman*, *Repository of Modern Literature*, 2 vols (London, 1823), II, 400.

29 This interpretation is developed in my articles, 'James Hogg's 'Singular Dream' and the *Confessions*' (*Scottish Literary Journal*, May 1983, pp. 54-66), and 'James Hogg's *Confessions* and the Vale of Soul-Making' (*Studies in Scottish Fiction: Nineteenth Century*, ed. Horst W. Drescher and Joachim Schwend (Frankfurt am Main, 1985), pp.29-41).

30 Hogg, *A Series of Lay Sermons*, pp. 272-73, 281. 'Sit down to your book as you would to conversation', the author continues; 'and never harbour an intention of triumph over the defects of your author; but divest yourself of all envy, and read to be pleased, and it is more than probable you will be so' (p. 285).

31 Hogg, *A Series of Lay Sermons*, pp. 274, 276.

32 J. H. [of Manchester], 'The Modern Poets: No. I; James Hogg, the Ettrick Shepherd', *Nepenthes*, 29 October 1825, p. 342.

33 Anon. rev. of Hogg's *Queen's Wake*, *Analectic Magazine*, February 1814, p. 109. This critique had first appeared in an issue of the *Scotish Review*, of which no copies apparently have survived.

34 Anon. rev., *Philomathic*, Spring 1825, p. 172.

35 Hogg, 'Memoir of the Author's Life', p. 36. Hogg goes on to say that 'Pilgrims of the Sun' 'was reprinted in two different towns in America, and ten thousand copies of it sold in that country'.

36 Anon. rev. of Hogg's 'Pilgrims of the Sun', *Eclectic Review*, March 1815, pp. 280-91; reprinted, *Analectic Magazine*, July 1815, pp. 36-46.

THE MISTAKES OF A NIGHT

TAK my advice, ye airy lads,
   That gang to see the lasses,
Keep weel your mind, for troth, the jads
   Tell ilka thing that passes.
Anither thing I wad advise,
   To gang on moon-light weather:
A friend o' mine, he was sae wise,
   He kiss't his lass's mither
            Ae Friday's Night.

She was a widow gaye an' douse,
   Liv'd o'er the hill frae Yarrow;
Her doughter Geordie lang had sought,
   And courtit for his marrow;
But 'twas in vain, she wadna do't
   Neither for gift nor fleechin;
Whilk sair provokit Geordie Scott,
   An' gart him slack the breechin,
            That Friday's night.

Awa' gaed Geordie hip and thigh,
   Out-o'er the muir to Maggy:
The night was neither warm nor dry,
   The road was rough an' haggy:
Wi' labour sair he reach'd the bit,
   By chance there stood her mither;
But Geordie ne'er observ'd the cheat,
   They spak sae sair like ither,
            That Friday's night.

He kiss't her o'er and o'er again,
   O'erjoy'd she was sae willin';
An' vow'd if she'd reject his flame,
   The very thought was killin'.
Then aff into the barn they hye,
   To spend the night in courtin';
The widow's heart did sing for joy,
   To think o' her good fortune,
            That Friday's night.

1

But when the cock began to cra',
  He left his saul's dear treasure,
And back the road he cam awa',
  He hugg'd himsel' wi' pleasure.
"The skittish elf was ay sae shy,
  "She fled whane'er I nam'd her:
"O! what a clever lad was I!
  "Faith, I trow I have tam'd her,
        "This lucky night."

At length the widow proves nae right,
  Whilk soon as e'er she sa' man,
She gangs and tells the hail affair,
  To rev'rend Doctor C——d:
Geordie appears on his defence,
  Hears a' his accusation;
But, conscious of his innocence,
  He laughs at the relation
        O' Friday's night.

Says he, " 'Tis false, this 'onest wife
  "May be a man for me, Sir."
Quo' she, "How dare ye for your life
  "Attest so great a lie, Sir!"
Says he, "If I a lie do tell,
  "To elders, priest, or bellman;
"Then may the miekle horned di'el,
  "Drive Geordie into hell, then,
        "This very night."

"I wish my lad," quo' Elder Tam,
  "Ye wadna speak sae rashly,
"You've surely done this woman wrang,
  "Or else she ne'er wad fash ye."
"Not I, Sir; I her ne'er did harm;
  "I never touch'd her skin yet;
"I own I kiss't her bonie bairn,
  "And hasna ru'd the sin yet,
        "That Friday's night."

The widow then began to state
  All that had pass'd between them;
Whilk soon clear'd up the grand mistake,
  Shew'd Geordie where he'd been then.

He curst himsel' for sik a deed;
   And for lak o' discretion;
He wish'd some frosty cauld dike-head,
   Had been his habitation
          That Friday's night.

What cou'd he do? the day approach'd
   His widow turn'd a mammy;
And weel he kend it wad mair cost
   Than ony whalp or lammie.
He married her, and brought her hame,
   Upon a gude grey naggy;
But often Geordie rues the time,
   He cross'd the muir to Maggie
          That Friday's night.

Now here's a health to 'onest Bess,
   And here's a health to Geordie;
And here's to ilka bony lass,
   That's constant to her wordie:
May peace and plenty be his lot,
   That loves his fellow-creature;
And warse than happen'd Geordie Scott,
   Meet ev'ry f——r,
          On ony night.

FROM
THE FOREST MINSTREL
DOCTOR MONRO

[Fairly brisk]

1 "Dear Doctor, be clever, and fling off your beaver; Come bleed me, and blister me, do not be slow: I'm sick, I'm exhausted, my schemes they are blasted, And all driven heels-o'er-head, Doctor Monro." "Be patient, dear fellow, you foster your fever; Pray what's the misfortune that bothers you so?" "O, Doctor! I'm ruin'd! I'm ruin'd for ever! My lass has forsaken me, Doctor Monro. [Fine]

2. I meant to have married, and tasted the pleasures, The sweets, the enjoyments, in wedlock that flow; But she's ta'en another, and broken my measures, And fairly confounded me, Doctor Monro." "I'll bleed and I'll blister you, over and over; I'll master your malady ere that I go: But raise up your head from below the bed cover, And give some attention to Doctor Munro.

[Repeat complete tune once, then again as far as Fine]

4

"DEAR Doctor, be clever, and fling off your beaver;
    Come bleed me, and blister me, do not be slow:
I'm sick, I'm exhausted, my schemes they are blasted,
    And all driven heels-o'er-head, Doctor Monro."
"Be patient, dear fellow, you foster your fever;
    Pray what's the misfortune that bothers you so?"
"O, Doctor! I'm ruin'd! I'm ruin'd for ever!
    My lass has forsaken me, Doctor Monro.

I meant to have married, and tasted the pleasures,
    The sweets, the enjoyments, in wedlock that flow;
But she's ta'en another, and broken my measures,
    And fairly confounded me, Doctor Monro."
"I'll bleed and I'll blister you, over and over;
    I'll master your malady ere that I go:
But raise up your head from below the bed cover,
    And give some attention to Doctor Monro.

If Christy had wed you, she would have misled you,
    And laugh'd at your love with some handsome young beau.
Her conduct will prove it; but how would you love it?"
    "I soon would have lam'd her, dear Doctor Monro."
"Each year brings a pretty young son, or a daughter;
    Perhaps you're the father; but how shall you know?
You hugg them—her gallant is bursting with laughter"—
    "That thought's like to murder me, Doctor Monro."

"The boys cost you many a penny and shilling;
    You breed them with pleasure, with trouble, and woe:
But one turns a rake, and another a villain."—
    "My heart could not bear it, dear Doctor Monro."
"The lasses are comely, and dear to your bosom;
    But virtue and beauty has many a foe!
O think what may happen; just nipt in their blossom!"—
    "Ah! merciful Heaven! cease, Doctor Monro.

Dear Doctor, I'll thank you to hand me my breeches;
    I'm better; I'll drink with you ere that you go;
I'll never more sicken for women or riches,
    But love my relations and Doctor Monro.
I plainly perceive, were I wedded to Christy,
    My peace and my pleasures I needs must forego."
He still lives a bachelor; drinks when he's thirsty;
    And sings like a lark, and loves Doctor Monro.

HOW FOOLISH ARE MANKIND

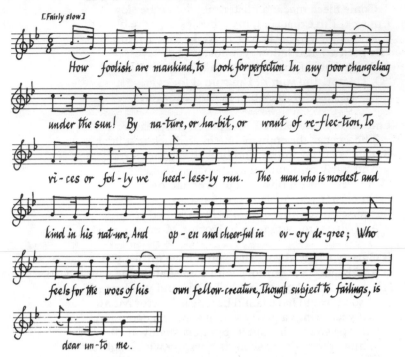

How foolish are mankind, to look for perfection
    In any poor changeling under the sun!
By nature, or habit, or want of reflection,
    To vices or folly we heedlessly run.
The man who is modest and kind in his nature,
    And open and cheerful in every degree;
Who feels for the woes of his own fellow-creature,
    Though subject to failings, is dear unto me.

Far dearer to me is the humble ewe-gowan,
    The sweet native violet, or bud of the broom,
Than fine foster'd flowers in the garden a-growing,
    Though sweet be their savour and bonny their bloom.
Far dearer to me is the thrush or the linnet,
    Than any fine bird from a far foreign tree;
And dearer my lad, with his plaid and blue bonnet,
    Than all our rich nobles or lords that I see.

LOVE'S LIKE A DIZZINESS

Tune—*Paddy's Wedding*

I LATELY liv'd in quiet case,
   An' never wish'd to marry, O;
But when I saw my Peggy's face,
   I felt a sad quandary, O.
Though wild as ony Athol deer,
   She has trapan'd me fairly, O;
Her cherry cheeks, an' een sae clear,
   Harass me late an' early, O.
              O! love! love! laddie.
                 Love's like a dizziness!
              It winna let a puir body
                Gang about his business!

To tell my feats this single week
   Wad mak a curious diary, O:
I drave my cart against a dyke,
   My horses in a miry, O:
I wear my stockings white an' blue,
   My love's sae fierce an' fiery, O:
I drill the land that I should plow,
   An' plow the drills entirely, O.——*O! love! &c.*

Soon as the dawn had brought the day,
   I went to theek the stable, O;
I coost my coat, an' ply'd away
   As fast as I was able, O.
I wrought a' morning out an' out
   As I'd been redding fire, O;
When I had done, and look'd about,
   Gude faith, it was the byre, O!—*O! love! &c.*

Her wily glance I'll ne'er forget;
   The dear, the lovely blinkin' o't,
Has pierc'd me through an' through the heart,
   An' plagues me wi' the prinklin' o't.
I try'd to sing, I try'd to pray,
   I try'd to drown't wi' drinkin' o't;
I try'd wi' toil to drive't away,
   But ne'er can sleep for thinkin' o't.—*O! love! &c.*

Were Peggy's love to hire the job,
  An' save my heart frae breakin', O,
I'd put a girdle round the globe,
  Or dive in Corryvrekin, O;
Or howk a grave at midnight dark
  In yonder vault sae eerie, O;
Or gang an' speir for Mungo Park
  Through Africa sae dreary, O.—*O! love! &c.*

Ye little ken what pains I prove!
  Or how severe my plisky, O!
I swear I'm sairer drunk wi' love
  Than e'er I was wi' whisky, O!
For love has rak'd me fore an' aft,
  I scarce can lift a leggy, O:
I first grew dizzy, then gaed daft,
  An' now I'll dee for Peggy, O.—*O! love! &c.*

THE DRINKIN', O;
A SANG FOR THE LADIES

[Fairly brisk]

O wae to the wearifu' drinkin', O! That foe to reflection an' thinkin', O! Our charms are gien in vain! Social conversation's game! For the rattlin' o' guns an' the drinkin', O. 2. O why will you ply at the drinkin', O? Which to weakness will soon lead you linkin', O; These eyes that shine sae bright Soon will be a weary sight, When ye're a' sittin' noddin' an' winkin', O! [Repeat entire tune twice]

8

O WAE to the wearifu' drinkin', O!
That foe to reflection an' thinkin', O!
 Our charms are gi'en in vain!
 Social conversation's gane!
For the rattlin' o' guns an' the drinkin', O.

O why will you ply at the drinkin', O?
Which to weakness will soon lead you linkin', O;
 These eyes that shine sae bright
 Soon will be a weary sight,
When ye're a' sittin' noddin' an' winkin', O!

Forever may we grieve for the drinkin', O!
The respect that is due daily sinkin', O!
 Our presence sair abused,
 An' our company refused,
An' it's a' for the wearifu' drinkin', O!

O drive us not away wi' your drinkin', O!
We like your presence mair than ye're thinkin', O!
 We'll gie ye another sang,
 An' ye're no to think it lang,
For the sake o' your wearifu' drinkin', O!

Sweet delicacy, turn to us blinkin', O!
For by day the guns and swords still are clinkin', O!
 An' at night the flowin' bowl
 Bothers ilka manly soul,
Then there's naething but beblin' an' drinkin', O!

Gentle Peace, come an' wean them frae drinkin', O!
Bring the little footy boy wi' you winkin', O!
 Gar him thraw at ilka man,
 An' wound as deep's he can,
Or we're ruin'd by the wearifu' drinkin', O!

BIRNIEBOUZLE

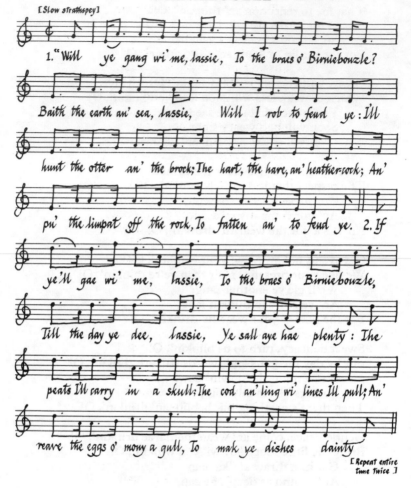

1. "Will ye gang wi' me, lassie, To the braes o' Birniebouzle?

Baith the earth an' sea, lassie, Will I rob to feud ye: I'll

hunt the otter an' the brock; The hart, the hare, an' heather-cock; An'

pu' the limpat off the rock, To fatten an' to feud ye. 2. If

ye'll gae wi' me, lassie, To the braes o' Birniebouzle,

Till the day ye dee, lassie, Ye sall aye hae plenty: The

peats I'll carry in a skull; The cod an' ling wi' lines I'll pull; An'

reave the eggs o' mony a gull, To mak ye dishes dainty

[Repeat entire
tune twice]

"WILL ye gang wi' me, lassie,
  To the braes o' Birniebouzle?
Baith the earth an' sea, lassie,
  Will I rob to fend ye:
I'll hunt the otter an' the brock;
The hart, the hare, an' heather-cock;
An' pu' the limpat off the rock,
  To fatten an' to fend ye.

If ye'll gae wi' me, lassie,
    To the braes o' Birniebouzle,
Till the day ye dee, lassie,
    Ye sall aye hae plenty:
The peats I'll carry in a skull;
The cod an' ling wi' lines I'll pull;
An' reave the eggs o' mony a gull,
    To mak ye dishes dainty.

Sae cheery will ye be, lassie,
    I' the braes o' Birniebouzle;
Donald Gun and me, lassie,
    Ever will attend ye.
Though we hae nouther milk nor meal,
Nor lamb nor mutton, beaf nor veal,
We'll fank the porpy an' the seal,
    An' that's the way to fend ye.

An' ye sal gang sae braw, lassie,
    At the kirk o' Birniebouzle;
Wi' littit brogs an' a', lassie,
    Wow but ye'll be vaunty:
An' ye sal wear, when you are wed,
The kirtle an' the Highland plaid,
An' sleep upon a heather bed,
    Sae cozy an' sae canty."

"If ye will marry me, laddie,
    At the kirk o' Birniebouzle,
My chiefest aim shall be, laddie,
    Ever to content ye:
I'll bait the line an' bear the pail,
An' row the boat an' spread the sail,
An' dadd the clotters wi' a flail,
    To mak our tatoes plenty."

"Then come awa wi' me, lassie,
    To the braes o' Birniebouzle;
An' since ye are sae free, lassie,
    Ye sall ne'er repent ye:
For ye sal hae baith tups an' ewes,
An' gaits an' swine, an' stots an' cows,
An' be the lady o' my house,
    An' that may weel content ye."

11

LIFE IS A WEARY COBBLE O' CARE

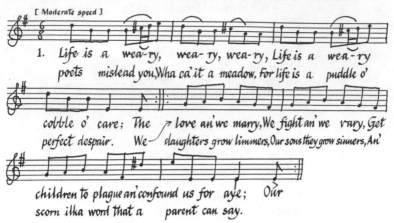

[Moderate speed]

1. Life is a wea-ry, wea-ry, wea-ry, Life is a wea-ry
poets mislead you, Wha ca' it a meadow, For life is a puddle o'

cobble o' care; The love an' we marry, We fight an' we vary, Get
perfect despair. We daughters grow limmers, Our sons they grow sinners, An'

children to plague an' confound us for aye; Our
scorn ilka word that a parent can say.

LIFE is a weary, weary, weary,
Life is a weary cobble o' care;
    The poets mislead you,
    Wha ca' it a meadow,
For life is a puddle o' perfect despair.
    We love an' we marry,
    We fight an' we vary,
Get children to plague an' confound us for aye;
    Our daughters grow limmers,
    Our sons they grow sinners,
An' scorn ilka word that a parent can say.

Man is a steerer, steerer, steerer,
Man is a steerer, life is a pool;
    We wrestle an' fustle,
    For riches we bustle,
Then drap in the grave, an' leave a' to a fool.
    Youth again could I see,
    Women should wilie be,
Ere I were wheedled to sorrow an' pain;
    I should take care o' them,
    Never to marry them;
Hang me if buckled in wedlock again.

THE QUEEN'S WAKE

THE WITCH OF FIFE

"Quhare haif ye been, ye ill womyne,
    These three lang nightis fra hame?
Quhat garris the sweit drap fra yer brow,
    Like clotis of the saut sea faem?

It fearis me muckil ye haif seen
    Quhat good man never knew;
It fearis me muckil ye haif been
    Quhare the gray cock never crew.

But the spell may crack, and the brydel breck,
    Then sherpe yer werde will be;
Ye had better sleipe in yer bed at hame,
    Wi yer deire littil bairnis and me."—

'Sit dune, sit dune, my leile auld man,
    Sit dune, and listin to me;
I'll gar the hayre stand on yer crown,
    And the cauld sweit blind yer e'e.

But tell nae wordis, my gude auld man,
    Tell never word again;
Or deire shall be yer courtisye,
    And driche and sair yer pain.

The first leet-night, quhan the new moon set,
    Quhan all was douffe and mirk,
We saddled ouir naigis wi the moon-fern leif,
    And rode fra Kilmerrin kirk.

Some horses ware of the brume-cow framit,
    And some of the greine bay tree;
But mine was made of ane humloke schaw,
    And a stout stallion was he.

We raide the tod doune on the hill,
    The martin on the law;
And we huntyd the hoolet out of brethe,
    And forcit him doune to fa.'—

"Quhat guid was that, ye ill womyn?
    Quhat guid was that to thee?
Ye wald better haif bein in yer bed at hame,
    Wi yer deire littil bairnis and me."—

And ay we raide, and se merrily we raide,
    Throw the merkist gloffis of the night;
And we swam the floode, and we darnit the woode,
    Till we cam to the Lommond height.

And quhen we cam to the Lommond height,
    Se lythlye we lychtid doune;
And we drank fra the hornis that never grew,
    The beer that was never browin.

Than up there rase ane wee wee man,
    Franethe the moss-gray stane;
His fece was wan like the collifloure,
    For he nouthir had blude nor bane.

He set ane reid-pipe till his muthe,
    And he playit se bonnilye,
Till the grey curlew, and the black-cock, flew
    To listen his melodye.

It rang se sweet through the green Lommond,
    That the nycht-winde lowner blew;
And it soupit alang the Loch Leven,
    And wakinit the white sea-mew.

It rang se sweet through the grein Lommond,
    Se sweitly butt and se shill,
That the wezilis laup out of their mouldy holis,
    And dancit on the mydnycht hill.

The corby craw cam gledgin near,
    The ern gede veeryng bye;
And the troutis laup out of the Leven Louch,
    Charmit with the melodye.

And ay we dancit on the green Lommond,
 Till the dawn on the ocean grew:
Ne wonder I was a weary wycht
 Quhan I cam hame to you."—

"Quhat guid, quhat guid, my weird weird wyfe,
 Quhat guid was that to thee?
Ye wald better haif bein in yer bed at hame,
 Wi yer deire littil bairnis and me."—

'The second nychte, quhan the new moon set,
 O'er the roaryng sea we flew;
The cockle-shell our trusty bark,
 Our sailis of the grein sea-rue.

And the bauld windis blew, and the fire flauchtis flew,
 And the sea ran to the skie;
And the thunner it growlit, and the sea dogs howlit,
 As we gaed scouryng bye.

And ay we mountit the sea green hillis,
 Quhill we brushit thro' the cludis of the hevin;
Than sousit dounright like the stern-shot light,
 Fra the liftis blue casement driven.

But our taickil stood, and our bark was good,
 And se pang was our pearily prowe;
Quhan we culdna speil the brow of the wavis,
 We needilit them throu belowe.

As fast as the hail, as fast as the gale,
 As fast as the midnycht leme,
We borit the breiste of the burstyng swale,
 Or fluffit i' the flotyng faem.

And quhan to the Norraway shore we wan,
 We muntyd our steedis of the wynd,
And we splashit the floode, and we darnit the woode,
 And we left the shouir behynde.

Fleet is the roe on the green Lommond,
 And swift is the couryng grew;
The rein deir dun can eithly run,
 Quhan the houndis and the hornis pursue.

But nowther the roe, nor the rein-deir dun,
    The hinde nor the couryng grew,
Culde fly owr muntaine, muir, and dale,
    As owr braw steedis they flew.

The dales war deep, and the Doffrinis steep,
    And we rase to the skyis ee-bree;
Quhite, quhite was ouir rode, that was never trode,
    Owr the snawis of eternity!

And quhan we cam to the Lapland lone
    The fairies war all in array,
For all the genii of the north
    War keepyng their holeday.

The warlock men and the weerd wemyng,
    And the fays of the wood and the steep,
And the phantom hunteris all war there,
    And the mermaidis of the deep.

And they washit us all with the witch-water,
    Distillit fra the moorland dew,
Quhill our beauty blumit like the Lapland rose,
    That wylde in the foreste grew.'—

"Ye lee, ye lee, ye ill womyne,
    Se loud as I heir ye lee!
For the warst-faurd wyfe on the shoris of Fyfe
    Is cumlye comparet wi thee.'—

'Then the mer-maidis sang and the woodlandis rang,
    Se sweetly swellit the quire;
On every cliff a herpe they hang,
    On every tree a lyre.

And ay they sang, and the woodlandis rang,
    And we drank, and we drank se deep;
Then soft in the armis of the warlock men,
    We laid us dune to sleep.'—

"Away, away, ye ill womyne,
    An ill deide met ye dee!
Quhan ye hae pruvit se false to yer God,
    Ye can never pruve trew to me."—

16

'And there we lernit fra the fairy foke,
    And fra our master true,
The wordis that can beire us throu the air,
    And lokkis and baris undo.

Last nycht we met at Maisry's cot;
    Richt weil the wordis we knew;
And we set a foot on the black cruik-shell,
    And out at the lum we flew.

And we flew owr hill, and we flew owr dale,
    And we flew owr firth and sea,
Until we cam to merry Carlisle,
    Quhar we lightit on the lea.

We gaed to the vault beyound the towir,
    Quhar we enterit free as ayr;
And we drank, and we drank of the bishopis wine
    Quhill we culde drynk ne mair.'—

"Gin that be trew, my gude auld wyfe,
    Whilk thou hast tauld to me,
Betide my death, betide my lyfe,
    I'll beire thee companye.

Neist tyme ye gaung to merry Carlisle
    To drynk of the blude-reid wine,
Beshrew my heart, I'll fly with thee,
    If the diel shulde fly behynde."—

'Ah! littil do ye ken, my silly auld man,
    The daingeris we maun dree;
Last nichte we drank of the bishopis wyne,
    Quhill near near taen war we.

Afore we wan to the sandy ford,
    The gor-cockis nichering flew;
The lofty crest of Ettrick Pen
    Was wavit about with blew,
And, flichtering throu the air, we fand
    The chill chill mornyng dew.

As we flew owr the hillis of Braid,
    The sun rase fair and clear;
There gurly James, and his baronis braw,
    War out to hunt the deere.

Their bowis they drew, their arrowis flew,
  And peircit the ayr with speede,
Quhill purpil fell the mornyng dew
  With witch-blude rank and reide.

 Littil do ye ken, my silly auld man,
  The dangeris we maun dree;
Ne wonder I am a weary wycht
  Quhan I come hame to thee.'—

"But tell me the *word*, my gude auld wyfe,
  Come tell it me speedilye;
For I lang to drink of the gude reide wyne,
  And to wyng the ayr with thee.

Yer hellish horse I wilna ryde,
  Nor sail the seas in the wynd;
But I can flee as well as thee,
  And I'll drynk quhill ye be blynd."—

'O fy! O fy! my leil auld man,
  That word I darena tell;
It wald turn this warld all upside down,
  And make it warse than hell.

For all the lasses in the land
  Wald munt the wynd and fly;
And the men wald doff their doublets syde,
  And after them wald ply.'—

But the auld gudeman was ane cunnyng auld man,
  And ane cunnyng auld man was he;
And he watchit, and he watchit for mony a night,
  The witches' flychte to see.

Ane nychte he darnit in Maisry's cot;
  The fearless haggs came in;
And he heard the word of awsome weird,
  And he saw their deedis of synn.

Then ane by ane, they said that word,
  As fast to the fire they drew;
Then set a foot on the black cruik-shell,
  And out at the lum they flew.

The auld gude-man cam fra his hole
  With feire and muckil dreide,
But yet he culdna think to rue,
  For the wyne came in his head.

He set his foot in the black cruik-shell,
  With ane fixit and ane wawlyng ee;
And he said the word that I darena say,
  And out at the lum flew he.

The witches skalit the moon-beam pale;
  Deep groanit the trembling wynde;
But they never wist till our auld gude-man
  Was hoveryng them behynde.

They flew to the vaultis of merry Carlisle,
  Quhair they enterit free as ayr;
And they drank and they drank of the byshopis wyne
  Quhill they culde drynk ne mair.

The auld gude-man he grew se crouse,
  He dancit on the mouldy ground,
And he sang the bonniest sangis of Fife,
  And he tuzzlit the kerlyngs round.

And ay he percit the tither butt,
  And he suckit, and he suckit se lang,
Quhill his een they closit, and his voice grew low,
  And his tongue wold hardly gang.

The kerlyngs drank of the bishopis wyne
  Quhill they scentit the mornyng wynde;
Then clove again the yielding ayr,
  And left the auld man behynde.

And ay he slepit on the damp damp floor,
  He slepit and he snorit amain;
He never dremit he was far fra hame,
  Or that the auld wyvis war gane.

And ay he slepit on the damp damp floor
  Quhill past the mid-day highte,
Quhan wakenit by five rough Englishmen,
  That trailit him to the lychte.

"Now quha are ye, ye silly auld man,
　　That sleepis se sound and se weil?
Or how gat ye into the bishopis vault
　　Throu lokkis and barris of steel?"—

The auld gude-man he tryit to speak,
　　But ane word he culdna fynde;
He tryit to think, but his head whirlit round,
　　And ane thing he culdna mynde:—
"I cam fra Fyfe," the auld man cryit,
　　"And I cam on the midnycht wynde."

They nickit the auld man, and they prickit the auld man,
　　And they yerkit his limbis with twine,
Quhill the reid blude ran in his hose and shoon,
　　But some cryit it was wyne.

They lickit the auld man, and they prickit the auld man,
　　And they tyit him till ane stone;
And they set ane bele-fire him about,
　　And they burnit him skin and bone.

Now wae be to the puir auld man
　　That ever he saw the day!
And wae be to all the ill wemyng,
　　That lead puir men astray!

Let never ane auld man after this
　　To lawless greide inclyne;
Let never an auld man after this
　　Rin post to the diel for wyne.

REVISED ENDING
TO
THE WITCH OF FIFE

They lickit the auld man, and they prickit the auld man,
　　And they tyit him till ane stone;
And they set ane bele-fire him about,
　　To burn him skin and bone.

"O wae to me!" said the puir auld man,
  "That ever I saw the day!
And wae be to all the ill wemyng
  That lead puir men astray!

"Let nevir ane auld man after this
  To lawless greide inclyne;
Let nevir ane auld man after this
  Rin post to the deil for wyne.":

The reike flew up in the auld manis face,
  And choukit him bitterlye;
And the lowe cam up with ane angry blese,
  And it syngit his auld breek-nee.

He lukit to the land fra whence he came,
  For lukis he culde get ne mae;
And he thochte of his deire littil bairnis at hame,
  And O the auld man was wae!

But they turnit their facis to the sun,
  With gloffe and wonderous glair,
For they saw ane thing beth lairge and dun,
  Comin swaipin down the aire.

That burd it cam fra the landis o' Fife,
  And it cam rycht tymeouslye,
For quha was it but the auld manis wife,
  Just comit his dethe to see.

Scho pat ane reide cap on his heide,
  And the auld gudeman lookit fain,
Then whisperit ane word intil his lug,
  And tovit to the aire again.

The auld gudeman he gae ane bob
  I' the mids o' the burnyng lowe;
And the sheklis that band him to the ring,
  They fell fra his armis like towe.

He drew his breath, and he said the word,
  And he said it with muckle glee,
Then set his fit on the burnyng pile,
  And away to the aire flew he.

Till aince he cleirit the swirlyng reike,
 He lukit beth ferit and sad;
But whan he wan to the lycht blue aire,
 He lauchit as he'd been mad.

His armis war spred, and his heide was hiche,
 And his feite stack out behynde;
And the laibies of the auld manis cote
 War wauffyng in the wynde.

And aye he neicherit, and aye he flew,
 For he thochte the ploy se raire;
It was like the voice of the gainder blue,
 Whan he flees throu the aire.

He lukit back to the Carlisle men
 As he borit the norlan sky;
He noddit his heide, and gae ane girn,
 But he nevir said gude-bye.

They vanisht far i' the liftis blue wale,
 Ne maire the English saw,
But the auld manis lauche cam on the gale,
 With a lang and a loud gaffa.

May everilke man in the land of Fife
 Read what the drinkeris dree;
And nevir curse his puir auld wife,
 Rychte wicked altho scho be.

KILMENY

Bonny Kilmeny gaed up the glen;
But it wasna to meet Duneira's men,
Nor the rosy monk of the isle to see,
For Kilmeny was pure as pure could be.
It was only to hear the yorlin sing,
And pu' the cress-flower round the spring;
The scarlet hypp and the hindberrye,
And the nut that hang frae the hazel tree;

For Kilmeny was pure as pure could be.
But lang may her minny look o'er the wa',
And lang may she seek i' the green-wood shaw;
Lang the laird of Duneira blame,
And lang, lang greet or Kilmeny come hame!

When many a day had come and fled,
When grief grew calm, and hope was dead,
When mess for Kilmeny's soul had been sung,
When the bedes-man had prayed, and the dead-bell rung,
Late, late in a gloamin, when all was still,
When the fringe was red on the westlin hill,
The wood was sere, the moon i' the wane,
The reek o' the cot hung over the plain,
Like a little wee cloud in the world its lane;
When the ingle lowed with an eiry leme,
Late, late in the gloaming Kilmeny came hame!

"Kilmeny, Kilmeny, where have you been?
Lang hae we sought baith holt and den;
By linn, by ford, and green-wood tree,
Yet you are halesome and fair to see.
Where gat you that joup o' the lilly scheen?
That bonny snood of the birk sae green?
And these roses, the fairest that ever were seen?
Kilmeny, Kilmeny, where have you been?"—

Kilmeny looked up with a lovely grace,
But nae smile was seen on Kilmeny's face;
As still was her look, and as still was her ee,
As the stillness that lay on the emerant lea,
Or the mist that sleeps on a waveless sea.
For Kilmeny had been she knew not where,
And Kilmeny had seen what she could not declare;
Kilmeny had been where the cock never crew,
Where the rain never fell, and the wind never blew.
But it seemed as the harp of the sky had rung,
And the airs of heaven played round her tongue,
When she spake of the lovely forms she had seen,
And a land where sin had never been;
A land of love, and a land of light,
Withouten sun, or moon, or night:
Where the river swa'd a living stream,
And the light a pure celestial beam:
The land of vision it would seem,
A still, an everlasting dream.

In yon green-wood there is a waik,
And in that waik there is a wene,
   And in that wene there is a maike,
That neither has flesh, blood, nor bane;
   And down in yon green-wood he walks his lane.

   In that green wene Kilmeny lay,
Her bosom happed wi' the flowerits gay;
But the air was soft and the silence deep,
And bonny Kilmeny fell sound asleep.
She kend nae mair, nor opened her ee,
Till waked by the hymns of a far countrye.

   She 'wakened on couch of the silk sae slim,
All striped wi' the bars of the rainbow's rim;
And lovely beings round were rife,
Who erst had travelled mortal life;
And aye they smiled, and 'gan to speer,
"What spirit has brought this mortal here?"—

   "Lang have I journeyed the world wide,"
A meek and reverend fere replied;
"Baith night and day I have watched the fair,
Eident a thousand years and mair.
Yes, I have watched o'er ilk degree,
Wherever blooms femenitye;
But sinless virgin, free of stain
In mind and body, fand I nane.
Never, since the banquet of time,
Found I virgin in her prime,
Till late this bonny maiden I saw
As spotless as the morning snaw:
Full twenty years she has lived as free
As the spirits that sojourn this countrye.
I have brought her away frae the snares of men,
That sin or death she never may ken."—

   They clasped her waiste and her hands sae fair,
They kissed her cheek, and they kemed her hair,
And round came many a blooming fere,
Saying, "Bonny Kilmeny, ye're welcome here!
Women are freed of the littand scorn:
O, blessed be the day Kilmeny was born!
Now shall the land of the spirits see,
Now shall it ken what a woman may be!
Many a lang year in sorrow and pain,

Many a lang year thro' the world we've gane,
Commissioned to watch fair womankind,
For it's they who nurice th' immortal mind.
We have watched their steps as the dawning shone,
And deep in the green-wood walks alone;
By lilly bower and silken bed,
The viewless tears have o'er them shed;
Have soothed their ardent minds to sleep,
Or left the couch of love to weep.
We have seen! we have seen! but the time must come,
And the angels will weep at the day of doom!

"O, would the fairest of mortal kind
Aye keep the holy truths in mind,
That kindred spirits their motions see,
Who watch their ways with anxious ee,
And grieve for the guilt of humanitye!
O, sweet to heaven the maiden's prayer,
And the sigh that heaves a bosom sae fair!
And dear to heaven the words of truth,
And the praise of virtue frae beauty's mouth!
And dear to the viewless forms of air,
The minds that kyth as the body fair!

"O, bonny Kilmeny! free frae stain,
If ever you seek the world again,
That world of sin, of sorrow, and fear,
O, tell of the joys that are waiting here!
And tell of the signs you shall shortly see;
Of the times that are now, and the times that shall be."—

They lifted Kilmeny, they led her away,
And she walked in the light of a sunless day:
The sky was a dome of crystal bright,
The fountain of vision, and fountain of light:
The emerald fields were of dazzling glow,
And the flowers of everlasting blow.
Then deep in the stream her body they laid,
That her youth and beauty never might fade;
And they smiled on heaven, when they saw her lie
In the stream of life that wandered bye.
And she heard a song, she heard it sung,
She kend not where; but sae sweetly it rung,
It fell on her ear like a dream of the morn:
"O! blest be the day Kilmeny was born!
Now shall the land of the spirits see,

25

Now shall it ken what a woman may be!
The sun that shines on the world sae bright,
A borrowed gleid frae the fountain of light;
And the moon that sleeks the sky sae dun,
Like a gouden bow, or a beamless sun,
Shall wear away, and be seen nae mair,
And the angels shall miss them travelling the air.
But lang, lang after baith night and day,
When the sun and the world have elyed away;
When the sinner has gane to his waesome doom,
Kilmeny shall smile in eternal bloom!"—

They bore her away she wist not how,
For she felt not arm nor rest below;
But so swift they wained her through the light,
'Twas like the motion of sound or sight;
They seemed to split the gales of air,
And yet nor gale nor breeze was there.
Unnumbered groves below them grew,
They came, they past, and backward flew,
Like floods of blossoms gliding on,
In moment seen, in moment gone.
O, never vales to mortal view
Appeared like those o'er which they flew!
That land to human spirits given,
The lowermost vales of the storied heaven;
From thence they can view the world below,
And heaven's blue gates with sapphires glow,
More glory yet unmeet to know.

They bore her far to a mountain green,
To see what mortal never had seen;
And they seated her high on a purple sward,
And bade her heed what she saw and heard,
And note the changes the spirits wrought,
For now she lived in the land of thought.
She looked, and she saw nor sun nor skies,
But a crystal dome of a thousand dies.
She looked, and she saw nae land aright,
But an endless whirl of glory and light.
And radiant beings went and came
Far swifter than wind, or the linked flame.
She hid her een frae the dazzling view;
She looked again and the scene was new.

She saw a sun on a summer sky,
And clouds of amber sailing bye;
A lovely land beneath her lay,
And that land had glens and mountains gray;
And that land had vallies and hoary piles,
And marled seas, and a thousand isles:
Its fields were speckled, its forests green,
And its lakes were all of the dazzling sheen,
Like magic mirrors, where slumbering lay
The sun and the sky and the cloudlet gray;
Which heaved and trembled and gently swung,
On every shore they seemed to be hung;
For there they were seen on their downward plain
A thousand times and a thousand again;
In winding lake and placid firth,
Little peaceful heavens in the bosom of earth.

Kilmeny sighed and seemed to grieve,
For she found her heart to that land did cleave;
She saw the corn wave on the vale,
She saw the deer run down the dale;
She saw the plaid and the broad claymore,
And the brows that the badge of freedom bore;
And she thought she had seen the land before.

She saw a lady sit on a throne,
The fairest that ever the sun shone on!
A lion licked her hand of milk,
And she held him in a leish of silk;
And a liefu' maiden stood at her knee,
With a silver wand and melting ee;
Her sovereign shield till love stole in,
And poisoned all the fount within.

Then a gruff untoward bedeman came,
And hundit the lion on his dame;
And the guardian maid wi' the dauntless ee,
She dropped a tear, and left her knee;
And she saw till the queen frae the lion fled,
Till the bonniest flower of the world lay dead.
A coffin was set on a distant plain,
And she saw the red blood fall like rain:
Then bonny Kilmeny's heart grew sair,
And she turned away, and could look nae mair.

Then the gruff grim carle girned amain,
And they trampled him down, but he rose again;
And he baited the lion to deeds of weir,
Till he lapped the blood to the kingdom dear;
And weening his head was danger-preef,
When crowned with the rose and clover leaf,
He gowled at the carle and chased him away,
To feed wi' the deer on the mountain gray.
He gowled at the carle, and he gecked at heaven,
But his mark was set, and his arles given.
Kilmeny a while her een withdrew;
She looked again, and the scene was new.

She saw below her fair unfurled
One half of all the glowing world,
Where oceans rolled, and rivers ran,
To bound the aims of sinful man.
She saw a people, fierce and fell,
Burst frae their bounds like fiends of hell;
There lillies grew, and the eagle flew,
And she herked on her ravening crew,
Till the cities and towers were wrapt in a blaze,
And the thunder it roared o'er the lands and the seas.
The widows they wailed, and the red blood ran,
And she threatned an end to the race of man:
She never lened, nor stood in awe,
Till claught by the lion's deadly paw.
Oh! then the eagle swinked for life,
And brainzelled up a mortal strife;
But flew she north, or flew she south,
She met wi' the gowl of the lion's mouth.

With a mooted wing and waefu' maen,
The eagle sought her eiry again;
But lang may she cour in her bloody nest,
And lang, lang sleek her wounded breast,
Before she sey another flight,
To play wi' the norland lion's might.

But to sing the sights Kilmeny saw,
So far surpassing nature's law,
The singer's voice wad sink away,
And the string of his harp wad cease to play.
But she saw till the sorrows of man were bye,
And all was love and harmony;

Till the stars of heaven fell calmly away,
Like the flakes of snaw on a winter day.

Then Kilmeny begged again to see
The friends she had left in her own country,
To tell of the place where she had been,
And the glories that lay in the land unseen;
To warn the living maidens fair,
The loved of heaven, the spirits' care,
That all whose minds unmeled remain
Shall bloom in beauty when time is gane.

With distant music, soft and deep,
They lulled Kilmeny sound asleep;
And when she awakened, she lay her lane,
All happed with flowers in the green-wood wene.
When seven lang years had come and fled;
When grief was calm, and hope was dead;
When scarce was remembered Kilmeny's name,
Late, late in a gloamin Kilmeny came hame!

And O, her beauty was fair to see,
But still and stedfast was her ee!
Such beauty bard may never declare,
For there was no pride nor passion there;
And the soft desire of maidens' een
In that mild face could never be seen.
Her seymar was the lilly flower,
And her cheek the moss-rose in the shower;
And her voice like the distant melodye,
That floats along the twilight sea.
But she loved to raike the lanely glen,
And keeped afar frae the haunts of men;
Her holy hymns unheard to sing,
To suck the flowers, and drink the spring.
But wherever her peaceful form appeared,
The wild beasts of the hill were cheered;
The wolf played blythly round the field,
The lordly byson lowed and kneeled;
The dun deer wooed with manner bland,
And cowered aneath her lilly hand.
And when at even the woodlands rung,
When hymns of other worlds she sung,
In extacy of sweet devotion,
O, then the glen was all in motion.
The wild beasts of the forest came,

Broke from their bughts and faulds the tame,
And goved around, charmed and amazed;
Even the dull cattle crooned and gazed,
And murmured and looked with anxious pain
For something the mystery to explain.
The buzzard came with the thristle-cock;
The corby left her houf in the rock;
The blackbird alang wi' the eagle flew;
The hind came tripping o'er the dew;
The wolf and the kid their raike began,
And the tod, and the lamb, and the leveret ran;
The hawk and the hern attour them hung,
And the merl and the mavis forhooyed their young;
And all in a peaceful ring were hurled:
It was like an eve in a sinless world!

When a month and a day had come and gane,
Kilmeny sought the greenwood wene;
There laid her down on the leaves sae green,
And Kilmeny on earth was never mair seen.
But O, the words that fell from her mouth,
Were words of wonder, and words of truth!
But all the land were in fear and dread,
For they kendna whether she was living or dead.
It wasna her hame, and she couldna remain;
She left this world of sorrow and pain,
And returned to the land of thought again.

MIDSUMMER NIGHT DREAMS

A Pupil in the many chambered school
Where Superstition weaves her airy dreams.

Wordsworth.

To the
Right Hon. Lord Byron

Not for thy crabbed state-creed, wayward wight,
Thy noble lineage, nor thy virtues high,
(God bless the mark!) do I this homage plight;
No—'tis thy bold and native energy;
Thy soul that dares each bound to overfly,
Ranging thro' Nature on erratic wing—
These do I honour—and would fondly try
With thee a wild aërial strain to sing:
Then, O! round Shepherd's head thy charmed mantle fling.

THE PILGRIMS OF THE SUN

Part First

OF all the lasses in fair Scotland,
That lightly bound o'er muir and lea,
There's nane like the maids of Yarrowdale,
Wi' their green coats kilted to the knee.

O! there shines mony a winsom face,
And mony a bright and beaming ee;
For rosy health blooms on the cheek,
And the blink of love plays o'er the bree.

But ne'er by Yarrow's sunny braes,
  Nor Ettrick's green and wizzard shaw,
Did ever maid so lovely won
  As Mary Lee of Carelha'.*

O! round her fair and sightly form
  The light hill-breeze was blythe to blow,
For the virgin hue her bosom wore
  Was whiter than the drifted snow.

The dogs that wont to growl and bark,
  Whene'er a stranger they could see,
Would cower, and creep along the sward,
  And lick the hand of Mary Lee.

On form so fair, or face so mild,
  The rising sun did never gleam;
On such a pure untainted mind,
  The dawn of truth did never beam.

She never had felt the stounds of love,
  Nor the waefu' qualms that breed o' sin;
But ah! she shewed an absent look,
  And a deep and thoughtfu' heart within.

She looked with joy on a young man's face,
  The downy chin, and the burning eye,
Without desire, without a blush,
  She loved them, but she knew not why.

She learned to read, when she was young,
  The books of deep divinity;
And she thought by night, and she read by day,
  Of the life that is, and the life to be.

And the more she thought, and the more she read,
  Of the ways of Heaven and Nature's plan,
She feared the half that the bedesmen said
  Was neither true nor plain to man.

Yet she was meek, and bowed to Heaven
  Each morn beneath the shady yew,
Before the laverock left the cloud,
  Or the sun began his draught of dew.

* Now vulgarly called Carterhaugh.

32

And when the gloaming's gouden veil
  Was o'er Blackandro's summit flung,
Among the bowers of green Bowhill
  Her hymn she to the virgin sung.

And aye she thought, and aye she read,
  Till mystic wildness marked her air;
For the doubts that on her bosom preyed
  Were more than maiden's mind could bear.

And she grew weary of this world,
  And yearned and pined the next to see;
Till Heaven in pity earnest sent,
  And from that thraldom set her free.

One eve when she had prayed and wept
  Till daylight faded on the wold—
The third night of the waning moon!
  Well known to hind and matron old!

For then the fairies boun' to ride,
  And the elves of Ettrick's greenwood shaw;
And aye their favourite rendezvous
  Was green Bowhill and Carelha'.

There came a wight to Mary's knee,
  With face, like angel's, mild and sweet;
His robe was like the lilly's bloom,
  And graceful flowed upon his feet.

He did not clasp her in his arms,
  Nor showed he cumbrous courtesy;
But took her gently by the hand,
  Saying, "Maiden, rise and go with me.

"Cast off, cast off these earthly weeds,
  They ill befit thy destiny;
I come from a far distant land
  To take thee where thou long'st to be."

She only felt a shivering throb,
  A pang defined that may not be;
And up she rose, a naked form,
  More lightsome, pure, and fair than he.

He held a robe in his right hand,
    Pure as the white rose in the bloom;
That robe was not of earthly make,
    Nor sewed by hand, nor wove in loom.

When she had donned that light seymar,
    Upward her being seemed to bound;
Like one that wades in waters deep,
    And scarce can keep him to the ground.

Tho' rapt and transient was the pause,
    She scarce could keep to ground the while;
She felt like heaving thistle down,
    Hung to the earth by viewless pile.

The beauteous stranger turned his face
    Unto the eastern streamers sheen,
He seemed to eye the ruby star
    That rose above the Eildon green.

He spread his right hand to the heaven,
    And he bade the maid not look behind,
But keep her face to the dark blue even;
    And away they bore upon the wind.

She did not linger, she did not look,
    For in a moment they were gone;
But she thought she saw her very form
    Stretched on the greenwood's lap alone.

As ever you saw the meteor speed,
    Or the arrow cleave the yielding wind,
Away they sprung, and the breezes sung,
    And they left the gloaming star behind,

And eastward, eastward still they bore,
    Along the night's grey canopy;
And the din of the world died away,
    And the landscape faded on the ee.

They had marked the dark blue waters lie
    Like curved lines on many a vale;
And they hung on the shelve of a saffron cloud,
    That scarcely moved in the slumbering gale.

They turned their eyes to the heaven above,
  And the stars blazed bright as they drew nigh;
And they looked to the darksome world below,
  But all was grey obscurity.

They could not trace the hill nor dale,
  Nor could they ken where the greenwood lay;
But they saw a thousand shadowy stars,
  In many a winding watery way;
And they better knew where the rivers ran
  Than if it had been the open day.

They looked to the western shores afar,
  But the light of day they could not see;
And the halo of the evening star
  Sank like a crescent on the sea.

Then onward, onward fast they bore
  On the yielding winds so light and boon,
To meet the climes that bred the day,
  And gave the glow to the gilded moon.

Long had she chambered in the deep,
  To spite the maidens of the main,
But now frae the merman's couch she sprung,
  And blushed upon her still domain.

When first from out the sea she peeped,
  She kythed like maiden's gouden kemb,
And the sleepy waves washed o'er her brow,
  And belled her cheek wi' the briny faem.

But the yellow leme spread up the lift,
  And the stars grew dim before her e'e,
And up arose the Queen of Night
  In all her solemn majesty.

O! Mary's heart was blythe to lie
  Above the ocean wastes reclined,
Beside her lovely guide so high,
  On the downy bosom of the wind.

She saw the shades and gleams so bright
  Play o'er the deep incessantly,
Like streamers of the norland way,
  The lights that danced on the quaking sea.

She saw the wraith of the waning moon,
  Trembling and pale it seemed to lie;
It was not round like golden shield,
  Nor like her moulded orb on high.

Her image cradled on the wave,
  Scarce bore similitude the while;
It was a line of silver light,
  Stretched on the deep for many a mile.

The lovely youth beheld with joy
  That Mary loved such scenes to view;
And away, and away they journeyed on,
  Faster than wild bird ever flew.

Before the tide, before the wind,
  The ship speeds swiftly o'er the faem;
And the sailor sees the shores fly back,
  And weens his station still the same.

Beyond that speed ten thousand times,
  By the marled streak and the cloudlet brown,
Past our aerial travellers on
  In the wan light of the waning moon.

They keeped aloof as they passed her bye,
  For their views of the world were not yet done;
But they saw her mighty mountain form
  Like Cheviot in the setting sun.

And the stars and the moon fled west away,
  So swift o'er the vaulted sky they shone;
They seemed like fiery rainbows reared,
  In a moment seen, in a moment gone.

Yet Mary Lee as easy felt
  As if on silken couch she lay;
And soon on a rosy film they hung,
  Above the beams of the breaking day.

And they saw the chambers of the sun,
  And the angels of the dawning ray,
Draw the red curtains from the dome,
  The glorious dome of the God of Day.

And the youth a slight obeisance made,
  And seemed to bend upon his knee:
The holy vow he whispering said
  Sunk deep in the heart of Mary Lee.
I may not say the prayer he prayed,
  Nor of its wondrous tendency;
But it proved that the half the bedesmen said
  Was neither true nor ever could be.

Sweet breaks the day o'er Harlaw cairn,
  On many an ancient peel and barrow,
On braken hill, and lonely tarn,
  Along the greenwood glen of Yarrow.

Oft there had Mary viewed with joy
  The rosy streaks of light unfurled:
O! think how glowed the virgin's breast
  Hung o'er the profile of the world.

On battlement of storied cloud
  That floated o'er the dawn serene,
To pace along with angel tread,
  And on the rainbow's arch to lean.

Her cheek lay on its rosy rim,
  Her bosom pressed the yielding blue,
And her fair robes of heavenly make
  Were sweetly tinged with every hue.

And there they lay, and there beheld
  The glories of the opening morn
Spread o'er the eastern world afar,
  Where winter wreath was never borne.

And they saw the blossom-loaded trees,
  And gardens of perennial blow,
Spread their fair bosoms to the day,
  In dappled pride, and endless glow.

These came and passed, for the earth rolled on,
  But still on the brows of the air they hung;
The scenes of glory they now beheld
  May scarce by mortal bard be sung.

It was not the hues of the marbled sky,
  Nor the gorgeous kingdoms of the East,
Nor the thousand blooming isles that lie
  Like specks on the mighty ocean's breast:

It was the dwelling of that God
  Who ope'd the welling springs of time;
Seraph and cherubim's abode;
  The Eternal's throne of light sublime.

The virgin saw her radiant guide
  On nature look with kindred eye;
But whenever he turned him to the sun,
  He bowed with deep solemnity.

And ah! she deemed him heathen born,
  Far from her own nativity,
In lands beneath the southern star,
  Beyond the sun, beyond the sea.

And aye she watched with wistful eye,
  But durst not question put the while;
He marked her mute anxiety,
  And o'er his features beamed the smile.

He took her slender hand in his,
  And swift as fleets the stayless mind,
They scaled the glowing fields of day,
  And left the elements behind.

When past the firmament of air,
  Where no attractive influence came;
There was no up, there was no down,
  But all was space, and all the same.

The first green world that they passed bye
  Had 'habitants of mortal mould;
For they saw the rich men, and the poor,
  And they saw the young, and they saw the old.

But the next green world the twain past bye
  They seemed of some superior frame;
For all were in the bloom of youth,
  And all their radiant robes the same.

And Mary saw the groves and trees,
    And she saw the blossoms thereupon;
But she saw no grave in all the land,
    Nor church, nor yet a church-yard stone.

That pleasant land is lost in light,
    To every searching mortal eye;
So nigh the sun its orbit sails,
    That on his breast it seems to lie.

And, though its light be dazzling bright,
    The warmth was gentle, mild, and bland,
Such as on summer days may be,
    Far up the hills of Scottish land.

And Mary Lee longed much to stay
    In that blest land of love and truth,
So nigh the fount of life and day;
    That land of beauty, and of youth.

"O maiden of the wistful mind,
    Here it behoves not to remain;
But Mary, yet the time will come
    When thou shalt see this land again.

"Thou art a visitant beloved
    Of God, and every holy one;
And thou shalt travel on with me,
    Around the spheres, around the sun,
To see what maid hath never seen,
    And do what maid hath never done."

Thus spoke her fair and comely guide,
    And took as erst her lily hand;
And soon in holy ecstacy,
    On mountains of the sun they stand.

Here I must leave the beauteous twain,
    Casting their raptured eyes abroad,
Around the vallies of the sun,
    And all the universe of God.

And I will bear my hill-harp hence,
    And hang it on its ancient tree;
For its wild warblings ill become
    The scenes that ope'd to Mary Lee.

Thou holy harp of Judah's land,
    That hung the willow boughs upon,
O leave the bowers on Jordan's strand,
    And cedar groves of Lebanon:

That I may sound thy sacred string,
    Those chords of mystery sublime,
That chimed the songs of Israel's King,
    Songs that shall triumph over time.

Pour forth the trancing notes again,
    That wont of yore the soul to thrill,
In tabernacles of the plain,
    Or heights of Zion's holy hill.

O come, etherial timbrel meet,
    In Shepherd's hand thou dost delight;
On Kedar hills thy strain was sweet,
    And sweet on Bethle'm's plain by night.

And when thy tones the land shall hear,
    And every heart conjoins with thee,
The mountain lyre that lingers near
    Will lend a wandering melody.

Part Second

HARP of Jerusalem! how shall my hand
Awake thy Halelujahs!—How begin
The song that tells of light ineffable,
And of the dwellers there! The fountain pure,
And source of all—Where bright Archangels dwell,
And where, in unapproached pavilion, framed
Of twelve deep veils, and every veil composed
Of thousand thousand lustres, sits enthroned
The God of Nature!—O thou harp of Salem,
Where shall my strain begin!

    Soft let it be,
And simple as its own primeval airs;

And, Minstrel, when on angel wing thou soar'st,
Then will the harp of David rise with thee.

In that fair heaven the mortal virgin stood,
Beside her lovely guide, Cela his name.
Yes deem it heaven, for not the ample sky,
As seen from earth, could slight proportion bear
To those bright regions of eternal day,
Once they are gained.—So sweet the breeze of life
Breathed through the groves of amarynth—So sweet
The very touch of that celestial land.
Soon as the virgin trode thereon, she felt
Unspeakable delight—Sensations new
Thrilled her whole frame—As one, who his life long
Hath in a dark and chilly dungeon pined,
Feels when restored to freedom and the sun.

Upon a mount they stood of wreathy light
Which cloud had never rested on, nor hues
Of night had ever shaded—Thence they saw
The motioned universe, that wheeled around
In fair confusion—Raised as they were now
To the high fountain head of light and vision,
Where'er they cast their eyes abroad, they found
The light behind, the object still before;
And on the rarified and pristine rays
Of vision borne, their piercing sight passed on
Intense and all unbounded—Onward!—onward!
No cloud to intervene! no haze to dim!
Or nigh, or distant, it was all the same;
For distance lessened not.—O what a scene,
To see so many goodly worlds upborne!
Around!—around!—all turning their green bosoms
And glittering waters to that orb of life
On which our travellers stood, and all by that
Sustained and gladdened! By that orb sustained!
No—by the mighty everlasting one
Who in that orb resides, and round whose throne
Our journeyers now were hovering. But they kept
Aloof upon the skirts of heaven; for, strange
Though it appears, there was no heaven beside.
They saw all nature—All that was they saw;
But neither moon, nor stars, nor firmament,
Nor clefted gallaxy, was any more.
Worlds beyond worlds, with intermundane voids,
That closed and opened as those worlds rolled on,

Were all that claimed existence: Each of these,
From one particular point of the sun's orb,
Seemed pendent by some ray or viewless cord,
On which it twirled and swung with endless motion.

O! never did created being feel
Such rapt astonishment, as did this maid
Of earthly lineage, when she saw the plan
Of GOD's fair universe!—Himself enthroned
In light she dared not yet approach!—From whence
He viewed the whole, and with a father's care
Upheld and cherished.—Wonder seemed it none
That Godhead should discern each thing minute
That moved on his creation, when the eyes
Which he himself had made could thus perceive
All these broad orbs turn their omniferous breasts,
And sun them in their maker's influence.
O! it was sweet to see their ample vales
Their yellow mountains, and their winding streams,
All basking in the beams of light and life!

Each one of all these worlds seemed the abode
Of intellectual beings; but their forms,
Their beauty, and their natures, varied all.
And in these worlds there were broad oceans rolled,
And branching seas.—Some wore the hues of gold,
And some of emerald or of burnished glass.
And there were seas that keel had never plowed,
Nor had the shadow of a veering sail
Scared their inhabitants—for slumbering shades
And spirits brooded on them.

"Cela speak,"
Said the delighted but inquiring maid,
"And tell me which of all these worlds I see
Is that we lately left? For I would fain
Note how far more extensive 'tis and fair
Than all the rest—little, alas! I know
Of it, save that it is a right fair globe,
Diversified and huge, and that afar,
In one sweet corner of it lies a spot
I dearly love—where Tweed from distant moors
Far travelled flows in murmuring majesty;
And Yarrow rushing from her bosky banks,
Hurries with headlong haste to the embrace
Of her more stately sister of the hills.

42

Ah! yonder 'tis!—Now I perceive it well,"
Said she with ardent voice, bending her eye
And stretching forth her arm to a broad globe
That basked in the light—"Yonder it is!
I know the Caledonian mountains well,
And mark the moony braes and curved heights
Above the lone St Mary.—Cela, speak;
Is not that globe the world where I was born;
And yon the land of my nativity?"
She turned around her beauteous earnest face,
With asking glance, but soon that glance withdrew,
And silent looked abroad on glowing worlds;
For she beheld a smile on Cela's face,
A smile that might an angel's face become,
When listening to the boasted, pigmy skill,
Of high presuming man.—She looked abroad,
But nought distinctly marked—nor durst her eye
Again meet his, although that way her face
So near was turned, one glance might have read more;
But yet that glance was staid. Pleased to behold
Her virgin modesty, and simple grace,
His hand upon her flexile shoulder pressed,
In kind and friendly guise, he thus began:

"My lovely ward, think not I deem your quest
Impertinent or trivial—well aware
Of all the longings of humanity
Toward the first, haply the only scenes
Of nature e'er beheld or understood;
Where the immortal and unquenched mind
First op'ed its treasures; and the longing soul
Breathed its first yearnings of eternal hope.
I know it all; nor do I deem it strange,
In such a wilderness of moving spheres,
Thou shouldst mistake the world that gave thee birth.
Prepare to wonder, and prepare to grieve:
For I perceive that thou hast deemed the earth
The fairest, and the most material part
Of God's creation. Mark yon cloudy spot,
Which yet thine eye hath never rested on;
And tho' not long the viewless golden cord
That chains it to this heaven, ycleped the sun,
It seems a thing subordinate—a sphere
Unseemly and forbidding—'Tis the earth.
What think'st thou now of thy Almighty maker,
And of this goodly universe of his?"

Down sunk the virgin's eye—her heart seemed warped
Deep deep in meditation—while her face
Denoted mingled sadness.—'Twas a thought
She trembled to express. At length with blush,
And faltering tongue, she mildly thus replied:

"I see all these fair worlds inhabited
By beings of intelligence and mind.
O! Cela, tell me this—Have they all fallen,
And sinned like us? And has a living God
Bled in each one of all these peopled worlds?
Or only on yon dank and dismal spot
Hath one Redeemer suffered for them all?"

"Hold, hold;—No more!—Thou talkest thou know'st not
  what,"
Said her conductor with a fervent mien;
"More thou shalt know hereafter.—But meanwhile
This truth conceive, that God must ever deal
With men as men—Those things by him decreed,
Or compassed by permission, ever tend
To draw his creatures, whom he loves, to goodness;
For he is all benevolence, and knows
That in the paths of virtue and of love
Alone, can final happiness be found.
More thou shalt know hereafter.—Pass we on
Around this glorious heaven, till by degrees
Thy frame and vision are so subtilised
As that thou may'st the inner regions near
Where dwell the holy angels—where the saints
Of God meet in assembly—seraphs sing,
And thousand harps, in unison complete,
With one vibration sound Jehovah's name."

Far far away, thro' regions of delight
They journeyed on—not like the earthly pilgrim,
Fainting with hunger, thirst, and burning feet,
But, leaning forward on the liquid air,
Like twin-born eagles, skimmed the fields of light,
Circling the pales of heaven. In joyous mood,
Sometimes thro' groves of shady depth they strayed,
Arm linked in arm, as lovers walk the earth;
Or rested in the bowers where roses hung,
And flow'rets holding everlasting sweetness.
And they would light upon celestial hills
Of beauteous softened green, and converse hold

With beings like themselves in form and mind;
Then, rising lightly from the velvet breast
Of the green mountain, down upon the vales
They swooped amain by lawns and streams of life;
Then over mighty hills an arch they threw
Formed like the rainbow.—Never since the time
That God outspread the glowing fields of heaven
Were two such travellers seen!—In all that way
They saw new visitants hourly arrive
From other worlds, in that auspicious land
To live for ever.—These had sojourned far
From world to world more pure—till by degrees
After a thousand years progression, they
Stepped on the confines of that land of life,
Of bliss unspeakable and evermore.

Yet, after such probation of approach,
So exquisite the feelings of delight
Those heavenly regions yielded, 'twas beyond
Their power of sufferance.—Overcome with bliss,
They saw them wandering in amazement on,
With eyes that took no image on their spheres,
Misted in light and glory, or laid down,
Stretched on the sward of heaven in ecstacy.

Yet still their half-formed words, and breathings, were
Of one that loved them, and had brought them home
With him in full felicity to dwell.

To sing of all the scenes our travellers saw
An angel's harp were meet, which mortal hand
Must not assay.—These scenes must be concealed
From mortal fancy, and from mortal eye,
Until our weary pilgrimage is done.

They kept the outer heaven, for it behoved
Them so to do; and in that course beheld
Immeasurable vales, all colonized
From worlds subjacent.—Passing inward still
Toward the centre of the heavens, they saw
The dwellings of the saints of ancient days
And martyrs for the right—men of all creeds,
Features, and hues! Much did the virgin muse,
And much reflect on this strange mystery,
So ill conform to all she had been taught
From infancy to think, by holy men;

Till looking round upon the spacious globes
Dependent on that heaven of light—and all
Rejoicing in their God's beneficence,
These words spontaneously burst from her lips:
"Child that I was, ah! could my stinted mind
Harbour the thought, that the Almighty's love,
Life, and salvation, could to single sect
Of creatures be confined, all his alike!"

　　Last of them all, in ample circle spread
Around the palaces of heaven, they past
The habitations of these radiant tribes
That never in the walks of mortal life
Had sojourned, or with human passions toiled.
Pure were they framed; and round the skirts of heaven
At first were placed, till other dwellers came
From other spheres, by human beings nursed.
Then inward those withdrew, more meet to dwell
In beatific regions. These again
Followed by more, in order regular,
Neared to perfection. It was most apparent
Thro' all created nature, that each being,
From the archangel to the meanest soul
Cherished by savage, caverned in the snow,
Or panting on the brown and sultry desert,
That all were in progression—moving on
Still to perfection. In conformity
The human soul is modelled—hoping still
In something onward! Something far beyond,
It fain would grasp!—Nor shall that hope be lost!
The soul shall hold it—she shall hope, and yearn,
And grasp, and gain, for times and ages, more
Than thought can fathom, or proud science climb!

　　At length they reached a vale of wonderous form
And dread dimensions, where the tribes of heaven
Assembly held, each in its proper sphere
And order placed. That vale extended far
Across the heavenly regions, and its form
A tall gazoon, or level pyramid.
Along its borders palaces were ranged,
All fronted with the thrones of beauteous seraphs,
Who sat with eyes turned to the inmost point
Leaning upon their harps; and all those thrones
Were framed of burning chrystal, where appeared
In mingled gleam millions of dazzling hues!

46

Still, as the valley narrowed to a close,
These thrones increased in grandeur and in glory,
On either side, until the inmost two
Rose so sublimely high, that every arch
Was ample as the compass of that bow
That, on dark cloud, bridges the vales of earth.

The columns seemed ingrained with gold, and branched
With many lustres, whose each single lamp
Shone like the sun as from the earth beheld;
And each particular column, placed upon
A northern hill, would cap the polar wain.
There sat half shrouded in incessant light
The great Archangels, nighest to the throne
Of the Almighty—for—O dreadful view!
Betwixt these two, closing the lengthened files,
Stood the pavilion of the eternal God!
Himself unseen, in tenfold splendours veiled,
The least unspeakable, so passing bright,
That even the eyes of angels turned thereon
Grow dim, and round them transient darkness swims.

Within the verge of that extended region
Our travellers stood. Farther they could not press,
For round the light and glory threw a pale,
Repellent, but to them invisible;
Yet myriads were within of purer frame.

Ten thousand thousand messengers arrived
From distant worlds, the missioners of heaven,
Sent forth to countervail malignant sprites
That roam existence. These gave their report,
Not at the throne, but at the utmost seats
Of these long files of throned seraphims,
By whom the word was passed. Then fast away
Flew the commissioned spirits, to renew
Their watch and guardship in far distant lands.
They saw them, in directions opposite,
To every point of heaven glide away
Like flying stars; or, far adown the steep,
Gleam like small lines of light.

                              Now was the word
Given out, from whence they knew not, that all tongues,
Kindreds, and tribes, should join, with one accord,
In hymn of adoration and acclaim,

To him that sat upon the throne of heaven,
Who framed, saved, and redeemed them to himself!

Then all the countless hosts obeisance made,
And, with their faces turned unto the throne,
Stood up erect, while all their coronals
From off their heads, were reverendly upborne.
Our earth-born visitant quaked every limb.
The angels touched their harps with gentle hand
As prelude to begin—then, all at once,
With full o'erwhelming swell the strain arose;
And pealing high rolled o'er the throned lists
And tuneful files, as if the sun itself
Welled forth the high and holy symphony!
All heaven beside was mute—the streams stood still
And did not murmur—the light wandering winds
Withheld their motion in the midst of heaven,
Nor stirred the leaf, but hung in breathless trance
Where first the sounds assailed them!—Even the windows
Of God's pavilion seemed to open wide
And drink the harmony!

                          Few were the strains
The virgin pilgrim heard, for they o'erpowered
Her every sense; and down she sunk entranced
By too supreme delight, and all to her
Was lost—She saw nor heard not!—It was gone!

Long did she lie beside a cooling spring
In her associate's arms, before she showed
Motion or life—and when she first awoke
In was in dreaming melody—low strains
Half sung half uttered hung upon her breath.

"O! is it past?" said she; "Shall I not hear
That song of heaven again?—Then all beside
Of being is unworthy—Take me back,
Where I may hear that lay of glory flow,
And die away in it.—My soul shall mix
With its harmonious numbers, and dissolve
In fading cadence at the gates of light."

Back near the borders of that sacred vale
Cautious they journeyed; and at distance heard
The closing anthem of that great assembly
Of saints and angels.—First the harps awoke

48

A murmuring tremulous melody, that rose
Now high—now seemed to roll in waves away.
And aye between this choral hymn was sung,
"O! holy! holy! holy! just, and true,
Art thou, Lord God Almighty! thou art he
Who was, and is, and evermore shall be!"
Then every harp, and every voice, at once
Resounded *Haleluiah!* so sublime,
That all the mountains of the northern heaven,
And they are many, sounded back the strain.

O! when the voices and the lyres were strained
To the rapt height, the full delirious swell,
Then did the pure elastic mounds of heaven
Quiver and stream with flickering radiance,
Like gossamers along the morning dew.
Still paused the choir, till the last echo crept
Into the distant hill—O it was sweet!
Beyond definement sweet! and never more
May ear of mortal list such heavenly strains,
While linked to erring frail humanity.

After much holy converse with the saints
And dwellers of the heaven, of that concerned
The ways of God with man, and wonderous truths
But half revealed to him, our sojourners
In holy awe withdrew. And now, no more
By circular and cautious route they moved,
But straight across the regions of the blest,
And storied vales of heaven, did they advance,
On rapt ecstatic wing; and oft assayed
The seraph's holy hymn. As they past bye,
The angels paused; and saints, that lay reposed
In bowers of paradise, upraised their heads
To list the passing music; for it went
Swift as the wild-bee's note, that on the wing
Bombs like unbodied voice along the gale.

At length upon the brink of heaven they stood;
There lingering, forward on the air they leaned
With hearts elate, to take one parting look
Of nature from its source, and converse hold
Of all its wonders. Not upon the sun,
But on the halo of bright golden air
That fringes it they leaned, and talked so long,
That from contiguous worlds they were beheld

And wondered at as beams of living light.

There all the motions of the ambient spheres
Were well observed, explained, and understood.
All save the mould of that mysterious chain
Which bound them to the sun—that God himself,
And he alone could comprehend or wield.

While thus they stood or lay (for to the eyes
Of all, their posture seemed these two between,
Bent forward on the wind, in graceful guise,
On which they seemed to press, for their fair robes
Were streaming far behind them) there passed bye
A most erratick wandering globe, that seemed
To run with troubled aimless fury on.
The virgin, wondering, inquired the cause
And nature of that roaming meteor world.

When Cela thus.—"I can remember well
When yon was such a world as that you left;
A nursery of intellect, for those
Where matter lives not.—Like these other worlds,
It wheeled upon its axle, and it swung
With wide and rapid motion. But the time
That God ordained for its existence run.
Its uses in that beautiful creation,
Where nought subsists in vain, remained no more!
The saints and angels knew of it, and came
In radiant files, with awful reverence,
Unto the verge of heaven where we now stand,
To see the downfall of a sentenced world.
Think of the impetus that urges on
These ponderous spheres, and judge of the event.
Just in the middle of its swift career,
Th' Almighty snapt the golden cord in twain
That hung it to the heaven—Creation sobbed!
And a spontaneous shriek rang on the hills
Of these celestial regions. Down amain
Into the void the outcast world descended,
Wheeling and thundering on! Its troubled seas
Were churned into a spray, and, whizzing, flurred
Around it like a dew.—The mountain tops,
And ponderous rocks, were off impetuous flung,
And clattered down the steeps of night for ever.

50

"Away into the sunless starless void
Rushed the abandoned world; and thro' its caves,
And rifted channels, airs of chaos sung.
The realms of night were troubled—for the stillness
Which there from all eternity had reigned
Was rudely discomposed; and moaning sounds,
Mixed with a whistling howl, were heard afar
By darkling spirits!—Still with stayless force,
For years and ages, down the wastes of night
Rolled the impetuous mass!—of all its seas
And superfices disencumbered
It boomed along, till by the gathering speed,
Its furnaced mines and hills of walled sulphur
Were blown into a flame—When meteor-like,
Bursting away upon an arching track,
Wide as the universe, again it scaled
The dusky regions.—Long the heavenly hosts
Had deemed the globe extinct—nor thought of it,
Save as an instance of Almighty power:
Judge of their wonder and astonishment,
When far as heavenly eyes can see, they saw
In yon blue void, that hideous world appear!
Showering thin flame, and shining vapour forth
O'er half the breadth of heaven!—The angels paused!
And all the nations trembled at the view.

"But great is he who rules them!—He can turn
And lead it all unhurtful thro' the spheres,
Signal of pestilence, or wasting sword,
That ravage and deface humanity.

"The time will come, when, in likewise, the earth
Shall be cut off from God's fair universe;
Its end fulfilled.—But when that time shall be,
From man, from saint, and angel is concealed."

Here ceased the converse.—To a tale like this
What converse could succeed?—They turned around,
And kneeling on the brow of heaven, there paid
Due adoration to that holy one,
Who framed and rules the elements of nature.
Then like two swans that far on wing hath scaled
The Alpine heights to gain their native lake,
At length, perceiving far below their eye
The beauteous silvery speck—they slack their wings,
And softly sink adown the incumbent air:

51

So sunk our lovely pilgrims, from the verge
Of the fair heaven, down the streamered sky;
Far other scenes, and other worlds to view.

Part Third

IMPERIAL England, of the ocean born,
Who from the isles beyond the dawn of morn,
To where waste oceans wash Peruvia's shore,
Hast from all nations drawn thy boasted lore.
Helm of the world, whom seas and isles obey,
Tho' high thy honours, and though far thy sway,
Thy harp I crave, unfearful of thy frown;
Well may'st thou lend what erst was not thine own.

   Come thou old bass—I loved thy lordly swell,
With Dryden's twang, and Pope's malicious knell;
But now, so sore thy brazen chords are worn,
By peer, by pastor, and by bard forlorn;
By every grub that harps for venal ore,
And crabbe that grovels on the sandy shore:
I wot not if thy maker's aim has been
A harp, a fiddle, or a tambourine.

   Come, leave these lanes and sinks beside the sea;
Come to the silent moorland dale with me;
And thou shalt pour, along the mountain hoar,
A strain its echoes never waked before;
Thou shalt be strung where green-wood never grew,
Swept by the winds, and mellowed by the dew.

   Sing of the globes our travellers viewed, that lie
Around the Sun, enveloped in the sky;
Thy music slightly must the veil withdraw,
From lands they visited, and scenes they saw;
From lands, where love and goodness ever dwell;
Where famine, blight, or mildew never fell;
Where face of man is ne'er o'erspread with gloom,
And woman smiles for ever in her bloom:
And thou must sing of wicked worlds beneath,
Where flit the visions, and the hues of death.

   The first they saw, though different far the scene,
Compared with that where they had lately been,
To all its dwellers yielded full delight;

Long was the day, and long and still the night;
The groves were dark and deep, the waters still;
The raving streamlets murmured from the hill:
It was the land where faithful lovers dwell,
Beyond the grave's unseemly sentinel;
Where, free of jealousy, their mortal bane,
And all the ills of sickness and of pain,
In love's delights they bask without alloy;
The night their transport, and the day their joy.
The broadened sun, in chamber and alcove,
Shines daily on their morning couch of love;
And in the evening grove, while linnets sing,
And silent bats wheel round on flittering wing,
Still in the dear embrace their souls are lingering.

"O! tell me, Cela," said the earthly maid,
"Must all these beauteous dames like woman fade?
In our imperfect world, it is believed
That those who most have loved the most have grieved;
That love can every power of earth controul,
Can conquer kings, and chain the hero's soul;
While all the woes and pains that women prove,
Have each their poignance and their source from love;
What law of nature has reversed the doom,
If these may always love, and always bloom?"

"Look round thee, maid beloved, and thou shalt see,
As journeying o'er this happy world with me,
That no decrepitude nor age is here;
No autumn comes the human bloom to sere;
For these have lived in worlds of mortal breath,
And all have passed the dreary bourn of death:
Can'st thou not mark their purity of frame,
Though still their forms and features are the same?"

Replied the maid: "No difference I can scan,
Save in the fair meridian port of man,
And woman fresh as roses newly sprung:
If these have died, they all have died when young."

"Thou art as artless as thy heart is good;
This in thy world is not yet understood;
But wheresoe'er we wander to and fro,
In heaven above, or in the deep below,
What thou misconstruest I shall well explain,

Be it in angel's walk, or mortal reign,
In sun, moon, stars, in mountain, or in main.

"Know then, that every globe which thou hast seen,
Varied with vallies, seas, and forests green,
Are all conformed, in subtilty of clime,
To beings sprung from out the womb of time;
And all the living groups, where'er they be,
In worlds which thou hast seen, or thou may'st see,
Wherever sets the eve and dawns the morn,
Are all of mankind—all of woman born.
The globes, from heaven, which most at distance lie,
Are nurseries of life to these so nigh,
In those, the minds for evermore to be,
Must dawn and rise with smiling infancy.

"Thus 'tis ordained—these grosser regions yield
Souls, thick as blossoms of the vernal field,
Which after death, in relative degree,
Fairer, or darker, as their minds may be,
To other worlds are led, to learn and strive,
Till to perfection all at last arrive.
This once conceived, the ways of God are plain,
But thy unyielding race in errors will remain.

"These beauteous dames, who glow with love unstained,
Like thee were virgins, but not so remained.
Not to thy sex this sere behest is given;
They are the garden of the God of heaven;
Of beauties numberless and woes the heir;
The tree was reared immortal fruit to bear;
And she, all selfish chusing to remain,
Nor share of love the pleasures and the pain,
Was made and cherished by her God in vain;
She sinks into the dust a nameless thing,
No son the requiem o'er her grave to sing.
While she who gives to human beings birth,
Immortal here, is living still on earth;
She in her offspring lives, to fade and bloom,
Flourish and spread thro' ages long to come.

"Now mark me, maiden—why that wistful look?
Though woman must those pains and passions brook,
Beloved of God, and fairest of his plan,
Note how she smiles, superior still to man;
As well it her behoves; for was not he

54

Lulled on her breast, and nursed upon her knee:
Her foibles and her failings may be rife,
While toiling thro' the snares and ills of life,
But he who framed her nature, knows her pains,
Her heart dependent, and tumultuous veins,
And many faults the world heap on her head,
Will never there be harshly visited.
Proud haughty man, the nursling of her care,
Must more than half her crimes and errors bear;
If flow'rets droop and fade before their day;
If others sink neglected in the clay;
If trees, too rankly earthed, too rathly blow,
And others neither fruit nor blossom know,
Let human reason equal judgment frame,
Is it the flower, the tree, or gardener's blame?

Thou see'st them lovely—so they will remain;
For when the soul and body meet again,
No 'vantage will be held, of age, or time,
United at their fairest fullest prime.
The form when purest, and the soul most sage,
Beauty with wisdom shall have heritage,
The form of comely youth, th' experience of age.

"When to thy kindred thou shalt this relate,
Of man's immortal and progressive state,
No credit thou wilt gain, for they are blind,
And would, presumptuous, the Eternal bind,
Either perpetual blessings to bestow,
Or plunge the souls he framed in endless woe.

"This is the land of lovers, known afar,
And named the Evening and the Morning star;
Oft, with rapt eye, thou hast its rising seen,
Above the holy spires of old Lindeen;
And marked its tiny beam diffuse a hue
That tinged the paleness of the morning blue;
Ah! did'st thou deem it was a land so fair?
Or that such peaceful 'habitants were there?

"See'st thou yon gloomy sphere, thro' vapours dun,
That wades in crimson like the sultry sun?
There let us bend our course, and mark the fates
Of mighty warriors, and of warriors' mates;
For there they toil 'mid troubles and alarms,
The drums and trumpets sounding still to arms;

55

Till by degrees, when ages are outgone,
And happiness and comfort still unknown,
Like simple babes, the land of peace to win,
The task of knowledge sorrowful begin.
By the enlightened philosophic mind,
More than a thousand ages left behind.

"O what a world of vanity and strife!
For what avails the stage of mortal life!
If to the last the fading frame is worn,
The same unknowing creature it was born!
Where shall the spirit rest! where shall it go!
Or how enjoy a bliss it does not know?
It must be taught in darkness and in pain,
Or beg the bosom of a child again.
Knowledge of all, avails the human kind,
For all beyond the grave are joys of mind."

So swift and so untroubled was their flight,
'Twas like the journey of a dream by night;
And scarce had Mary ceased, with thought sedate,
To muse on woman's sacred estimate,
When on the world of warriors they alight,
Just on the confines of its day and night;
The purple light was waning west away,
And shoally darkness gained upon the day.

"I love that twilight," said the pilgrim fair,
"For more than earthly solemness is there.
See how the rubied waters winding roll;
A hoary doubtful hue involves the pole!
Uneasy murmurs float upon the wind,
And tenfold darkness rears its shades behind!

"And lo! where, wrapt in deep vermilion shroud,
The daylight slumbers on the western cloud!
I love the scene!—O let us onward steer,
The light our steeds, the wind our charioteer!
And on the downy cloud impetuous hurled,
We'll with the twilight ring this warrior world!"

Along, along, along the nether sky!
The light before, the wreathed darkness nigh!
Along, along, thro' evening vapours blue,
Thro' tinted air, and racks of drizzly dew,
The twain pursued their way, and heard afar

56

The moans and murmurs of the dying war;
The neigh of battle-steeds by field and wall,
That missed their generous comrades of the stall,
Which, all undaunted, in the ranks of death,
Yielded, they knew not why, their honest breath;
And, far behind, the hill-wolf's hunger yell,
And watchword past from drowsy sentinel.

Along, along, thro' mind's unwearied range,
It flies to the vicissitudes of change.
Our pilgrims of the twilight weary grew,
Transcendent was the scene, but never new;
They wheeled their rapid chariot from the light,
And pierced the bosom of the hideous night.

So thick the darkness, and its veil so swarth,
All hues were gone of heaven and of the earth!
The watch-fire scarce like gilded glow-worm seemed;
No moon nor star along the concave beamed!
Without a halo flaming meteors flew;
Scarce did they shed a sullen sulphury blue;
Whizzing they past, by folded vapours crossed,
And in a sea of darkness soon were lost.

Like pilgrim birds that o'er the ocean fly,
When lasting night and polar storms are nigh,
Enveloped in a rayless atmosphere,
By northern shores uncertain course they steer;
O'er thousand darkling billows flap the wing,
Till far is heard the welcome murmuring
Of mountain waves, o'er waste of waters tossed,
In fleecy thunder fall on Albyn's coast.

So passed the pilgrims through impervious night,
Till, in a moment, rose before their sight
A bound impassable of burning levin!
A wall of flame, that reached from earth to heaven!
It was the light, shed from the bloody sun,
In bootless blaze upon that cloud so dun;
Its gloom was such as not to be oppressed,
That those perturbed spirits might have rest.

Now op'ed a scene, before but dimly seen,
A world of pride, of havock, and of spleen;
A world of scathed soil, and sultry air;
For industry and culture was not there;

The hamlets smoked in ashes on the plain,
The bones of men were bleaching in the rain,
And, piled in thousands, on the trenched heath,
Stood warriors bent on vengeance and on death.

"Ah!" said the youth, "we timely come to spy
A scene momentous, and a sequel high!
For late arrived, on this disquiet coast,
A fiend, that in Tartarian gulf was tossed,
And held in tumult, and commotion fell,
The gnashing legions through the bounds of hell,
For ages past—but now, by heaven's decree,
The prelude of some dread event to be,
Is hither sent like desolating brand,
The scourge of God, the terror of the land!
He seems the passive elements to guide,
And stars in courses fight upon his side.

"On yon high mountain will we rest, and see
The omens of the times that are to be;
For all the wars of earth, and deeds of weir,
Are first performed by warrior spirits here;
So linked are souls by one eternal chain,
What these perform, those needs must do again;
And thus th' Almighty weighs each kingdom's date,
Each warrior's fortune, and each warrior's fate,
Making the future time with that has been,
Work onward, rolling like a vast machine."

They sat them down on hills of Alpine form,
Above the whirlwind and the thunder storm;
For in that land contiguous to the sun,
The elements in wild obstruction run;
They saw the bodied flame the cloud impale,
Then river like fleet down the sultry dale.
While, basking in the sun-beam, high they lay,
The hill was swathed in dark unseemly gray;
The downward rainbow hung across the rain,
And leaned its glowing arch upon the plain.

While thus they staid, they saw in wonderous wise,
Armies and kings from out the cloud arise;
They saw great hosts and empires over-run,
War's wild extreme, and kingdoms lost and won;
The whole of that this age has lived to see,
With battles of the east long hence to be,

They saw distinct and plain, as human eye
Discerns the forms and objects passing bye.
Long yet the time, ere wasting war shall cease,
And all the world have liberty and peace!

The pilgrims moved not—word they had not said,
While this mysterious boding vision staid;
But now the virgin, with disturbed eye,
Besought solution of the prodigy.

"These all are future kings of earthly fame;
That wolfish fiend, from hell that hither came,
Over thy world, in ages yet to be,
Must desolation spread and slavery,
Till nations learn to know their estimate:
To be unanimous is to be great!
When right's own standard calmly is unfurled,
The people are the sovereigns of the world!

"Like one machine a nation's governing,
And that machine must have a moving spring,
But of what mould that moving spring should be,
'Tis the high right of nations to decree.
This mankind must be taught, though millions bleed,
That knowledge, truth, and liberty, may spread."

"What meant the vision 'mid the darksome cloud;
Some spirits rose as from unearthly shroud,
And joined their warrior brethren of the free;
Two souls inspired each, and some had three?"

"These were the spirits of their brethren slain,
Who, thus permitted, rose and breathed again;
For still let reason this high truth recal,
The body's but a mould, the soul is all;
Those triple minds that all before them hurled,
Are called Silesians in this warrior world."

"O tell me, Cela, when shall be the time,
That all the restless spirits of this clime,
Erring so widely in the search of bliss,
Shall win a milder happier world than this?"

"Not till they learn, with humbled hearts, to see
The falsehood of their fuming vanity.
What is the soldier but an abject fool!

A king's, a tyrant's, or a stateman's tool!
Some patriot few there are—but ah! how rare!
For vanity or interest still is there;
Or blindfold levity directs his way;
A licenced murderer that kills for pay!
Though fruitless ages thus be overpast,
Truth, love, and knowledge, must prevail at last!"

The pilgrims left that climate with delight,
Weary of battle and portentous sight.

It boots not all their wanderings to relate,
By globes immense, and worlds subordinate;
For still my strain in mortal guise must flow,
Though swift as winged angels they might go;
The palled mind would meet no kind relay,
And dazzled fancy 'wilder by the way.

They found each clime with mental joys replete,
And all for which its 'habitants were meet.
They saw a watery world of sea and shore,
Where the rude sailor swept the flying oar,
And drove his bark like lightning o'er the main,
Proud of his prowess, of her swiftness vain;
Held revel on the shore with stormy glee,
Or sung his boisterous carol on the sea.

They saw the land where bards delighted stray,
And beauteous maids that love the melting lay;
One mighty hill they clomb with earnest pain,
For ever clomb, but higher did not gain;
Their gladsome smiles were mixed with frowns severe;
For all were bent to sing and none to hear.

Far in the gloom they found a world accursed,
Of all the globes the dreariest and the worst!
But there they could not sojourn, though they would,
For all the language was of mystic mood,
A jargon, nor conceived, nor understood;
It was of deeds, respondents, and replies,
Dark quibbles, forms, and condescendencies;
And they would argue, with vociferous breath,
For months and days, as if the point were death,
And when at last enforced to agree,
'Twas only how the argument should be!

They saw the land of bedesmen discontent,
Their frames their god, their tithes their testament!
And snarling critics bent with aspect sour,
T' applaud the great, and circumvent the poor;
And knowing patriots, with important face,
Raving aloud with gesture and grimace,
Their prize a land's acclaim, or proud and gainful place.
Then by a land effeminate they passed,
Where silks and odours floated in the blast;
A land of vain and formal compliment,
Where won the flippant belles, and beaux magnificent.

They circled nature on their airy wain,
From God's own throne, unto the realms of pain;
For there are prisons in the deep below,
Where wickedness sustains proportioned woe,
Nor more nor less; for the Almighty still
Suits to our life the goodness and the ill.

O! it would melt the living heart with woe,
Were I to sing the agonies below;
The hatred nursed by those who cannot part;
The hardened brow, the seared and sullen heart;
The still defenceless look, the stifled sigh,
The writhed lip, the staid despairing eye,
Which ray of hope may never lighten more,
Which cannot shun, yet dares not look before.
O! these are themes reflection would forbear,
Unfitting bard to sing, or maid to hear;
Yet these they saw, in downward realms prevail,
And listened many a sufferer's hapless tale,
Who all allowed that rueful misbelief
Had proved the source of their eternal grief;
And all th' Almighty punisher arraigned
For keeping back that knowledge they disdained.

"Ah!" Cela said, as up the void they flew,
"The axiom's just—the inference is true;
Therefore no more let doubts thy mind enthral,
Thro' nature's range thou seest a God in all:
Where is the mortal law that can restrain
The athiest's heart, that broods o'er thoughts profane?
Soon fades the soul's and virtue's dearest tie,
When all the future closes from the eye."
By all, the earth-born virgin plainly saw
Nature's unstaid, unalterable law;

That human life is but the infant stage
Of a progressive, endless pilgrimage,
To woe, or state of bliss, by bard unsung,
At that eternal fount where being sprung.

When these wild wanderings all were past and done,
Just in the red beam of the parting sun,
Our pilgrims skimmed along the light of even',
Like flitting stars that cross the nightly heaven,
And lighting on the verge of Phillip plain,
They trode the surface of the world again.

Arm linked in arm, they walked to green Bowhill;
At their approach the woods and lawns grew still!
The little birds to brake and bush withdrew,
The merl away unto Blackandro flew;
The twilight held its breath in deep suspense,
And looked its wonder in mute eloquence!

They reached the bower, where first at Mary's knee,
Cela arose her guide through heaven to be.
All, all was still—no living thing was seen!
No human footstep marked the daisied green!
The youth looked round, as something were unmeet,
Or wanting there, to make their bliss complete.
They paused—they sighed—then with a silent awe,
Walked onward to the halls of Carelha'.

They heard the squires and yeomen, all intent,
Talking of some mysterious event!
They saw the maidens in dejection mourn,
Scarce daring glance unto a yeoman turn!
Straight to the inner chamber they repair,
Mary beheld her widowed mother there,
Flew to her arms, to kiss her and rejoice;
Alas! she saw her not, nor heard her voice!
But sat unmoved with many a bitter sigh,
Tears on her cheek, and sorrow in her eye!
In sable weeds, her lady form was clad,
And the white lawn waved mournful round her head!
Mary beheld, arranged in order near,
The very robes she last on earth did wear,
And shrinking from the disregarded kiss,
"Oh, tell me Cela!—tell me, what is this?"

"Fair maiden of the pure and guileless heart,
As yet thou knowest not how, nor what thou art;
Come, I will lead thee to yon hoary pile,
Where sleep thy kindred in their storied isle:
There I must leave thee, in this world below;
'Tis meet thy land these holy truths should know:
But Mary, yield not thou to bootless pain,
Soon we shall meet, and never part again."

He took her hand, she dared not disobey,
But, half reluctant, followed him away.
They paced along on Ettrick's margin green,
And reached the hoary fane of old Lindeen;
It was a scene to curdle maiden's blood!
The massy church-yard gate wide open stood!
The stars were up!—the valley steeped in dew!
The baleful bat in silent circles flew!
No sound was heard, except the lonely rail,
Harping his ordinal adown the dale;
And soft, and slow, upon the breezes light,
The rush of Ettrick breathed along the night!
Dark was the pile, and green the tombs beneath!
And dark the gravestones on the sward of death!

Within the railed space appeared to view,
A grave new opened—thitherward they drew;
And there beheld, within its mouldy womb!
A living, moving tenant of the tomb!
It was an aged monk, uncouth to see,
Who held a sheeted corse upon his knee,
And busy, busy, with the form was he!
At their approach he uttered howl of pain,
Till echoes groaned it from the holy fane,
Then fled amain—Ah! Cela too, is gone!
And Mary stands within the grave alone!
With her fair guide, her robes of heaven are fled,
And round her fall the garments of the dead!

Here I must seize my ancient harp again,
And chaunt a simple tale, a most uncourtly strain.

Part Fourth

THE night-wind is sleeping—the forest is still,
The blair of the heath-cock has sunk in the hill,

Beyond the gray cairn of the moor is his rest,
On the red heather bloom he has pillowed his breast;
There soon with his note the gray dawning he'll cheer,
But Mary of Carel' that note will not hear!

The night-wind is still, and the moon in the wane,
The river-lark sings on the verge of the plain;
So lonely his plaint, by the motionless reed,
It sounds like an omen or tale of the dead;
Like a warning of death, it falls on the ear
Of those who are wandering the woodlands in fear;
For the maidens of Carelha' wander, and cry
On their young lady's name, with the tear in their eye.
The gates had been shut, and the mass had been sung,
But Mary was missing, the beauteous and young;
And she had been seen in the evening still,
By woodman, alone, in the groves of Bowhill.

O were not these maidens in terror and pain!
They knew the third night of the moon in the wane!
They knew on that night that the spirits were free;
That revels of fairies were held on the lea;
And heard their small bugles, with eirysome croon,
As lightly they rode on the beam of the moon!
O! woe to the wight that abides their array!
And woe to the maiden that comes in their way!

The maidens returned all hopeless and wan;
The yeomen they rode, and the pages they ran;
The Ettrick and Yarrow they searched up and down,
The hamlet, the cot, and the old borough town;
And thrice the bedesman renewed the host,
But the dawn returned and Mary was lost!

Her lady mother, distracted and wild,
For the loss of her loved, her only child,
With all her maidens tracked the dew—
Well Mary's secret bower she knew!
Oft had she traced, with fond regard,
Her darling to that grove, and heard
Her orisons the green bough under,
And turned aside with fear and wonder.

O! but their hearts were turned to stone,
When they saw her stretched on the sward alone;
Prostrate, without a word or motion,

As if in calm and deep devotion!
They called her name with trembling breath;
But ah! her sleep was the sleep of death!
They laid their hands on her cheek composed;
But her cheek was cold and her eye was closed.
They laid their hands upon her breast,
But the playful heart had sunk to rest;
And they raised an eldrich wail of sorrow,
That startled the hinds on the braes of Yarrow.

And yet, when they viewed her comely face,
Each line remained of beauty and grace;
No death-like features it disclosed,
For the lips were met, and the eyes were closed.
'Twas pale—but the smile was on the cheek;
'Twas modelled all as in act to speak!
It seemed as if each breeze that blew,
The play of the bosom would renew;
As nature's momentary strife
Would wake that form to beauty and life.

It is borne away with fear and awe
To the lordly halls of Carelha',
And lies on silken couch at rest—
The mother there is constant guest,
For hope still lingers in her breast.

O! seraph Hope! that here below
Can nothing dear to the last forego!
When we see the forms we fain would save
Wear step by step adown to the grave,
Still hope a lambent gleam will shed,
Over the last, the dying bed.
And even, as now, when the soul's away,
It flutters and lingers o'er the clay!
O Hope! thy range was never expounded!
'Tis not by the grave that thou art bounded!

The leech's art, and the bedesman's prayer,
Are all misspent—no life is there!
Between her breasts they dropped the lead,
And the cord in vain begirt her head;
Yet still on that couch her body lies,
Though another moon has claimed the skies.
For once the lykewake maidens saw,
As the dawn arose on Carelha',

A movement soft the sheets within,
And a gentle shivering of the chin!

All earthly hope at last outworn,
The body to the tomb was borne;
The last pale flowers in the grave were flung;
The mass was said, and the requiem sung;
And the turf that was ever green to be,
Lies over the dust of Mary Lee.

Deep fell the eve on old Lindeen!
Loud creaked the rail in the clover green!
The new moon from the west withdrew.—
O! well the monk of Lindeen knew
That Mary's winding-sheet was lined
With many fringe of the gold refined!
That in her bier behoved to be
A golden cross and a rosary;
Of pearl beads full many a string,
And on every finger a diamond ring.
The holy man no scruples staid;
For within that grave was useless laid
Riches that would a saint entice;—
'Twas worth a convent's benefice!

He took the spade, and away he is gone
To the church-yard, darkling and alone;
His brawny limbs the grave bestride,
And he shovelled the mools and the bones aside;
Of the dust, nor the dead, he stood not in fear,
But he stooped in the grave and he opened the bier;
And he took the jewels, of value high,
And he took the cross, and the rosary,
And the golden heart on the lid that shone,
And he laid them carefully on a stone.

Then down in the depth of the grave sat he,
And he raised the corpse upon his knee;
But in vain to gain the rings he strove,
For the hands were cold, and they would not move.
He drew a knife from his baldrick gray,
To cut the rings and fingers away.

He gave one cut—he gave but one—
It scarcely reached unto the bone:
Just then the soul, so long exiled,

Returned again from its wanderings wild;
By the stars and the sun it ceased to roam,
And entered its own, its earthly home.
Loud shrieked the corse at the wound he gave,
And rising, stood up in the grave.

The hoary thief was chilled at heart
Scarce had he power left to depart;
For horror thrilled through every vein;
He did not cry, but he roared amain;
For hues of dread and death were rife
On the face of the form he had woke to life:
His reason fled from off her throne,
And never more dawned thereupon.

Aloud she called her Cela's name,
And the echoes called, but no Cela came!
O! much she marvelled that he had gone,
And left her thus in the grave alone.
She knew the place, and the holy dome;
Few moments hence she had thither come;
And thro' the hues of the night she saw
The woods and towers of Carelha'.
'Twas mystery all—She did not ween
Of the state or the guise in which she had been;
She did not ween that while travelling afar,
Away by the sun and the morning star,
By the moon, and the cloud, and aerial bow,
That her body was left on the earth below.

But now she stood in grievous plight;
The ground was chilled with the dews of the night;
Her frame was cold and ill at rest,
The dead-rose waved upon her breast;
Her feet were coiled in the sheet so wan,
And fast from her hand the red blood ran.

'Twas late, late on a Sabbath night!
At the hour of the ghost, and the restless sprite!
The mass at Carelha' had been read,
And all the mourners were bound to bed,
When a foot was heard on the paved floor,
And a gentle rap came to the door.

O God! that such a rap should be
So fraught with ambiguity!

A dim haze clouded every sight;
Each hair had life and stood upright;
No sound was heard throughout the hall,
But the beat of the heart and the cricket's call;
So deep the silence imposed by fear,
That a vacant buzz sung in the ear.

The lady of Carelha' first broke
The breathless hush, and thus she spoke.
"Christ be our shield!—who walks so late,
And knocks so gently at my gate?
I felt a pang—it was not dread—
It was the memory of the dead!
O! death is a dull and dreamless sleep!
The mould is heavy, the grave is deep!
Else I had weened that foot so free
The step and the foot of my Mary Lee!
And I had weened that gentle knell
From the light hand of my daughter fell!
The grave is deep, it may not be!
Haste porter—haste to the door and see."

He took the key with an eye of doubt,
He lifted the lamp and he looked about;
His lips a silent prayer addressed,
And the cross was signed upon his breast;
Thus mailed within the armour of God,
All ghostly to the door he strode.
He wrenched the bolt with grating din,
He lifted the latch—but none came in!
He thrust out his lamp, and he thrust out his head,
And he saw the face and the robes of the dead!
One sob he heaved, and tried to fly,
But he sunk on the earth, and the form came bye.

She entered the hall, she stood in the door,
Till one by one dropt on the floor,
The blooming maiden, and matron old,
The friar gray, and the yeoman bold.
It was like a scene on the Border green,
When the arrows fly and pierce unseen;
And nought was heard within the hall,
But Aves, vows, and groans withal.
The lady of Carel' stood alone,
But moveless as a statue of stone.

"O! lady mother, thy fears forego;
Why all this terror and this woe?
But late when I was in this place,
Thou would'st not look me in the face;
O! why do you blench at sight of me?
I am thy own child, thy Mary Lee."

"I saw thee dead and cold as clay;
I watched thy corpse for many a day;
I saw thee laid in the grave at rest;
I strewed the flowers upon thy breast;
And I saw the mould heaped over thee—
Thou art not my child, my Mary Lee."

O'er Mary's face amazement spread;
She knew not that she had been dead;
She gazed in mood irresolute:
Both stood agast, and both were mute.

"Speak thou loved form—*my* glass is run,
I nothing dread beneath the sun,
Why come'st thou in thy winding-sheet,
Thy life-blood streaming to thy feet?
The grave-rose that my own hands made,
I see upon thy bosom spread;
The kerchief that my own hands bound,
I see still tied thy temples round;
The golden rings, and bracelet bands,
Are still upon thy bloody hands.
From earthly hope all desperate driven,
I nothing fear beneath high heaven;
Give me thy hand and speak to me,
If thou art indeed my Mary Lee.

That mould is sensible and warm,
It leans upon a parent's arm.
The kiss is sweet, and the tears are sheen,
And kind are the words that pass between;
They cling as never more to sunder,
O! that embrace was fraught with wonder!

Yeoman, and maid, and menial poor,
Upraised their heads from the marble floor;
With lengthened arm, and forward stride,
They tried if that form their touch would bide;

They felt her warm!—they heard!—they saw
And marvel reigns in Carelha'!

The twain into their chamber repair;
The wounded hand is bound with care;
And there the mother heard with dread
The whole that I to you have said,
Of all the worlds where she had been,
And of all the glories she had seen.
I pledge no word that all is true,
The virgin's tale I have told to you;
But well 'tis vouched, by age and worth,
'Tis real that relates to earth.

'Twas trowed by every Border swain,
The vision would full credence gain.
Certes 'twas once by all believed,
Till one great point was misconceived;
For the mass-men said, with fret and frown,
That thro' all space it well was known,
By moon, or stars, the earth or sea,
An up and down there needs must be;
This error caught their minds in thrall;
'Twas dangerous and apocryphal!
And this nice fraud unhinged all.
So grievous is the dire mischance
Of priest-craft and of ignorance!

Belike thou now can'st well foresee,
What after hap'd to Mary Lee—
Then thou may'st close my legend here.
But ah! the tale to some is dear!
For though her name no more remains,
Her blood yet runs in Minstrel veins.

In Mary's youth, no virgin's face
Wore such a sweet and moving grace;
Nor ever did maiden's form more fair
Lean forward to the mountain air;
But now, since from the grave returned,
So dazzling bright her beauty burned,
The eye of man could scarcely brook
With steady gaze thereon to look:
Such was the glow of her cheek and eyes,
She bloomed like the rose of paradise!

Though blyther than she erst had been,
In serious mood she oft was seen.
When rose the sun o'er mountain grey,
Her vow was breathed to the east away;
And when low in the west he burned,
Still there her duteous eye was turned.
For she saw that the flowerets of the glade
To him unconscious worship paid;
She saw them ope their breasts by day,
And follow his enlivening ray,
Then fold them up in grief by night,
Till the return of the blessed light.
When daylight in the west fell low,
She heard the woodland music flow,
Like farewel song, with sadness blent,
A soft and sorrowful lament;
But when the sun rose from the sea,
O! then the birds from every tree
Poured forth their hymn of holiest glee!
She knew that the wandering spirits of wrath
Fled from his eye to their homes beneath,
But when the God of glory shone
On earth, from his resplendent throne,
In valley, mountain, or in grove,
Then all was life, and light, and love.
She saw the new born infant's eye
Turned to that light incessantly;
Nor ever was that eye withdrawn
Till the mind thus carved began to dawn.
All Nature worshipped at one shrine,
Nor knew that the impulse was divine.

The Chiefs of the Forest the strife begin,
Intent this lovely dame to win;
But the living lustre of her eye
Balked every knight's pretensions high;
Abashed they sunk before her glance,
Nor farther could their claims advance;
Though love thrilled every heart with pain,
They did not ask, and they could not gain.

There came a Harper out of the east;
A courteous and a welcome guest
In every lord and baron's tower;
He struck his harp of wond'rous power;
So high his art, that all who heard

Seemed by some magic spell ensnared;
For every heart, as he desired,
Was thrilled with woe—with ardour fired;
Roused to high deeds his might above,
Or soothed to kindness and to love.
No one could learn from whence he came,
But Hugo of Norroway hight his name.

One day, when every Baron came,
And every maid, and noble dame,
To list his high and holy strain
Within the choir of Melrose fane,
The lady of Carelha' joined the band,
And Mary, the flower of all the land.

The strain rose soft—the strain fell low—
O! every heart was steeped in woe!
Again as it pealed a swell so high,
The round drops stood in every eye;
And the aisles and the spires of the hallowed fane,
And the caves of Eildon, sung it again.

O Mary Lee is sick at heart!
That pang no tongue can ever impart!
It was not love, nor joy, nor woe,
Nor thought of heaven, nor earth below;
'Twas all conjoined in gleam so bright—
A poignant feeling of delight!
The throes of a heart that sought its rest,
Its stay—its home in another's breast!
Ah! she had heard that holy strain
In a land she hoped to see again!
And seen that calm benignant eye
Above the spheres and above the sky!
And though the strain her soul had won,
She yearned for the time that it was done,
To greet the singer in language bland,
And call him Cela, and clasp his hand.

It was yon ancient tombs among
That Mary glided from the throng,
Smiled in the fair young stranger's face,
And proffered her hand with courteous grace.
He started aloof—he bent his eye—
He stood in a trance of ecstacy!
He blessed the power that had impelled

Him onward till he that face beheld;
For he knew his bourn was gained at last,
And all his wanderings then were past.

She called him Cela, and made demand
Anent his kindred, and his land;
But his hand upon his lip he laid,
He lifted his eye, and he shook his head!
No—Hugo of Norroway is my name,
Ask not from whence or how I came:
But since ever memory's ray was borne
Within this breast of joy forlorn,
I have sought for thee, and only thee;
For I ween thy name is Mary Lee.
My heart and soul with thine are blent,
My very being's element—
O! I have wonders to tell to thee,
If thou art the virgin Mary Lee!

The border chiefs were all amazed,
They stood at distance round and gazed;
They knew her face he never had seen,
But they heard not the words that past between.
They thought of the power that had death beguiled;
They thought of the grave, and the vision wild!
And they found that human inference failed;
That all in mystery was veiled;
And they shunned the twain in holy awe.
The flower of the forest, and Carelha',
Are both by the tuneful stranger won,
And a new existence is begun.

Sheltered amid his mountains afar,
He kept from the bustle of Border war;
For he loved not the field of foray and scathe,
Nor the bow, nor the shield, nor the sword of death;
But he tuned his harp in the wild unseen,
And he reared his flocks on the mountain green.

He was the foremost the land to free
Of the hart, and the hind, and the forest tree;
The first who attuned the pastoral reed
On the mountains of Ettrick, and braes of Tweed;
The first who did to the land impart
The shepherd's rich and peaceful art,
To bathe the fleece, to cherish the dam,

73

To milk the ewe, and to wean the lamb;
And all the joys ever since so rife
In the shepherd's simple, romantic life.
More bliss, more joy, from him had birth,
Than all the conquerors of the earth.

They lived in their halls of Carelha'
Until their children's sons they saw;
There Mary closed a life refined
To purity of soul and mind,
And at length was laid in old Lindeen,
In the very grave where she erst had been.
Five gallant sons upbore her bier,
And honoured her memory wth a tear;
And her stone, though now full old and grey,
Is known by the hinds unto this day.

From that time forth, on Ettrick's shore,
Old Hugo the harper was seen no more!
Some said he died as the morning rose;
But his body was lost ere the evening close!
He was not laid in old Lindeen;
For his grave nor his burial never were seen!

Some said that eve a form they saw
Arise from the tower of Carelha'
Aslant the air, and hover a while
Above the spires of the hallowed pile,
Then sail away in a snow-white shroud,
And vanish afar in the eastern cloud.

But others deemed that his grave was made
By hands unseen in the greenwood glade.
Certes that in one night there grew
A little mound of an ashen hue,
And some remains of gravel lay
Mixed with the sward at the break of day;
But the hind past bye with troubled air,
For he knew not what might be slumbering there:
And still above that mound there grows,
Yearly, a wond'rous fairy rose.

Beware that cairn and dark green ring!
For the elves of eve have been heard to sing
Around that grave with eldritch croon,
Till trembled the light of the waning moon!

74

And from that cairn, at midnight deep,
The shepherd has heard from the mountain steep
Arise such a mellowed holy strain
As if the Minstrel had woke again!

Late there was seen, on summer tide,
A lovely form that wont to glide
Round green Bowhill, at the fall of even',
So like an angel sent from heaven,
That all the land believed and said
Their Mary Lee was come from the dead;
For since that time no form so fair
Had ever moved in this earthly air:
And whenever that beauteous shade was seen
To visit the walks of the forest green,
The joy of the land ran to excess,
For they knew that it boded them happiness;
Peace, love, and truth, for ever smiled
Around that genius of the wild.

Ah me! there is omen of deep dismay,
For that saintlike form has vanished away!
I have watched her walks by the greenwood glade,
And the mound where the Harper of old was laid;
I have watched the bower where the woodbine blows,
And the fairy ring, and the wonderous rose,
And all her haunts by Yarrow's shore,
But the heavenly form I can see no more!
She comes not now our land to bless,
Or to cherish the poor and the fatherless,
Who lift to heaven the tearful eye
Bewailing their loss—and well may I!
I little weened when I struck the string,
In fancy's wildest mood to sing,
That sad and low the strain should close,
'Mid real instead of fancied woes!

CONNEL OF DEE

Connel went out by a blink of the moon
   To his light little bower in the deane;
He thought they had gi'en him his supper owr soon,
   And that still it was long until e'en
   Oh the air was so sweet and the sky so serene
And so high his soft languishment grew
   That visions of happiness danced oer his mind
   He longed to leave parent and sisters behind
   For he thought that his maker to him was unkind
For that high were his merits he knew.

Sooth Connel was halesome, and stalwart to see,
   The bloom of fayir yudith he wore;
But the lirk of displeasure hung over his bree
   Nae glisk of contentment it bore.
   He langit for a wife with a mailin, and store;
He grevit in idless to lie,
   Afar from his cottage he wished to remove
   To wassail and waik, and unchided to rove,
   And beik in the cordial transports of love
All undyr a kindlier sky.

O sweet was the fa' of that gloaming to view.
   The day-lighte crap laigh on the doon,
And left it's pale borders abeigh on the blue
   To mix wi the beams of the moon.
   The hill hang it's skaddaw the greinwood aboon
The houf of the bodyng benshee
   Slow oer him were sailing the cloudlets of June
   The be'ttle began his wild airel to tune,
   And sang on the wynde with ane eirysome croon
Away on breeze of the Dee!

With haffat on lufe poor Connel lay lorn!
   He languishit for muckle and mair!
His bed of greine hether he eynit to scorn,
   The bygane he doughtna weel bear!
   Atour him the greine leife was fannyng the air,
In noiseless and flychtering play;
   The hush of the water fell saft on his ear
   And he fand as gin sleep, wi her gairies, war near
   Wi her freaks and her ferlies and phantoms of fear
But he eidently wysit hir away.

Short time had he sped in that sellible strife
   Ere he saw a young maiden stand by,
Who seemed in the bloom and the bell of hir life;
   He wist not that ane was sae nigh!
   But sae sweet was her look, and sae saft was her eye,
That his heart was all quaking with love;
   And then there was kythin a dimple sae sly
   At play on her cheek of the moss-rose's dye
   That kindled the heart of poor Connel on high
With ravishment deadlye to prove.

He deemed her a beautifull spirit of night,
   And eiry was he to assay;
But he found she was mortal with thrilling delight,
   For her breath was like zephyr of May;
   Her eye was the dew-bell, the beam of the day,
And her arm it was softer than silk;
Her hand was so warm, and her lip was so red,
Her slim taper waiste so enchantingly made!
   And some beauties moreover that cannot be said
   Of a bosom far whiter than milk!

Poor Connel was reaved of all power and of speech,
   His frame grew all powerless and weak;
He neither could stir, nor caress her, nor fleech,
   He trembled but word couldna speak!
But O when his lips touched her soft rosy cheek,
   The channels of feeling ran dry
   He found that like emmets his life-blood it crept
His liths turned as limber as dud that is steeped,
He streekit his limbs, and he moaned and he wept
   And for love he was just gaun to die.

The damsel beheld and she raised him so kind,
   And she said "my dear beautifull swain,
Take heart till I tell you the hark of my mind,
   I'm weary of lying my lane;
I have castles, and lands, and flocks of my ain,
   But want ane my gillour to share;
A man that is hale as the hart on the hill;
As stark, and as kind, is the man to my will,
   Who has slept on the heather and drank of the rill
   And, like you, gentle, amorous and fair.

I often hae heard that like you there was nane,
   And I aince got a glisk of thy face;
Now far have I ridden, and far have I gane,
   In hopes thou wilt nurice the grace,
To make me thy ain—O come to my embrace!
   For I love thee as dear as my life!
I'll make thee a laird of the boonmost degree,
My castles and lands I'll give freely to thee,
   Though rich and abundant thine own they shall be,
   If thou wilt but make me thy wife."

Oh never was man sae delighted and fain!
   He bowed a consent to her will,
Kind providence thankit again and again;
   And 'gan to display his rude skill
In leifu' endearment, and thought it nae il!
   To kiss the sweet lips of the fair
And press her to lie, in that gloamin sae still,
Adown by his side in the howe of the hill,
   For the heath-flower was sweet and the sound of the rill
   Would soothe every sorrow and care

No—she wadna lie by the side of a man
   Till the rites of the marriage were bye.
Away they hae sped; but soon Connel began,
   For his heart it was worn to a sigh
To fondle, and simper and look in her eye,
   Oh dreadful to bear was his wound
When on her fair neck fell his fingers sae dun—
He felt as the sand of existence were run
It strak thro' his breast like the shot of a gun!
   He trembled and fell to the ground.

O Connel, dear Connel, be patient a while!
   These wounds of thy bosom will heal,
And thou with thy love may'st walk many a mile
   Nor transport nor passion once feel.
Thy spirits once broke on electerick wheel,
   Cool reason her empire shall gain;
And haply, repentance in dowy array,
And laithly disgust may arise in thy way,
Encumb'ring the night, and o'ercasting the day
   And turn all those pleasures to pain.

The mansion is gained, and the bridal is past,
    And the transports of wedlock prevail;
The lot of poor Connel the Shepherd is cast
    Mid pleasures that never can fail;
The balms of Arabia sweeten the gale,
    The tables for ever are spread
With damask, and viands, and heart-cheering wine,
Their splendour and elegance fully combine
His lawns they are ample, his bride is divine,
    And of goud-fringed silk is his bed.

The transports of love gave rapture and flew;
    The banquet soon sated and cloyed;
Nae mair they delighted, nae langer were new,
    They could not be ever enjoyed!
He felt in his bosom a fathomless void,
    A yearning again to be free;
Than all that voluptuous sickening store,
The wine that he drank and the robes that he wore
His diet of milk had delighted him more
    Afar on the hills of the Dee.

O oft had he sat by the clear springing well,
    And dined from his wallet full fain!
Then sweet was the scent of the blue heather bell,
    And free was his bosom of pain;
The laverock was lost in the lift, but her strain
    Came trilling so sweetly from far,
To rapture the hour he would wholly resign
He would listen, and watch, till he saw her decline,
And the sun's yellow beam on her dappled breast shine
    Like some little musical star.

And then he wad lay his blue bonnet aside,
    And turn his rapt eyes to the heaven,
And bless his kind maker who all did provide,
    And beg that he might be forgiven,
For his sins were like crimson!—all bent and uneven
    The path he had wilsomely trode!
Then who the delight of his bosom could tell
Sweet was that meal by his pure mountain well,
And sweet was its water he drank from the shell,
    And peacefull his moorland abode!

But now was he deaved and babbled outright,
  By gossips in endless array,
Who thought not of sin nor of Satan aright,
  Nor the dangers that mankind belay;
Who joked about heaven, and scorned to pray,
  And gloried in that was a shame.
O Connel was troubled at things that befel!
So different from scenes he had once loved so well
He deemyt he was placed on the confines of Hell,
  And fand like the saur of its flame!

Of bonds and of law-suits he still was in doubt,
  And old debts coming due every day;
And a thousand odd things he kend naething about
  Kept him in continued dismay.
At board he was awkward, nor wist what to say,
  Nor what his new honours became;
His guests they wad mimic and laugh in their sleeve,
He blushed, and he faultered, and scarce dought believe
That men were so base as to smile and decieve
  Or eynied of him to make game!

Still franker and freer his gossipers grew,
  And preyed upon him and his dame;
Their jests and their language to Connel were new,
  It was slander, and cursing, and shame!
He groaned in his heart, and he thought them to blame
  For revel and rout without end;
He saw himself destined to pamper and feed
A race whom he hated, a profligate breed,
The scum of existence to vengeance decreed
  Who laughed at their god and their friend.

He saw that in wickedness all did delight,
  And he kendna what length it might bear;
They drew him to evil by day and by night,
  To scenes that he trembled to share!
His heart it grew sick and his head it grew sair,
  And he thought what he dared not to tell!
He thought of the far distant hills of the Dee!
Of his cake, and his cheese, and his lair on the lea!
Of the laverock that hung on the heaven's ee-bree,
  His prayer and his clear mountain well!

His breast he durst sparingly trust wi' the thought,
    Of the virtuous days that were fled!
Yet still his kind lady he loved as he ought,
    Or soon from that scene he had fled.
It now was but rarely she honoured his bed—
    'Twas modesty heightening her charms!
A delicate feeling that man cannot ween
O heaven!—each night from his side she had been—
He found it at length—Nay he saw't with his een,
    She slept in a paramour's arms!!!

It was the last pang that the spirit could bear!
    Destruction and death was the meed.
For forfeited vows there was nought too severe,
    Even Conscience applauded the deed.
His mind was decided, her doom was decreed;
    He led her to chamber apart
To give her to know of his wrongs he had sense
To chide and upbraid her in language intense,
And kill her, at least, for her heinous offence,
    A crime at which demons would start

With grievous reproaches, in agonized zeal,
    Stern Connel his lecture began.
He mentioned her crime!—She turned on her heel,
    And her mirth to extremity ran.
"Why that was the fashion!—no sensible man
    Could e'er of such freedom complain.
What was it to him? there were maidens enow
Of the loveliest forms, and the loveliest hue
Who blithely would be his companions he knew
    If he wearied of lying his lane."

How Connel was shocked!—but his fury still rose,
    He shivered from toe to the crown!
His hair stood like heath on the mountain that grows
    And each hair had a life of its own!
"O thou most—" —But whereto his passion had flown
    No man to this day can declare,
For his dame, with a frown, laid her hand on his mouth
That hand once as sweet as the breeze of the south!
That hand that gave pleasures and honours and routh
    And she said with a dignified air,

"Peace booby!—if life thou regardest beware!
　　I have had some fair husbands ere now!
They wooed and they flattered, they sighed and they sware,
　　At length they grew irksome like you.
Come hither one moment, a sight I will show
　　That will teach thee some breeding and grace."
She opened a door, and there Connel beheld
A sight that to trembling his spirit impelled
A man standing chained, who nor 'plained, nor rebelled,
　　And that man had a sorrowfull face

Down creaked a trap-door on which he was placed,
　　Right softly and slowly it fell!
And the man seemed in terror, and strangely amazed,
　　But why Connel could not then tell.
He sunk and he sunk as the vice did impel,
　　At length, as far downward he drew,
Good lord! in a trice with the pull of a string
A pair of dread shears, like the thunder-bolt's wing,
Came snap on his neck with a terrible spring
　　And severed it neatly in two.

Adown fell the body—the head lay in sight,
　　The lips in a moment grew wan!
The temple just quivered—the eye it grew white,
　　And upward the purple threads span!
The dark crooked streamlets along the boards ran,
　　Thin pipings of reek could be seen!
Poor Connel was blinded—his lugs how they sung!
He looked once again and he saw like the tongue
That motionless out twixt the livid lips hung
　　Then mirkness set over his een.

He turned and he dashed his fair lady aside;
　　And off like the lightening he broke,
By staircase and gallery, with horrified stride,
　　He turned not, he staid not, nor spoke!
The iron-spiked court-gate he would not unlock,
　　His haste was beyond that of man!
He stop'd not to rap and he staid not to call,
With ram-race he cleared at a bensil the wall,
And headlong beyond got a grieveous fall,
　　But he rose, and he ran! and he ran!

As stag of the forest, when fraudfully coiled,
    And mured up in barn for a prey,
Sees his dappled comerades dishonoured and soiled
    In their blood on some festival day,
Bursts all intervension and hies him away,
    Like the wind over holt over lea,
So Connel pressed on—all encumbrance he threw,
Over height, over hollow, he lessened to view,
It may not be said that he ran for he flew,
    Straight on for the hills of the Dee.

The contrair of all other runners in life
    His swiftness increased as he flew,
But be it remembered he ran from a wife,
    And a trap-door that sunk on a screw.
'Tis told to this day, and believed as true,
    So much did his swiftness excel,
That he skimm'd the wild paths like a thing of the mind
And the stour from each footstep was seen on the wind,
Distinct by itself for a furlong behind,
    Before that it mingled or fell!

He came to a hill—the ascent it was steep!
    And much did he fear for his breath.
He halted—he ventured behind him to peep—
    The sight was a vision of death!
His wife and her paramours came on the path,
    Well mounted with devilish speed!
O Connel! poor Connel! thy hope is a wreck!
Sir, run for thy life! without stumble or check!
It is thy only stake, the last chance for thy neck!
    Strain Connel, or death is thy meed!

O wend to the right, to the woodland betake;
    Gain that and yet safe thou may'st be!
How fast they are gaining!—O stretch to the brake!
    Poor Connel! 'tis over with thee!!
In the breath of the horses his yellow locks flee,
    The voice of his wife's in the van!
Even that was not needfull to heighten his fears,
He sprang o'er the bushes, he dashed thro' the briers,
For he thought of the trap-door and d——ble shears,
    And he cried to his god and he ran.

Thro' gallwood and bramble he floundered amain
    No bar his advancement could stay
Tho' heels-o'er-head whirled again and again
    Still faster he gained on his way
This moment on swinging bough powerless he lay
    The next he was rolling along
So lightly he scarce made the green leaf to quake
Impetous he splashed thro the bog and the lake
He rainbowed the hawthorn he needled the brake
    With power supernaturally strong

The riders are foiled and far lagging behind
    Poor Connel has leisure to pray
He hears their dread voices around on the wind
    Still farther and farther away
"O thou who sit'st throned o'er the fields of the day
    Have pity this once upon me
Deliver from those that are hunting my life
From *traps* of the wicked that round me are rife
And O above all from the rage of a wife
    And guide to the hills of the Dee

And if ever I grumble at providence more
    Or scorn my own mountains of heath
If ever I yearn for that sin-breeding ore
    Or shape to complaining a breath
Then may I be nipt with the scissors of death—"
    No further could Connel proceed
He thought of the trap that he saw in the nook
Of the tongue that came out and the temple that shook
Of the blood and the reek and the deadening look
It was more than his heart or his feelings could brook
    He lifted his bonnet and fled

He wandered and wandered thro' woodlands of gloom
    And sorely he sobbed and he wept.
At chirk of the pyat or bee's passing boomb
    He started, he listened—he leaped.
With eye and with ear a strick guardship he kept;
    No scene could his sorrows beguile.
At length he stood lone by the side of the Dee,
It was placid and deep and as broad as a sea;
O could he get over, how safe he might be,
    And gain his own mountains the while!

'Twas dangerous to turn but proceeding was worse
　　For the country grew open and bare
No forest appeared neither broomwood nor gorse
　　Nor furze that would shelter a hare
Ah! could he get over how safe he might fare
　　At length he resolved to try
At worst 'twas but drowning and what was a life
Compared to confinement in sin and in strife
Beside a trap-door and a scandalous wife
　　'Twas nothing!—he'd swim or he'd die

Ah he could not swim, and was loth to resign
　　This life for a world unknown!
For he had been sinning, and misery condign
　　Would sure be his portion alone.
How sweetly the sun on the green mountain shone!
　　And the flocks they were resting in peace,
Or bleating along on each parallel path;
The lambs they were skipping on fringe of the heath;
How different might kythe the lone vallies of death,
　　And cheerfulness evermore cease!

All wistfull he stood on the brink of the pool,
　　And dropt on its surface the tear;
He started at something that boded him dool,
　　And his mouth fell wide open with fear;
The trample of gallopers fell on his ear;
　　One look was too much for his eye;
For there was his wife, and her paramours twain,
With whip and with spur coming over the plain,
Bent forward, revengefull, they galloped amain—
　　They hasten—they quicken—they fly

Short time was there now to deliberate I ween,
　　And shortly did Connel decree;
He shut up his mouth, and he closed his een,
　　And he pointed his arms like a V;
And like a scared otter he dived in the Dee,
　　His heels pointed up to the sky;
Like bolt from the firmament downward he bears,
The still liquid element startled uprears,
It bubbled and bullered and roared in his ears,
　　Like thunder that gallows on high.

He soon found the symptoms of drowning begin,
   And painfull the feeling be sure!
For his breath it gaed out, and the water gaed in,
   With drumble and mudwort impure;
It was most unpleasant, and hard to endure,
   And he struggled its inroads to wear;
But it rushed by his mouth, and it rushed by his nose,
His joints grew benumbed, all his fingers and toes,
And his een turned they neither would open nor close
   And he found his departure was near

One time he came up like a porpoise above,
   He breathed and he lifted his eye;
It was the last glance of the land of his love,
   Of the world and the beautifull sky!
How bright looked the sun from his window on high,
   Thro' furs of the light golden grain!
O Connel was sad but he thought with a sigh,
That far above yon peacefull vales of the sky,
In bowers of the morning he shortly might lie,
   Tho' very unlike it just then!

He sunk to the bottom no more he arose,
The waters for ever his body inclose;
The horse-mussel clasped on his fingers and toes;
   All passive he suffered the scathe.
But O there was one thing his heart could not brook,
Even in his last struggles his spirit it shook,
The eels, with their cursed equivocal look,
   Redoubled the horrors of death!
O aye since the time that he was but a bairn,
When catching his trouts in the Cluny, or Gairn,
At sight of an eel he would shudder and darn;
   It almost deprived him of breath.

He died—but he found that he never would be
   So dead to all feeling and smart,
No, not though his flesh were consumed in the Dee,
   But that eels would some horror impart.
With all other fishes he yielded to mart,
   Resistance became not the dead;
The minnow, with gushet se gouden and braw,
The siller-ribbed perch, and the indolent craw,
And the ravenous ged with his teeth like a saw,
   Came all on poor Connel to feed!

They rave and they rugged—he cared not a speal,
　　Though they preyed on his vitals alone!
But lord! when he felt the cold nose of an eel,
　　A quaking seized every bone.
Their slid slimy forms lay his bosom upon;
　　His mouth, that was ope, they came near;
They guddled his loins, and they bored thro' his side,
They warped all his bowels about on the tide.
One snapt him on place he no longer would bide;
　　It was more than a dead man could bear!

　　　　★　★　★　★　★　★　★

Young Connel was missed, and his mother was sad,
　　But his sisters consoled her mind;
And said, he was wooing some favourite maid,
　　For Connel was amorous and kind.
Ah! little weened they that their Connel reclined
　　On a couch that was lothfull to see!
Twas mud!—and the water-bells o'er him did heave;
The lampreys passed thro' him without law or leave,
And windowed his frame like a riddle or sieve
　　Afar in the deeps of the Dee!

It was but a night, and a midsummer night,
　　And next morning when rose the red sun,
His sisters in haste their fair bodies bedight,
　　And ere the days work was begun
They sought for their Connel, for they were undone
　　If aught should their brother befal:
And first they went straight to the bower in the dean,
For there he of late had been frequently seen;
For nature he loved, and her evening scene,
　　To him was the dearest of all.

And when within view of his bowrak they came,
　　It lay in the skaddow so still,
They lift up their voices and called his name,
　　And their forms they shone white on the hill;
When trow you that hallo so erlich and shrill
　　Arose from those maids on the heath?
It was just as poor Connel most poignant did feel,
As reptiles he loved not of him made a meal,
Just when the misleered and unmannerly eel
　　Waked him from the slumbers of death.

He opened his eyes and with wonder beheld
    The sky and the hills once again;
But still he was haunted, for over the field
    Two females came running amain.
No form but his spouse's remained on his brain;
    His sisters to see him were glad;
But he started bolt upright in horror and fear,
He deemyt that his wife and her minions were near,
He flung off his plaid, and he fled like a deer,
    And they thought their poor brother was mad.

He scaped; but he halted on top of the rock,
    And his wonder and pleasure still grew;
For his clothes were not wet, and his skin was unbroke,
    But he scarce could believe it was true
That no eels were within; and too strictly he knew
    He was married and buckled for life.
It could not be a dream; for he slept, and awoke;
Was drunken, and sober; had sung, and had spoke;
For months and for days he had dragged in the yoke
    With an unconscientious wife.

However it was, he was sure he was there
    On his own native cliffs of the Dee.
O never before looked a morning so fair,
    Or the sun-beam so sweet on the lea!
The song of the merl from her old hawthorn tree,
    And the blackbird's melodious lay,
All sounded to him like an anthem of love,
A song that the spirit of nature did move,
A kind little hymn to their maker above,
    Who gave them the beauties of day.

So deep the impression was stamped on his brain
    The image was never defaced,
Whene'er he saw riders that galloped amain,
    He darned in some bush till they passed.
At kirk or at market sharp glances he cast,
    Lest haply his wife might be there;
And once, when the liquor had kindled his ee,
It never was known who or what he did see,
But he made a miraculous flight from Dundee,
    The moment he entered the fair.

But never again was his bosom estranged,
   From his simple and primitive fare;
No longer his wishes or appetite ranged
   With the gay and voluptous to share.
He viewed every luxury of life as a snare;
   He drank of his pure mountain spring;
He watched all the flowers of the wild as they sprung;
He blessed his sweet laverock, like fairy that sung,
Aloft on the hem of the morning cloud hung,
   Light fanning its down with her wing.

And oft on the shelve of the rock he reclined
   Light carolling humoursome rhyme
Of his midsummer dream, of his feelings refined,
   Or some song of the good olden time.
And even in age was his spirit in prime,
   Still reverenced on Dee is his name!
His wishes were few, his enjoyments were rife,
He loved and he cherished each thing that had life
With two small exceptions, an eel, and a wife,
   Whose commerce he dreaded the same.

SUPERSTITION

In Caledonia's glens there once did reign
   A Sovereign of supreme unearthly eye;
No human power her potence could restrain,
   No human soul her influence deny:
   Sole Empress o'er the mountain homes, that lie
Far from the busy world's unceasing stir:
   But gone is her mysterious dignity,
And true Devotion wanes away with her;
While in loose garb appears Corruption's harbinger.

Thou sceptic leveller—ill-framed with thee
   Is visionary bard a war to wage:
Joy in thy light thou earth-born Saducee,
   That earth is all thy hope and heritage:
   Already wears thy front the line of age;
Thou see'st a heaven above—a grave before;
   Does that lone cell thy wishes all engage?
Say, does thy yearning soul not grasp at more?
Woe to thy grovelling creed—thy cold ungenial lore!

Be mine to sing of visions that have been,
    And cherish hope of visions yet to be;
Of mountains clothed in everlasting green,
    Of silver torrent and of shadowy tree,
    Far in the ocean of eternity.
Be mine the faith that spurns the bourn of time;
    The soul whose eye can future glories see;
The converse here with things of purer clime,
And hope above the stars that soars on wing sublime.

But she is gone that thrilled the simple minds
    Of those I loved and honoured to the last;
She who gave voices to the wandering winds,
    And mounted spirits on the midnight blast:
    At her behest the trooping fairies past,
And wayward elves in many a glimmering band;
    The mountains teemed with life, and sore aghast
Stood maid and matron 'neath her mystic wand,
When all the spirits rose and walked at her command.

And she could make the brown and careless boy
    All breathless stand, unknowing what to fear;
Or panting deep beneath his co'erlet lie,
    When midnight whisper stole upon his ear.
    And she could mould the vision of the seer
To aught that rankled breast of froward wight;
    Or hang the form of cerement or of bier
Within the cottage fire—O woful sight!
That called forth many a prayer and deepened groan by night.

O! I have bowed to her resistless sway,
    When the thin evening vapours floated nigh;
When the grey plover's wailings died away,
    And the tall mountains melted into sky;
    The note of gloaming bee that journeyed bye
Sent thro' my heart a momentary knell;
    And sore I feared in bush or brake might lie
Things of unearthly make—for I knew well
That hour with danger fraught more than when midnight fell.

But O! if ancient cemetry was near,
    Or cairn of harper murdered long ago,
Or wandering pedlar for his hoarded gear,
    Of such, what glen of Scotland doth not know?

Or grave of suicide (upon the brow
Of the bleak mountain) withered all and grey;
   From these I held as from some deadly foe:
There have I quaked by night and mused by day;
But chiefly where I weened the bard or warrior lay.

For many a wild heart-thrilling Scottish bard,
   In lowland dale the lyre of heaven that wooed,
Sleeps 'neath some little mound or lonely sward,
   Where humble dome of rapt devotion stood;
   'Mid heathy wastes by Mary's silent flood,
Or in the moorland glen of dark Buccleuch;
   There o'er their graves the heath-fowl's mottled brood,
Track with light feathery foot the morning dew;
There plays the gamesome lamb, or bleats the yeaning ewe.

Yet, there still meet the thoughtful shepherd's view
   The marble fount-stone, and the rood so grey;
And often there he sees with changeful hue
   The snow-white scull washed by the burn away:
   And O! if 'tis his chance at eve to stray,
Lone by the place where his forefathers sleep;
   At bittern's whoop or gor-cock's startling bay,
How heaves his simple breast with breathings deep;
He mutters vow to heaven, and speeds along the steep.

For well he knows, along that desert room,
   The spirits nightly watch the sacred clay;
That, cradled on the mountain's purple bloom,
   By him they lie companions of the day,
   His guardian friends, and listening to his lay:
And many a chaunt floats on the vacant air,
   That spirit of the bard or warrior may
Hear the forgotten names perchance they bare:
For many a warrior wight, and nameless bard lies there!

Those were the times for holiness of frame;
   Those were the days when fancy wandered free;
That kindled in the soul the mystic flame,
   And the rapt breathings of high poesy;
   Sole empress of the twilight—Woe is me!
That thou and all thy spectres are outworn;
   For true devotion wanes away with thee.
All thy delirious dreams are laughed to scorn,
While o'er our hills has dawned a cold saturnine morn.

Long did thy fairies linger in the wild,
  When vale and city wholly were resigned;
Where hoary cliffs o'er little holms were piled,
  And torrents sung their music to the wind:
  The darksome heaven upon the hills reclined,
Save when a transient sun-beam, thro' the rain,
  Past like some beauteous phantom of the mind
Leaving the hind in solitude again—
These were their last retreats, and heard their parting strain.

But every vice effeminate has sped,
  Fast as the spirits from our hills have gone,
And all these light unbodied forms are fled,
  Or good or evil, save the ghost alone.
  True, when the kine are lowing in the lone,
An evil eye may heinous mischief brew;
  But deep enchantments to the wise are known,
That certainly the blasted herd renew,
And make the eldron crone her cantrips sorely rue.

O! I have seen the door most closely barred;
  The green turf fire where stuck was many a pin;
The rhymes of incantation I have heard,
  And seen the black dish solemnly laid in
  Amid the boiling liquid—Was it sin?
Ah! no—'twas all in fair defence of right.
  With big drops hanging at her brow and chin,
Soon comes the witch in sad and woeful plight;
Is cut above the breath, and yelling takes her flight!!

And I have seen, in gaunt and famished guise,
  The brindled mouser of the cot appear;
A haggard wildness darted from her eyes:
  No marvel was it when the truth you hear!
  That she is forced to carry neighbour near,
Swift thro' the night to countries far away;
  That still her feet the marks of travel bear;
And her broad back that erst was sleek and grey,
O! hapless beast!—all galled where the curst saddle lay!

If every creed has its attendant ills,
  How slight were thine!—a train of airy dreams!
No holy awe the cynic's bosom thrills;
  Be mine the faith diverging to extremes!

What, though upon the moon's distempered beams,
Erewhile thy matrons galloped thro' the heaven,
  Floated like feather on the foaming streams,
Or raised the winds by tenfold fury driven,
Till ocean blurred the sky, and hills in twain were riven.

Where fell the scathe?—The beldames were amused,
  Whom eld and poverty had sorely crazed;
What, though their feeble senses were abused
  By gleesome demon in the church-aisle raised,
  With lion tail and eyes that baleful blazed!
Whose bagpipe's blare made all the roof to quake!
  But ages yet unborn will stand amazed
At thy dread power, that could the wretches make
Believe these things all real, and swear them at the stake.

But ah! thou filled'st the guilty heart with dread,
  And brought the deeds of darkness to the day!
Who was it made the livid corse to bleed
  At murderer's touch, and cause the gelid clay
  By fancied movement all the truth betray?
Even from dry bones the drops of blood have sprung!
  'Twas thou Inquisitor!—whose mystic sway
A shade of terror over nature hung;
A feeling more sublime than poet ever sung.

Fearless the shepherd faced the midnight storm
  To save his flocks deep swathed amid the snow;
Though threatening clouds the face of heaven deform,
  The sailor feared not o'er the firth to row;
  Dauntless the hind marched forth to meet the foe:
For why, they knew, though earth and hell combined,
  In heaven were registered their days below;
That there was one well able and inclined
To save them from the sword, the wave, and stormy wind.

O! blissful thought to poverty and age,
  When troubles press and dangers sore belay!
This is their only stay, their anchorage;
  "It is the will of heaven, let us obey!
  "Ill it befits the creatures of a day,
"Beneath a father's chastening to repine."
  This high belief in Providence's sway,
In the eye of reason wears into decline;
And soon that heavenly ray must ever cease to shine.

Yet these were days of marvel—when our king,
   As chronicles and sapient sages tell,
Stood with his priests and nobles in a ring,
   Searching old beldame for the mark of hell,
   The test of witchcraft and of devilish spell;
And when I see a hag, the country's bane,
   With rancorous heart and tongue of malice fell,
Blight youth and beauty with a burning stain,
I wish for these old times and Stuarts back again.

Haply 'tis weened that Scotland now is free
   Of witchcraft, and of spell o'er human life.
Ah me!—ne'er since she rose out of the sea,
   Were they so deep, so dangerous, and so rife;
   The heart of man unequal to the strife
Sinks down before the lightning of their eyes.
   O! it is meet that every maid and wife
Some keen exorcist still should scrutinize,
And bring them to the test, for all their sorceries.

Much have I owed thee—Much may I repine,
   Great Queen! to see thy honours thus decay.
Among the mountain maids the power was thine,
   On blest Saint Valantine's or Hallow Day.
   Our's was the omen—their's was to obey:
Firm their belief, or most demurely feigned!
   Each maid her cheek on lover's breast would lay,
And, sighing, grant the kiss so long refrained;
'Twas sin to counteract what Providence ordained!

O! I remember, as young fancy grew,
   How oft thou spoke'st in voice of distant rill;
What sheeted forms thy plastic finger drew,
   Throned on the shadow of the moonlight hill;
   Or in the glade so motionless and still
That scarcely in this world I seemed to be;
   High on the tempest sing thine anthem shrill;
Across the heaven upon the meteor flee,
Or in the thunder speak with voice of majesty!

All these are gone—The days of vision o'er;
   The bard of fancy strikes a tuneless string.
O! if I wist to find thee here no more,
   My muse should wander on unwearied wing,

To find thy dwelling by some lonely spring,
Where Norway opes her forests to the gale;
The dell thy home, the cloud thy covering,
The tuneful sea maid, and the spectre pale,
Tending thy gloomy throne, amid heaven's awful veil.

Or shall I seek thee where the Tana rolls
Her deep blue torrent to the northern main;
Where many a shade of former huntsman prowls,
Where summer roses deck th' untrodden plain,
And beauteous fays and elves, a flickering train,
Dance with the foamy spirits of the sea.
O! let me quake before thee once again,
And take one farewel on my bended knee,
Great ruler of the soul, which none can rule like thee!

FINIS

THE POETIC MIRROR

JAMES RIGG

ON Tuesday morn, at half-past six o'clock,
I rose and dress'd myself, and having shut
The door o' the bed-room still and leisurely,
I walk'd down stairs. When at the outer-door
I firmly grasp'd the key that ere night-fall
Had turn'd the lock into its wonted niche
Within the brazen implement, that shone
With no unseemly splendour,—mellow'd light,
Elicited by touch of careful hand
On the brown lintel; and th' obedient door,
As at a potent necromancer's touch,
Into the air receded suddenly,
And gave wide prospect of the sparkling lake,
Just then emerging from the snow-white mist
Like angel's veil slow-folded up to heaven.
And lo! a vision bright and beautiful
Sheds a refulgent glory o'er the sand,
The sand and gravel of my avenue!
For, standing silent by the kitchen-door,
Tinged by the morning sun, and in its own
Brown natural hide most lovely, two long ears
Upstretching perpendicularly, then
With the horizon levell'd—to my gaze
Superb as horn of fabled Unicorn,
Each in its own proportions grander far
Than the frontal glory of that wandering beast,
Child of the Desert! Lo! a beauteous Ass,
With panniers hanging silent at each side!
Silent as cage of bird whose song is mute,
Though silent yet not empty, fill'd with bread
The staff of life, the means by which the soul
By fate obedient to the powers of sense,
Renews its faded vigour, and keeps up
A proud communion with the eternal heavens.
Fasten'd to a ring it stood, while at its head
A boy of six years old, as angel bright,
Patted its neck, and to its mouth applied
The harmless thistle that his hand had pluck'd
From the wild common, melancholy crop.

Not undelightful was that simple sight,
For I at once did recognize that ass
To be the property of one James Rigg,
Who for the last seven years had managed,
By a firm course of daily industry,
A numerous family to support, and clothe
In plain apparel of our shepherd's grey.
On him a heavy and calamitous lot
Had fallen. For working up among the hills
In a slate-quarry, while he fill'd the stone,
Bored by his cunning with the nitrous grain,
It suddenly exploded, and the flash
Quench'd the bright lustre of his cheerful eyes
For ever, so that now they roll in vain
To find the searching light that idly plays
O'er the white orbs, and on the silent cheeks
By those orbs unillumined calm and still.

Quoth I, I never see thee and thy ass,
My worthy friend, but I methinks behold
The might of that unconquerable spirit,
Which, operating in the ancient world
Before the Flood, when fallen man was driven
From paradise, accompanied him to fields
Bare and unlovely, when the sterile earth
Oft mock'd the kindly culture of the hand
Of scientific agriculture—mock'd
The shepherd's sacrifice, and even denied
A scanty pittance to the fisherman,
Who by the rod or net sought to supply
His natural wants from river or from mere.
Blind were these people to the cunning arts
Of smooth civility—men before the Flood,
And therefore in the scriptures rightly call'd
Antediluvians!
                    While thus I spake
With wisdom, that industrious blind old man,
Seemingly flatter'd by those words of mine,
Which, judging by myself, I scarcely think
He altogether understood, replied,
While the last thistle slowly disappear'd
Within the jaws of that most patient beast:
"Master!" quoth he,—and while he spake his hat
With something of a natural dignity
Was holden in his hand—"Master," quoth he,
"I hear that you and Mrs Wordsworth think

97

Of going into Scotland, and I wish
To know if, while the family are from home,
I shall supply the servants with their bread,
For I suppose they will not all be put
Upon board-wages."
                              Something in his voice,
While thus he spake, of simplest articles
Of household use, yet sunk upon my soul,
Like distant thunder from the mountain-gloom
Wakening the sleeping echoes, so sublime
Was that old man, so plainly eloquent
His untaught tongue! though something of a lisp,
(Natural defect,) and a slight stutter too
(Haply occasion'd by some faint attack,
Harmless, if not renew'd, of apoplex)
Render'd his utterance most peculiar,
So that a stranger, had he heard that voice
Once only, and then travell'd into lands
Beyond the ocean, had on his return,
Met where they might, have known that curious voice
Of lisp and stutter, yet I ween withal
Graceful, and breathed from an original mind.

    Here let me be permitted to relate,
For sake of those few readers who prefer
A simple picture of the heart to all
Poetic imagery from earth or heaven
Drawn by the skill of bard,—let me, I say,
For sake of such few readers, be permitted
To tell, in plain and ordinary verse,
What James Rigg first experienced in his soul,
Standing amid the silence of the hills,
With both the pupils of his eyes destroyed.

    When first the loud explosion through the sky
Sent its far voice, and from the trembling rocks
That with an everlasting canopy
O'ershadow Stickle-Tarn the echoes woke,
So that the mountain-solitude was filled
With sound, as with the air! He stood awhile,
Wondering from whence that tumult might proceed,
And all unconscious that the blast had dimm'd
His eyes for ever, and their smiling blue
Converted to a pale and mournful grey.
Was it, he thought, some blast the quarrymen
Blasted at Conniston, or in that vale,
Called from its huge and venerable yew,

Yewdale? (though other etymologists
Derive that appellation from the sheep,
Of which the female in our English tongue
Still bears the name of ewe.) Or did the gun
Of fowler, wandering o'er the heathery wilds
In search of the shy gor-cock, yield that voice
Close to his ear, so close that through his soul
It rolled like thunder? Or had news arrived
Of Buonaparte's last discomfiture,
By the bold Russ, and that great heir of fame
Blucher, restorer of the thrones of kings?
And upon Lowood bowling-green did Laker
Glad of expedient to beguile the hours,
Slow moving before dinner, did he fire
In honour of that glorious victory,
The old two-pounder by the wind and rain
Rusted, and seemingly to him more old
Than in reality it was, though old,
And on that same green lying since the days
Of the last landlord, Gilbert Ormathwaite,
Name well-remember'd all the country round,
Though twenty summer suns have shed their flowers
On the green turf that hides his mortal dust.
Or was it, thought he, the loud signal-gun
Of pleasure-boat, on bright Winander's wave,
Preparing 'gainst some new antagonist
To spread her snowy wings before the wind,
Emulous of glory and the palmy wreath
Of inland navigation? graceful sport!
It next perhaps occur'd to him to ask,
Himself, or some one near him, if the sound
Was not much louder than those other sounds,
Fondly imagined by him,—and both he,
And that one near him, instantly replied
Unto himself, that most assuredly
The noise proceeded from the very stone,
Which they two had so long been occupied
In boring, and that probably some spark,
Struck from the gavelock 'gainst the treacherous flint,
Had fallen amid the powder, and so caused
The stone t' explode, as gunpowder will do,
With most miraculous force, especially
When close ramm'd down into a narrow bore,
And cover'd o'er with a thin layer of sand
To exclude the air, else otherwise the grain,
Escaping from the bore, would waste itself

In the clear sky, and leave the bored stone
Lying unmoved upon the verdant earth,
Like some huge creature stretch'd in lazy sleep
Amid the wilderness,—or lying dead
Beneath the silence of the summer sun.

This point establish'd, he was gently led
By the natural progress of the human soul,
Aspiring after truth, nor satisfied
Till she hath found it, wheresoever hid,
(Yea even though at the bottom of a well,)
To enquire if any mischief had been done
By that explosion; and while thus he stood
Enquiring anxiously for all around,
A small sharp boy, whose task it was to bring
His father's breakfast to him 'mid the hills,
Somewhat about eleven years of age,
Though less than some lads at the age of eight,
Exclaim'd—"Why, father, do you turn the white
Of your eyes up so?" At these simple words
Astonishment and horror struck the souls
Of all the quarrymen, for they descried,
Clear as the noon-day, that James Rigg had lost
His eyesight, yea his very eyes were lost,
Quench'd in their sockets, melted into air,
A moisture mournful as the cold dim gleam
Of water sleeping in some shady wood,
Screen'd from the sunbeams and the breath of heaven.

On that he lifted up his harden'd hands,
Harden'd by sun, and rain, and storm, and toil,
Unto the blasted eye-balls, and awhile
Stood motionless as fragment of that rock
That wrought him all his woe, and seem'd to lie,
Unwitting of the evil it had done,
Calm and serene, even like a flock of sheep,
Scatter'd in sunshine o'er the cheviot-hills.
I ween that, as he stood in solemn trance,
Tears flow'd for him who wept not for himself,
And that his fellow-quarrymen, though rude
Of soul and manner, not untouchingly
Deplored his cruel doom, and gently led
His footsteps to a green and mossy rock,
By sportive Nature fashion'd like a chair,
With seat, back, elbows,—a most perfect chair
Of unhewn living rock! There, hapless man,

He moved his lips, as if he inly pray'd,
And clasp'd his hands and raised his sightless face
Unto the smiling sun, who walk'd through heaven,
Regardless of that fatal accident,
By which a man was suddenly reduced
From an unusual clear long-sightedness
To utter blindness—blindness without hope,
So wholly were the visual nerves destroyed.
"I wish I were at home!" he slowly said,
"For though I ne'er must see that home again,
"I yet may hear it, and a thousand sounds
"Are there to gladden a poor blind man's heart."

He utter'd truth,—lofty, consoling truth!
Thanks unto gracious Nature, who hath framed
So wondrously the structure of the soul,
That though it live on outward ministry,
Of gross material objects, by them fed
And nourish'd, even as if th' external world
Were the great wet-nurse of the human race,
Yet of such food deprived, she doth not pine
And fret away her mystic energies
In fainting inanition; but, superior
To the food she fed on, in her charge retains
Each power, and sense, and faculty, and lives,
Cameleon-like, upon the air serene
Of her own bright imaginative will,
Desiderating nothing that upholds,
Upholds and magnifies, but without eyes
Sees—and without the vestige of an ear
Listens, and listening, hears—and without sense
Of touch (if haply from the body's surface
Have gone the sense of feeling) keenly feels,
And in despite of nose abbreviate
Smells like a wolf—wolf who for leagues can snuff
The scent of carrion, bird by fowler kill'd,
Kill'd but not found, or little vernal kid
Yean'd in the frost, and soon outstretch'd in death,
White as the snow that serves it for a shroud.

Therefore James Rigg was happy, and his face
Soon brighten'd up with smiles, and in his voice
Contentment spoke most musical; so when
The doctor order'd his most worthy wife
To loose the bandage from her husband's eyes,
He was so reconciled unto his lot,

That there almost appear'd to him a charm
In blindness—so that, had his sight return'd,
I have good reason to believe his happiness
Had been thereby scarcely at all increased.

While thus confabulating with James Rigg,
Even at that moment when such silence lay
O'er all my cottage, as by mystic power
Belonging to the kingdom of the ear,
O'erthrew at once all old remembrances—
Even at that moment, over earth, and air,
The waving forest, and the sleeping lake,
And the far sea of mountains that uplifted
Its stately billows through the clear blue sky,
Came such a sound, as if from her dumb trance
Awaken'd Nature, starting suddenly,
Were jealous of insulted majesty,
And sent through continent and trembling isle
Her everlasting thunders. Such a crash
Tore the foundations of the earth, and shook
The clouds that slumber'd on the breast of heaven!
It was the parlour-bell that suddenly
An unknown hand had rung. I cast my eyes
Up the long length of bell-rope, and I saw
The visible motion of its iron tongue,
By heaven I *saw* it tinkling. Fast at first,
O most unearthly fast, then somewhat slower,
Next very slow indeed, until some four
Or half-a-dozen minutes at the most,
By Time's hand cut from off the shorten'd hour,
It stopp'd quite of itself—and idly down,
Like the sear leaf upon th' autumnal bough
Dangled!   ⋆   ⋆   ⋆   ⋆
　　⋆   ⋆   ⋆   ⋆   ⋆

PETER OF BARNET

PETER of Barnet—know'st thou such a man?
'Tis meet thou should'st, for he's a manual
Which one may ever read,—I love old Peter!
Not for his genius or stupendous science,
For he has neither; while his outward man,

Mien, word, and manner, has no other gloss
Than that the stubborn hand of Nature framed
By mallet and by chisel,—but he is
A character distinct,—I ever love
A man that is so,—many have I known,
And many studied with poetic eye.

Peter is one—the slave of keen sensation.
So obviously affected is his heart,
By that he hears and sees, that passion there
Holds everlasting coil,—farther than these,
Peter makes no research,—they are enough
For any heart to brook. I oft have weened,
If Peter neither saw nor heard, he would
Be happier than he is.—What boy is that,
At whom you scold so much, said I, good Peter?

Rascal! said he,—he is as great a knave
As wags beneath the sun,—a saucy knave,
Whom I have reared and nourished as my own.
His mother was a vagrant—no good dame,
I ween was she—She came unto my house
One rainy summer eve, followed by him,
That naughty rogue—a little urchin then,
Not five years old—Brown with the sun he was,
And ragged as a colt!—his head was bare,
And weather-beaten like the tufted moss.

Far far behind he lagged, for he was lame,
And sore bedraggled,—by his foot still kept
A little dog, his fellow traveller
And bosom friend.—I felt I wot not how
For the young imp, for he came wading on
Through mud and mire, halting most wofully.
The guttered road his soal might not imprint,
For it was wounded,—but with dexterous skill
He placed his foot on edge, and ambled thus.

Then Peter walked across the field and back
With awkward limp, to show me how the boy
Walked out the way,—the fancy pleased him much,
For ever and anon he laughed at it,
And yet the tear was pacing down his cheek.
'Twas just this way he walked, poor soul, said Peter;
And then, with turned-up foot, and gait oblique,
Again he halted lamely o'er the ridge,

103

Laughing with shrilly voice, and all the while
Wiping his eyes.—I thought I saw, said Peter,
An independence in the child's blue eye,
A soul that seemed determined to outbrave
Reproach and sufferance,—and to work his way
Throughout the world, though scarce a ray of hope
Lay onward to allure or beckon him.

His supper with his faithful dog he shared;
To that alone he talked, nor heeded once
The tattle of the menials who assailed him.
Soon he was sound asleep; his dumb companion,
With head laid on his little master's breast,
Fell sound as he.—O it was such a picture
Of generous friendship as I ne'er again
Shall look upon!—Then Peter sobbed full hard,
And told it o'er again,—and then he laid
His head upon his shoulder,—stopped his breath
To shortened pant, and with an open mouth,
And face ludicrously demure, he showed me
The way the poor boy slept, and how the dog!
I could not chuse but laugh, and so did Peter;
For he assured me there was never aught
On earth seen like it,—then a second time
He sniff'd in mimic sleep, while from his breast
Issued a feeble dreaming sound of plaint.
That was the very way they slept, said Peter,
I thought my heart would burst,—yet she his mother
Ne'er look'd at them,—not she,—she heeded not.

I could not sleep a wink that night, said Peter,
Nor could I think of aught but the poor boy,
The little ragged pilgrim of the world!
Poor devil! said I, an hundred times I ween
And more,—and then I turned! and turned! and turned!
I sighed a prayer for the unfortunate,
And tried to think of others in distress.
I thought that many a fair and comely mother
Shed the salt tear o'er an unfathered boy,
Who, all unconscious, lay upon her breast,
His only shelter, while, alas! that breast
And beauteous head, no shelter had at all!
I tried such things to ponder,—'twas in vain!
My thoughts were on the boy.—I saw him still!
The little, sun-burnt, naked raggamuffian!
His round red lip and independent eye!

The tiny conscript on the field of life
The veteran of eternity!—I wept-
And turned! and turned!—Good God! said I, what's this!

His tale was never ended, nor would mine
Should I go on, and deftly follow him
Through every maze of feeling,—but the boy
Lives with old Peter,—they have never parted,
Nor ever will till death shall sunder them;
And on my troth, when my old head is laid
Low in the dust, said Peter, I do think
There is not one alive will miss me more,
Or think of me so much as that young knave.
Nor shall he then be destitute, or forced
To prowl in desperate guise throughout the world.
He's a dear boy! a noble generous boy!
But I have spoiled him—all my folk are spoiled.

This is most true,—I walked with Peter forth
Across the winter field, where his one hind
Drew the long furrow, who with lengthened *vo*
And *hie* vociferous urged on his steeds,
And gave harsh tones unto the chilly gale.

It chanced that on the cold wet field we found
A mountain daisy blooming all alone.
I paused, and spoke of Burns, the Scottish bard.
Peter had heard the name,—I then conned o'er
The lines unto the Daisy in a tone
Most tender and affecting.—Peter looked
As he would look me through,—he could not ween
Of feeling for a flower, and yet he felt
A kind of sympathy, that overpowered
All his philosophy.—He took a stone,
And placed it tall on end.—Herbert, said he,
When thou plough'st down this ridge, spare me this flower.
I charge thee note it well,—and for thy life
Do it no injury.—Pugh! said the clown,
Such stuff!—I shall not mind it—He went on
Whistling his tune.—Oh Peter was most wroth!
He run in hasty guise around, and looked
For a convenient stone, that he might throw
And smite the ploughman's head.—No one would suit.
Then, turning round to me, he gave full vent
To's rage against the hind, and all was o'er.
In his first heat, he cursed the menial race;

105

I told you they were all alike, said he,
A most provoking and ungracious set;
(Peter had never told *me* such a thing.)
Now did you ever see a wretch like that?
He's a good workman, and he knows it well,
But not one thing that I desire of him
Will he perform.—I'm an old fool, 'tis true,
But yet methinks the man that eats my bread
Might somewhat humour me.—I thought so too.
But ah! said Peter, when I think of this,
The freedom of the will, by man so valued,
Is not his own!—and that how proud he is
Sometimes to show it, then I give it him;
And when I do, I have not cause to rue.
What a discerning learned man is Peter!
He's nature's genuine, plain philosopher.

That night, at board, Peter sat silent long,
Thoughtful he was.—I think I've heard, said he,
That Burns, of whom you spake, was a bad man,
A man of a most vicious, tainted mind,
Fit to corrupt an age.—Was it not so?

Alas! said I, never was man abused
So much as he!—He was a good man, Peter;
A man of noble independent mind,
So high, that wealth's low minions envied it;
Exerting all their malice to assail
His only part that was assailable.
Keen were his feelings and his passions strong,
Such as your own—The vantage ground was gained.
The foes of genius came, in social guise,
Luring to gusts of blindfold levity
The bard that sore relented.—These were blabbed
With tenfold zest, until the injured heart
Of genius was wrung—It broke!—and then
The foes of humble and inherent worth,
O how they triumphed o'er the Poet's dust!

D—n them! said Peter,—he thrust back his chair,
Dashed one knee o'er the other furiously,
Took snuff a double portion,—swallowed down
His glass at once,—looked all around the room
With wrathful eye, and then took snuff again.

I love old Peter! I would rather see
Nature's strong workings in the human breast,
Than list the endless dogmas which define
Their operations and existing springs.
Peter's a living representative,
A glossary to many terms, that stand
In fair-cast characters upon the page
Of the philosopher,—in other form
To him unknown.—But these are fading all;
Impressed themselves, they no impression leave;
Peter's a stereotype,—that for an age
Will momently throw bold impressions off,
Ever demonstrative, and ever new.
When next I visit him, I'll copy forth
One other page from nature's manual.

Could this ill warld — Air. Mischievous woman.

Allegretto un poco scherzoso.

Could this ill warld have been contriv'd to stand without that

Mischief Woman   How peaceful bodies wou'd have liv'd Releas'd frae a' the

ills sae common   But since it is the waefu' case that man must have this

teasing crony Why such a sweet bewitching face O had they no been made sae bonnie

cres   cres   p

108

COULD THIS ILL WARLD HAVE BEEN CONTRIVED.

WRITTEN FOR THIS WORK

By *JAMES HOGG.*

THE AIR COMPOSED FOR THE WORDS BY A FRIEND OF THE EDITOR.

Could this ill warld have been contrived
  To stand without that mischief, woman!
How peacefu' bodies wou'd have liv'd,
  Releas'd frae a' the ills sae common.
But since it is the waefu' case,
  That man must have this teasing crony,
Why such a sweet bewitching face?
  O had they no been made sae bonnie!

I might have roam'd wi' cheerful mind,
  Nae sin nor sorrow to betide me,
As careless as the wand'ring wind,
  As happy as the lamb beside me.
I might have screw'd my tuneful pegs,
  And carol'd mountain airs fu' gaily,
Had we but wanted a' the Megs,
  Wi' glossy een sae dark and wily.

I saw the danger,—fear'd the dart,—
  The smile, the air, and a' sae taking!
Yet open laid my warless heart,
  And got the wound that keeps me waking!
My harp waves on the willow green,
  Of wild witch notes it has na ony,
Sin' e'er I saw that pawky quean,
  Sae sweet, sae wicked, and sae bonny!

I'LL NO WAKE WI' ANNIE.

Air, by James Hogg.

VOICE

O Mother tell the laird o't, Or sair_ly it will grieve meO,That

PIANO FORTE Slowly.

I'm to wake the ewes the night An' Annie's to gang wi' me O I'll

wake the ewes my night a_bout, But ne'er wi' ane sae sau_cy O nor

sit my lane the lee lang night wi' sic a scorn_fu' lass_ie O. I'll

no wake I'll no wake I'll no wake wi' Annie O Nor sit my lane o'er

night wi' ane sae thra-ward an' un-can-nie O.

Dear Son be wise an warie,
　But never be unmanly O,
I've heard you tell another tale,
　O young an' charming Annie O.
The ewes ye wake are fair enough,
　Upon the brae sae bonny O,
But the laird himsel wad gie them a,
　To wake the night wi' Annie O.
　　I'll no wake, &c.

I tauld ye ear', I tauld ye late,
　That lassie wad trapan ye O,
An' ilka word ye boud to say,
　When left your lane wi' Annie O.
Tak' my advice this night for ance,
　Or beauty's tongue will ban ye O.
An' sey your leel auld mother's skeel,
　Ayont the moor wi' Annie O.
　　He'll no wake, &c.

The night it was a simmer night,
　An' O the glen was lanely O,
For just ae sternie's gowden ee,
　Peep'd o'er the hill serenely O.
The twa are in the flow'ry heath,
　Ayont the moor sae flowy O,
An' but ae plaid atween them baith,
　An' wasna that right dowy O.
　　He maun wake, &c.

Neist morning at his mother's knee,
　He bless'd her love unfeign'dly O;
An' aye the tear fell frae his ee,
　An' aye he clasp'd her kindly O.
Of a' my griefs I've got amends,
　Up in yon glen sae grassy O,
A woman only woman kens,
　Your skill has won my lassie O.
　　I'll aye wake, I'll aye wake,
　　I'll aye wake, wi' Annie O,
　　I'll ne'er again keep wake wi' ane,
　　Sae sweet sae kind an' cannie O.

111

Air, by James Hogg.

O Sair_ly may I rue the day I fan_cy'd first the wo_men kind for aye sin_syne I ne'er can hae a quiet thought or peace o' mind. They hae plagued my heart an' pleas'd my ee An' teaz'd an' flat_ter'd me at will But aye for a' their witch_er_ye the

Chorus.

paw-ky things I lo'e them still O the wo-men fok O the wo-men fok, But they hae been the wreck o' me O wea—ry fa' the wo-men fok for they win—na let a bo-dy be.

I've thought, an' thought, but darna tell;
  I've studied them wi' a' my skill;
I've lo'ed them better than mysel';
  I've try'd again to like them ill.
Wha sairest strives will sairest rue,
  To comprehend what nae man can;
When he has done what man can do,
  He'll end at last where he began.
    O the women fok &c.

That they hae gentle forms and meet,
  A man wi' half a look may see;
An' graceful' airs an' faces sweet,
  An' wavin' curls aboon the bree,
An' smiles as saft as the young rose bud,
  An' een sae pawky bright an' rare,
Wad lure the laverock frae the clud
  But laddie seek to ken nae mair.
    O the women fok &c.

Even but this night nae farther gane,
  The date is nouther lost nor lang,
I tak' ye witness ilka ane,
  How fell they fought and fairly dang;
Their point they've carried, right or wrang,
  Without a reason rhyme or law,
An' forc'd a man to sing a sang,
  That ne'er could sing a verse ava.
    O the women fok, &c.

113

THE POOR MAN.

Slow with Expression.

Loose the yett an' let me in,

La - dy wi' the glist'ning ee, Dinna let your menial train

Drive an auld man out to dee. Cauld rife is the winter ev'n,

See the rime hangs at my chin; La - dy, for the sake of Heav'n,

114

Loose the yett an' let me in.

Ye shall gain a virgin hue
   Lady for your courtesy,
Ever bonny, ever new,
   Aye to bloom an' ne'er to dee.
Lady there's a lovely plain
   Lies beyond yon setting sun,
There we soon may meet again,
   Short the race we hae to run.

'Tis a land of love an' light,
   Rank or title is not there,
High an' low maun there unite,
   Poor man, prince, an' lady fair.
There, what thou on earth hast given,
   Doubly shall be paid again,
Lady for the sake of heaven,
   Loose the yett an' let me in.

Blessings rest upon thy head,
   Lady of this lordly ha'
That bright tear that thou did'st shed,
   Fell na down amang the snaw.
It is gane to heav'n aboon,
   To the fount of charitye,
When thy days on earth are done,
   O how it shall plead for thee.

THE LARK.

Bird of the wilderness, Blithsome an' cumberless, Sweet be thy martin o'er moorland an' lea, Emblem of happiness, Blest is thy dwelling place, O to abide in the desart with thee! Wild is thy lay an' loud, Far in the downy cloud;

Love gives it en-er-gy, love gave it birth. Where on thy dew-y wing,

Where art thou jour-ney-ing? Thy lay is in heav-en, Thy

love is on earth.

O'er fell an' fountain sheen,
O'er moor an' mountain green,
O'er the red streamer that heralds the day;
Over the cloudlet dim,
Over the rainbow's rim,
Musical cherubim, hie thee away.

Then when the gloaming comes,
Low in the heather blooms,
Sweet will thy welcome and bed of love be,
Emblem of happiness!
Blest is thy dwelling place!
O to abide in the desert with thee!

THE LAIRD O' LAMINGTON.

Air by James Hogg.

Can I bear to part wi' thee, Never mair your face to see, Can I bear to part wi' thee, Drun_ken laird o' Lam_ing_ton. Can_ty war ye o'er your kale, Tod_dy jugs an' caups o' ale, Heart aye kind an' leel an' hale,

ho - nest laird o' Lam - ing - ton.

He that swears is but so so,
He that lies to hell must go,
He that falls in bagnio,
    Falls in the devil's frying-pan.
Wha wasn't ne'er pat aith to word?
Never lied for duke nor lord?
Never sat at sinfu' board?
    The honest laird o' Lamington.

He that cheats can ne'er be just;
He that prays is ne'er to trust;
He that drinks to drauck his dust
    Wha can say that wrang is done?
Wha wasn't ne'er to fraud inclin'd?
Never pray'd sin' he can mind?
Ane wha's drouth there's few can find,
    The honest laird o' Lamington.

I like a man to tak' his glass,
Toast a friend or bonny lass;
He that winna is an ass,
    De'il send him ane to gallop on!
I like a man that's frank an' kind,
Meets me when I have a mind,
Sings his sang, an' drinks me blind,
    Like the laird o' Lamington.

So thou'lt not read my Tales, thou say'st, Horatio,
"Because, forsooth, such characters as those
That I have chosen should ne'er be defined,
For when they are,—where's the epitome,
The moral or conclusion? What may man
Profit or learn by studying such as these?"

Wo worth thy shallow, thy insidious wit,
Thy surface-skimming lore, Horatio!
Thou'rt a mere title-page philosopher;
A thing of froth and vapour, formed of all
The unsubstantialities of nature,
Nourished by concourse of the elements;
A man of woman born, of woman bred,
Of woman's mind, frame, fashion, and discourse,
A male blue-stocking!—Out upon thee, girl!
Nay, do not fume nor wince; for, on my soul,
Let but thy barber smooth that whiskered cheek,
With sterile but well-nourished crop besprent,
Scythe thy mustachio, and by this true hand,
I'll hire thee for a nurse, Horatio.

Dost thou not know, presuming as thou art,
That purest gold in smallest veins is found,
And with most rubbish mixed, which thou must sift,
And sorely dig for?—Treasures of the deep,
The mine, the vale, the mountain—Heaven itself,
Man needs must toil for, else he cannot win.
And wilt thou still be fashion's minion,
Reading alone what fashion warrants thee,
The calendar of women?—Wilt thou never
Learn for thyself to judge, and turn thine eye
Into that page of life, the human soul,
With all its rays, shades, and dependencies,
For ever varied, and for ever new?

O if thou dost, be this thy axiom,
Not to despise the slighest, most minute
Of all its shades and utterings, if they flow
Warm from the heart but cherish such in thine;
The day may come thou may'st think otherwise

Than thou dost now.—Ah, hast thou never seen,
The kindly flush and genial glow of spring,
And summer's flower nipt by the biting blast
Of chill unhealthful gale?—Yes, oft thou hast;
And could'st thou see as well into this breast,
And note the toil and warfare there maintained
By the fond weary sojourner within,
That pours this lay, its only anodyne!
Thou could'st not chuse but listen,—it is not
Thy nature to despise my rural lay.

I would be friends with thee, Horatio,
For I have weaknesses, and foibles too,
Worse than thine own, and heavier far to bear!
Then say not thou, by desk or counter placed,
Or haply on the gilded sofa set,
By board of drawing-room, while some fair dame
Stretches her lily hand, with careless mien,
To seize my little book—O say not thou,
"This is our friend again; poor man! he is
For ever publishing, and still the same,
The fairy's raide, the witch's embassy,
The spirit's voice, the mountain and the mist."
Spare the injurious speech—dost thou not see
That beauteous smirk, and that half-lifted eye,
How they bespeak the comely vacancy,
The void of soul within?—Yet that same dame
Leads and misleads one half of all the town.
Dost thou not know, Horatio, that one word,
The first word critical that is pronounced
On any trembling author's valued work,
Nay the first syllable, is like a spark
Set to the mountain, that will flame and spread
Even when the breezes rest; working its way,
And none can certify where it may end?
Beware then how thou kindlest such a flame,
To sear a soul and genius in the bloom!

Far rather say—for 'tis as easy said,
And haply nigher truth—"Madam, I have
Perused that work, and needs must own to you,
I deemed my time well spent—read it throughout,
Thou wilt not rue it."—This were friendlier far,
And more becoming thee;—but it is not
Thy cherished principle, for thou wilt talk
Of egotism, and drawing from one's self,

Chatter of mind, and nerve, and the effect
Of constitution, till the matrons yawn,
And green girls stare at thee—for shame, Horatio!

Of "Egotism and drawing from one's self!"
Does this befit thee?—I have heard thee talk
Three hours and thirty minutes by the clock
Of old Saint Giles, and ever of thyself!
Thyself and thine.—Yet thou wilt carp at me,
And say that I draw only from myself!
Well, be it so; he who draws otherwise
Than from his feelings never shall draw true.
I know my faults, Horatio, and can laugh
At them and thee, as thou shalt see anon.
Read thou the tale before thee—if it please
Not thee I care not; but I pledge my word
My next shall please thee worse—I have a mark
Will better suit,—for it shall be of thee.

There was a time, Horatio—but 'tis gone,
Would that we saw't again—when every hind
Of Scotland's southern dales tilled his own field;
When master, dame, and maid, servant and son,
At the same board eat of the same plain meal.
The health and happiness of that repast
Made every meal a feast.—In these good days
Of might and hardihood, there lived a man.
A wealthy, worthy, and right honest hind,
Hight John of Manor—He had ewes and lambs,
Kids and he-goats, more than he well could number,
Besides good breeding mares and playful colts,
Heifers and lazy bullocks, many a one.
But John had that, which better fits the song
Of rhyming bard and thee, Horatio,
Than kid or lamb, colt or unwieldy ox;
He had five daughters, all of them as fair
As roses in their prime—beshrew that heart
That would not leap and warm at such a sight
As John of Manor's daughters!—At that time
There lived in Lyne a shrewd discerning dame,
Who had an only son, Halbert his name.

One day she drew her chair close to the light,
For, ah! her seam was fine, and it was white
As the pure snow, while by her side reclined
Her darling son, just resting from his work.

122

His ruddy cheek was leant upon his hand,
His eyes fixed on the wall, in careless wise,
And all the while he was full earnestly
Whistling a tune, as if it did import
Greatly to him the masterly performance.

"Thou never dost remark," said the good dame,
And as she spoke she turned her prying eye
Right o'er the spectacles to look at Hab;
The eyes of glass were still upon the seam,
But the true eye peeped over them—it was
A mother's eye! aye fraught with kind concern
When turned on her own offspring!—"Look thou here,
Thou careless thing—thou never dost remark,
What beauteous linen I have bought this year
For my good son—but trow me, it has cost
Thy mother a round sum—yet though it has,
I have a meaning in't, which bodes thee well.—
List me, my son. What whillilu is that,
Thou keep'st a trilling at?"—Halbert went on,
Straight with his tune, there was a fall in it
He could not lose.—"List what I say, my son;
I'm wearing old and frail, and by the course
Of nature soon must leave thee—we have lived
Full happily and well, but slow decay
Steals on with silent foot, and we must part."

"Hush, hush," said Halbert, "talk not of that theme
For many years to come. I'd rather part
With all I have on earth than my dear mother."
She took her spectacles, and wiped them clean,
For a warm tear had dimm'd her aged eye,
Then went she on with theme she dearly loved,
Lauding her filial son—who by that time
Had made recovery of his favourite air
On a sweet minor key, and pour'd it forth,
Soft and delightful as a flageolet.
"When I have sew'd this sleeve my work is done,
And thou shalt go a-wooing in this shirt;
And, trust me, thou shalt not its marrow meet
In all the lands of Lyne, March, and Montgomery,
So fine, and yet so fair."—Halbert went on
Sheer with his tune—it was a lay of love,
An old and plaintive thing, and strangely was
Blent with some nameless feelings of delight,
Which Halbert keenly felt, but little knew

123

How to account for.—"List to me, my son:
Fain would I see thee settled rationally
In life as thee becomes, and fairly join'd
To virtuous daughter of an honest man.
My old acquaintance, John of Manor, has
Five winsome daughters—there is not in all
The bounds of Scotland five such lovely maids
As John of Manor's daughters—and he is
A man of wealth, which these fair maids must heir,
For son he hath not.—Would you go, my son,
And chuse a wife from Manor, it would glad
The heart of your old mother.—There is Ann,
The eldest born, who likely wilt share most
Of his wide wealth—O such a wife, my son,
As Ann of Manor, would become your house,
Your table head, your right hand at the church,
And when the cold long nights of winter come

    *   *   *   *
    *   *   *   *+

    This last description Halbert could not stand;
He gave his tune quite up, which of itself
Long ere that time had nearly died away;
He sigh'd, gave a short yawn, and rising up,
Look'd at the linen, praised its snowy hue
And beauteous texture—some inquiry made
What time it would be ready for the wear,
Then sat he down again to hear some more
Of lovely Ann of Manor:—"Ah! my son,
She is not one of the light-headed herd,
These gew-gaw, giddy-paced, green-sickly girls,
That mind nought but their gaudery and their glee.
Poor thriftless, shiftless, syrup-lipped shreds
That take men in to ruin.—No, she is
A sound man's child, an honest woman born,
And bred up in the paths of decency
And fear of Heaven—and then she is so fair,
So fresh and lovely!—and as sweet, my son,
As field of new-won hay."—Halbert arose,
Drew a long breath, stretch'd up his boardly frame
In guise of anxious solicitude,
Look'd at the shirt again, and went away.

    That day he thought of Ann, he sung of Ann,
He whistled the sweet air of *Bonny Ann*

+ Some lines wanting here.

124

Along the hay-field, and when came the night,
He lay and dream'd of lovely Ann of Manor.

Next morning Halbert found when he awoke
A fair new shirt, white as the lily's breast,
Well air'd and plaited with neat careful hand,
At his bed-head; proudly he put it on,
And in his heart he blest the kindred love
That had prepared it so while others slept.

Hab went away with ardent anxious breast
Across the moor to Manor—as he went,
He conned his deep-laid schemes of policy.
I am resolved, said Halbert to himself,
If these fair maidens please me, that I will
Be frank and generous—I'll not sue for dower,
For flock or herd, gelding, or sullen ox.
I'll win their favour well, and then I'll trust
To fortune for the rest—With the good-man
I'll talk of farming and the service work;
Of the improven breeds of sheep and wool;
Of crops and servants, and the foolish risk
Of selling aught on credit, till he say
When I walk out, "He's a shrewd fellow Hab,
One who knows more than many thrice his age;
Wife, give us of the best the house affords
At dinner-time—you, wenches, get you gone,
Put your new kirtles on, and make you clean;
Hab is the son of an old worthy friend,
I love him for his parents' sake as well
As for his own—He's a shrewd fellow Hab!"

"Then, when a chance occurs, I'll talk apart
With the old dame of prudence and of thrift,
The vices and the follies of the age;
I'll talk of sins, of sermons, and of faith,
Of Boston, and Ralph Erskine, and renounce
The slightest atom of dependency
Upon my own good works.—"Ah!" she will say,
"He is a sensible good Christian lad
That Halbert!—one who minds the thing that's good!"
Then will she look in her loved daughter's face
With wistful eye, and with a sigh exclaim,
"What pity should he throw himself away
On some light worthless jilflirt!—Ah! he is
A sensible good Christian lad that Halbert!"

"But then the maid, how shall I deal with her?
There lies the difficulty, should they not
Once leave us by ourselves—I never can
Ask her in public with as formal face
As I would buy a heifer or a mare.
No, by ourselves we needs must be; and then
O how I'll press, teaze, flatter, and caress her!
I'll clasp her waist, and kiss her comely cheek,
Steal by degrees to her soft moisten'd lip—
The sharp reproof will quickly grow more mild
Until it melt away—then will I sigh,
And say that it was cruel in th' extreme
To grant so sweet a kiss—for how can man
That has enjoy'd it ever more be happy,
Or live without the owner of such kiss!
Then she'll say to herself as I do now
"I like that Hab—he hath some spirit Hab."

By this time Hab had so wound up his thoughts
With visions of delight, that he had quitted
His common pace, and ran across the moor
Without perceiving it, while shepherds stood
And gazed afar with wonder—dreading sore
That Halbert was distraught, or something wrong
With the good folks of Lyne. He came at last
To the hall-door of Manor with a breast
Beating full hard, and little wist he then
What he should say.—Forth came the old goodman
With his white hosen and his broad blue bonnet;
Stout and well-framed he was, but in his eye
Lurk'd a discernment Halbert scarce could brook.

After good-morrow, question, and reply,
With downcast look Hab thus his errand said:
"I'm come in search of a much-valued ewe
Which I have lost, and she, it seems, was seen
Coming this way—a beautiful young ewe,
One which I may not and I must not lose."
"What are her marks and whither did she come?"
"She came from Lyne." "Ah, do I see the son
Of my old valued friend? Welcome, good youth;
I saw not your lost sheep, but all my flock
I'll put before you; if you find her not,
Chuse one from mine and welcome; you may find
Some ewes as young, as beautiful, and good,
As any bred on Lyne." Halbert look'd down,

Full sore abash'd, but made as fit reply
As he well could.—"My girls are out," said John,
"Milking the ewes, they will be here anon,
And they perchance may give you some account
Of your lost ewe.. 'Tis hard that a young man
Should lose his ewe—meanwhile let us go in,
See the goodwife, and taste her morning cheer."

Good ewe-milk whey, thick as the curdled breast
Of cauliflower, brose, butter, bread, and cheese,
Furnish'd the breakfast board of John of Manor.
Hard did he press his youthful guest to all,
Whose high resolves had faded into smoke.
He talked not of religion, nor the mode
Of farming to advantage, for old John
Failed not at every interval to hint,
With sly demeanour, something of his ewe.
"Who's that," said Halbert, "coming from the bught
With the five maids?"—"I know not," John replied;
"He seems a stranger,—some young man perchance
Seeking a ewe.—O these same ewes, my friend,
Are a precarious stock,—they go astray,
And will not stay with one, do as he will."

At length the maidens, decked all neat and clean,
Entered the little parlour one by one.
Ann was not tall, but lively and discreet,
And comely as a cherub,—Halbert weened
No woman ever born so beautiful
As Ann of Manor.—But when entered Jane,
Of fair delicious form, round pouting lips,
Cheeks like the damask rose, and liquid eye
That spoke unutterable things, her locks,
Fair as the morning, waving round her brow
Like light clouds curling o'er the rising sun,
Or, if you please, the mist-wreaths pale, Horatio.
Soon Halbert saw that all the world beside
Could never once compare with beauteous Jane.
Then came the third, young Douglas, with an eye
Dark and majestic as the eagle's, when
She looks down from the cliff.—Her form was tall,
Slender, and elegant, while from her tongue
Flowed such a spirit of melodious breath,
That thrilled the hearer,—not alone they seemed
The language of the soul, her tones and words
Were very soul itself.—Halbert was fixed—

127

Confirmed in this, that never mortal man,
Nor angel, had beheld a female form,
A face, an eye, nor listened to a voice
Like that of lovely Douglas.—Mary came,
The modest, diffident, and blushing Mary.
The mild blue eye, the joy of innocence
Beaming through every smile!—O Halbert's heart
Was wholly overpowered; till Barbara came,
The youngest and the loveliest of them all.

Halbert went home,—he went without his ewe,
And heart to boot,—that heart was lost for ever,
To whom he knew not! in the family
That heart had lingered, he wist not with whom.
Such grace, such purity of form and mind,
Appeared in all, Halbert was on the rack.
He took to bed, but sleep had flown from thence;
He thought of Ann, and sighed a prayer to Heaven;
Of young and blooming Barbara, and the smile
That shed a radiance o'er the maiden blush
Of gentle Mary; then a burning tear,
A tear of sympathy, crept o'er his cheek.
He thought of Jane, and turned him in his bed;
He thought of Douglas, and turned back again.

Day follow'd day, and week came after week,
Years past away, and Halbert all the while
Was wooing hard at Manor—sometimes one,
Sometimes another, as blind chance decreed;
Each of them was so good, so beautiful,
So far surpassing all of womankind,
That time, nor chance, nor reason, e'er could frame
A choice determinate; till at the last
Old Manor, in a kind but earnest way,
Enquiry made what his intentions were
That thus he haunted his fair family.

"Sooth, my good friend," said Halbert, "ne'er was man
On earth so hard beset—I love them all
With such a pure esteem and stainless love,
That though I well could give the preference
To any one, yet for my life and soul
There is not one of them I can reject.
I give the matter wholly up to you,
I know you wish me well, and all the maids
Alike to you are dear,—Whom shall I chuse?"

John set his bonnet in becoming mode,
That well betoken'd deep considerate thought;
One edge of it directed middle way
'Twixt the horizon and the cope of heaven,
And with the one hand in his bosom sheathed,
The other heaving slightly in the air
To humour what he said, he utter'd words
Which I desire you note—"My son," said he,
"I've one advice to give you, which through life
I rede you follow—when you make a choice
Of man or woman, beast, farm, fish, or fowl,
CHUSE EVER THAT WHICH HAS THE FEWEST FAULTS.
My girls have all their foibles and their faults—
Mary's are FEWEST AND LEAST DANGEROUS.
Take thou my Mary—if she prove to thee
As good a wife as she has ever been
A dutiful and loving child to me,
Thou never wilt repent it."—So it proved,
A happier pair ne'er travell'd through this vale
Of life together, than our Halbert
With his beloved Mary.—Peace to them,
And to their ashes!—and may every pair
Of happy lovers in their kindred dale
Cherish their memory, and be blest as they!

Now, dear Horatio, when thou makest choice
Of book, of friend, companion, or of wife,
Think of the sage advice of John of Manor;
CHUSE EVER THAT WHICH HAS THE FEWEST FAULTS.
AND THOSE LEAST DANGEROUS.—Take note of this:

All have their faults and foibles—all have too
The feelings that congenial minds will love;
And to each other genial minds will cling
Long as this world has being, and the shades
Of nature hold their endless variation.
I say no more Horatio, but this word:
In time to come, when thronged variety
Of books, and men, and women, on thee crowd,
When choice distracts thee, or when spleen misleads,
Think of the sage advice of John of Manor.

ne'er see a - gain; Fare - weel to my he - ro, the gal - lant and young, Fare -

Dol.

- weel to the lad I shall ne'er see again.

The Above Sym. & Accom by M. Geo. Jno. Edin.

The Moorcock that craws on the brows o' Ben—Connal,
    He kens o' his bed in a sweet mossy hame;
The Eagle that soars o'er the cliffs of Clan—Ronald
    Unawed and unhunted his eiry can claim,
The Solan can sleep on his shelve of the shore,
    The Cormorant roost on his rock of the sea;
But Oh! there is ane whose hard fate I deplore,
    Nor house, ha', nor hame in his country has he;
The conflict is past, and our name is no more,
    There's nought left but sorrow for Scotland and me!

The target is torn from the arms of the just,
    The helmet is cleft on the brow of the brave,
The claymore for ever in darkness must rust;
    But red is the sword of the stranger and slave;
The hoof of the horse, and the foot of the proud
    Have trode o'er the plumes on the bonnet of blue
Why slept the red bolt in the breast of the cloud
    When tyranny revelled in blood of the true,
Farewell my young hero, the gallant and good!
    The crown of thy Fathers is torn from thy brow

V. I. F.

131

THE HIGHLAND WATCH.

Beethoven.

Written for this work by J. HOGG on the Highlanders return from Waterloo.

Old Scotia wake thy mountain strain, In all its wild_est splendors; And wel_come back the lads a_gain, Your honour's dear de__fend___ers. Be ev'ry harp and vi_ol strung, 'Till all the woodlands qua__ver; Of many a band your Bards have sung, But ne_ver hail'd a bra__ver.

CHORUS.

Then raise the pibroch Donald Bane, We're all in key to cheer it; And

Then raise the pibroch Donald Bane, We're all in key to cheer it; And

Then raise the pibroch Donald Bane, We're all in key to cheer it; And

132

let it be a martial strain, That Warriors bold may hear it.

let it be a martial strain, That Warriors bold may hear it.

let it be a martial strain, That Warriors bold may hear it.

2.

Ye lovely maids, pitch high your notes,
 As virgin voice can sound them,
Sing of your brave, your noble Scots,
 For glory kindles round them.
Small is the remnant you will see,
 Lamented be the others!
But such a stem of such a tree,
 Take to your arms like brothers.

CHORUS.—Raise high the pibroch, Donald Bane,
 Strike all our glen with wonder;
 Let the chaunter yell, and the drone note swell,
 Till music speaks in thunder.

Vol: 5.

3.

What storm can rend your mountain rock,
 What wave your headlands shiver!
Long have they stood the tempest's shock,
 Thou know'st they will for ever.
Sooner your eye these cliffs shall view,
 Split by the wind and weather,
Than foeman's eye the bonnet blue,
 Behind the nodding feather.

CHO: O raise the pibroch, Donald Bane,
 Our caps to the sky we'll send them;
 Scotland, thy honour who can stain,
 Thy laurels who can rend them.

GOODNIGHT AN' JOY
BE WI' YOU A'

The year is wearin' to the wane, An' day is fadin'
west a-wa' Loud raves the torrent an' the rain, An' dark the cloud comes
down the shaw. But let the tempest tout an' blaw, U-
pon his loud-est win-ter horn, Goodnight an' joy be
wi' you a', We'll may-be meet a-gain the morn.

The year is wearin' to the wane,
    An' day is fadin' west awa'
Loud raves the torrent an' the rain,
    An' dark the cloud comes down the shaw.
But let the tempest tout an' blaw,
    Upon his loudest winter horn,
Goodnight an' joy be wi' you a',
    We'll maybe meet again the morn.

O we hae wander'd far an' wide,
    O'er Scotia's land of firth an' fell,
An' mony a simple flower we've cull'd,
    An' twined them wi' the heather-bell:
We've ranged the dingle an' the dell,
    The hamlet an' the baron's ha',
Now let us tak a kind farewell,
    Good night an' joy be wi' you a'.

Ye hae been kind as I was keen,
    And follow'd where I led the way,
Till ilka poet's lore we've seen
    Of this an' mony a former day.
If e'er I led your steps astray
    Forgie your minstrel ance for a'
A tear fa's wi' his parting lay
    Good night and joy be wi' you a'.

James Hogg

SELECTED
POEMS AND SONGS

Edited by
DAVID GROVES

Many of Hogg's songs were published with music during his lifetime, the music frequently being composed by Hogg himself.

Although often badly printed, these early publications are documents of exceptional interest and importance for the study of Hogg's career as a song-writer. A number of them are therefore reproduced in the present volume. Unfortunately, the poor quality of the printing of the originals sometimes produces problems of legibility.

For this reason, the words of two of these songs are reprinted overleaf and references are provided to the pages in the present volume in which the originals are reproduced.

SCOTTISH ACADEMIC PRESS
EDINBURGH

THE POOR MAN

Loose the yett an' let me in,
   Lady wi' the glist'ning ee;
Dinna let your menial train
   Drive an auld man out to dee.
Cauld rife is the winter ev'n,
   See the rime hangs at my chin;
Lady, for the sake of Heav'n,
   Loose the yett an' let me in.

Ye shall gain a virgin hue
   Lady for your courtesy,
Ever bonny, ever new,
   Aye to bloom an' ne'er to dee.
Lady there's a lovely plain
   Lies beyond yon setting sun,
There we soon may meet again,
   Short the race we hae to run.

'Tis a land of love an' light,
   Rank or title is not there,
High an' low maun there unite,
   Poor man, prince, an' lady fair.
There, what thou on earth hast given,
   Doubly shall be paid again,
Lady for the sake of heaven,
   Loose the yett an' let me in.

Blessings rest upon thy head,
   Lady of this lordly ha'
That bright tear that thou did'st shed,
   Fell na down amang the snaw.
It is gane to heav'n aboon,
   To the fount of charitye,
When thy days on earth are done,
   O how it shall plead for thee.

THE LAMENT
OF
FLORA MACDONALD

Far over yon hills of the heather so green,
   And down by the Correi that sings to the sea,
The bonny young Flora sat sighing her lane,
   The dew on her plaid and the tear in her ee.
She look'd at a boat with the breezes that swung
   Away on the wave, like a bird of the main,
And aye as it lessen'd she sigh'd and she sung,
   Fareweel to the lad I shall ne'er see again;
Fareweel to my hero, the gallant and young,
   Fareweel to the lad I shall ne'er see again.

The Moorcock that craws on the brows o' Ben-Connal,
   He kens o' his bed in a sweet mossy hame;
The Eagle that soars o'er the cliffs of Clan-Ronald
   Unawed and unhunted his eiry can claim,
The Solan can sleep on his shelve of the shore,
   The Cormorant roost on his rock of the sea;
But Oh! there is ane whose hard fate I deplore,
   Nor house, ha', nor hame in his country has he;
The conflict is past, and our name is no more,
   There's nought left but sorrow for Scotland and me!

The target is torn from the arms of the just,
   The helmet is cleft on the brow of the brave,
The claymore for ever in darkness must rust;
   But red is the sword of the stranger and slave;
The hoof of the horse, and the foot of the proud
   Have trode o'er the plumes on the bonnet of blue.
Why slept the red bolt in the breast of the cloud
   When tyranny revelled in blood of the true?
Fareweel my young hero, the gallant and good!
   The crown of thy Fathers is torn from thy brow.

Printed by Lindsay & Co. Ltd., Edinburgh

Come all ye jolly shepherds that whistle thro' the glen,
  I'll tell ye of a secret that courtiers dinna ken.
What is the greatest bliss that the tongue of man can name?
  'Tis to woo a bonny lassie when the kye comes hame.
    When the kye comes hame, when the kye comes hame,
      'Tween the gloaming an' the mirk, when the kye comes
      hame.

'Tis not beneath the burgonet, nor yet beneath the crown,
  'Tis not on couch of velvet, nor yet in bed of down—
'Tis beneath the spreading birch, in the dell without the name,
  Wi' a bonny, bonny lassie, when the kye comes hame.
    When the kye comes hame, when the kye comes hame,
      'Tween the gloaming an' the mirk, when the kye comes
      hame.

There the blackbird bigs his nest for the mate he lo'es to see,
  And up upon the topmost bough, oh, a happy bird is he!
There he pours his melting ditty, and love 'tis a' the theme,
  And he'll woo his bonny lassie when the kye comes hame.
    When the kye comes hame, &c.

When the bluart bears a pearl, and the daisy turns a pea,
  And the bonny lucken gowan has fouldit up his ee,

Then the lavrock frae the blue lift drops down, and thinks nae
    shame
  To woo his bonnie lassie when the kye comes hame.
    When the kye comes hame, &c.

Then the eye shines sae bright, the hale soul to beguile,
  There's love in every whisper, and joy in every smile:
O wha wad choose a crown, wi' its perils and its fame,
  And miss a bonny lassie when the kye comes hame?
    When the kye comes hame, &c.

See yonder pawky shepherd, that lingers on the hill,
  His ewes are in the fauld, and his lambs are lying still;
Yet he downa gang to bed, for his heart is in a flame,
  To meet his bonny lassie when the kye comes hame.
    When the kye comes hame, &c.

Away wi' fame and fortune, what comfort can they gie?
  And a' the arts that prey on man's life and liberty:
Gie me the highest joy that the heart o' man can frame,
  My bonny, bonny lassie, when the kye comes hame.
    When the kye comes hame, &c.

NEW CHRISTMAS CAROL

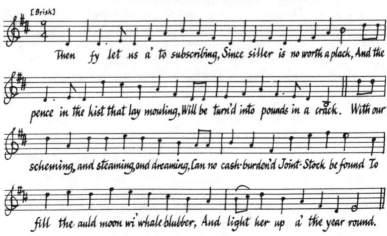

Then fy let us a' to subscribing, Since siller is no worth a plack, And the
pence in the kist that lay mouling, Will be turn'd into pounds in a crack. With our
scheming, and steaming, and dreaming, Can no cash-burden'd Joint-Stock be found To
fill the auld moon wi' whale-blubber, And light her up a' the year round.

THEN fy let us a' to subscribing,
  Since siller is no worth a plack,
And the pence in the kist that lay mouling,
  Will be turn'd into pounds in a crack.
With our scheming, and steaming, and dreaming,
  Can no cash-burden'd Joint-Stock be found
To fill the auld moon wi' whale blubber,
  And light her up a' the year round.

Now thieves will be nabb'd by the thousand;
  And houses insured by the street;
And share-holders will scarcely know whether
  They walk on their heads or their feet.
The Celtic will soon compass breeches;
  The shoe-black will swagger in pumps;
And phrenologists club for old perukes,
  To cover their assinine bumps.

Alack, for our grandfathers musty,
  Of such ongoings ne'er did they dream;
Soon our Jockies will bizz out, at gloaming,
  To court their kind Jennies by steam;
And the world shall be turn'd topsy-turvy;
  And the patients their doctors will bleed;
And the dandy, by true gravitation,
  Shall go waltz on the crown of his head.

Then fy let us a' to subscribing,
  And build up a tower to the moon;
And get fou on the tap, and, in daffing,
  Dad out the wee stars wi' our shoon;—
Then, hey fal de ray, fal de rady,
  Let's see a' how proud we can be,
And build ower a brig to Kirkaldy,
  And drown a' the French in the sea!

Gabriel.—Alas! Sir John, thou nothing know'st of love.
Would I could say the same!

Sir John.—   What? Gabriel, thou,
A pillar of the temple, a strong prop
In God's true Anti-burgher meetinghouse,
In love? Throwing thy sombre cloak aside,
Religion's cloak that covers many flaws,
Thy stern demeanor, and thy look severe,
And yielding to that lightsome dalliance
The love of women? I may not believe
That such a doure, staunch, rugged Antiburgher
Could fall into that crimson sin so deep.
Gabriel why dost thou sigh? I purpose not
To preach a sermon now. Or if I do,
Women shall be my text, and vanity,
Smiles, beauty, sin and suffering my doctrine.

Gabriel.—'Tis easy for a gentleman to talk
In folly's lightest strain of things that lie
Beyond his fathom. There are germs Sir John
Implanted in our natures—embryo sparks,
That need but kindling to set a whole world
In burning flame. Of all these energies,
The love of woman is the first, the greatest,
The most supreme, intense, and absolute,
That man's firm soul encounters. To my cost
I know this for a truth!

Sir John.—   Who can believe
That one so used to sit and grunt at church;
To make wry faces, wink, and shake the head;
Gather up halfpence in long-shafted ladles;
Hand the good elements, and pocket up
Stiff leaden coinage of unshapely mould
And sullen hue.—A fellow used to gape,
And sing "O mother dear Jerusalem"
In every saintly throng. A very slowhound
Upon the scent of sin—a terrier
Within the warren of iniquity
To tear up youthful crime, and it expose

To the anathemas of stern divine,
Of ancient maiden, and of matron grim
Yearning o'er blooming offspring.—Such a dog,
To bow at beauty's shrine! To sit and blink
Out through his fingers at the youthful bloom
Of virgin in her prime—O Gabriel fie!
I may not credit it, unless you give
All the particulars of that huge offence.

Gabriel.—O master, for my life I cannot say it.
I have not words, nor looks, nor countenance
For such an effort.

Sir John.—   Prithee Gabriel do,
I cannot live without the full detail
Of this great backsliding, this woful fall.
It must be piteous tale; and as I deem
One of most thrilling interest.

Gabriel.—Aye that it is.
Wilt thou not tell't again? Swear thou wilt not
And I'll essay it.

Sir John.—   I do.

Gabriel.—Well then Sir John, when thou wert far away
At the great English schools, there came a youth
Forth from the Border to be butler here.
By wayward fate our lots were cast together;
We messed, work'd, walk'd, and went to church,
Sung, waked, and slept still by each other's sides.
Now not any thought was in that fellow's mind,
Nor theme nor subject ever on his tongue
But one, and that was WOMEN.—Women, women!
He talked of women when he woke at morn,
He talked of women till he went to rest
And then he dreamed of them, and raved and laughed
In weak and treble quavers; sighed, and wept,
And named their thrilling names. There was not aught
Lovely in nature that he would not liken
To something about women; and all in them
Lovely or not to something heavenly.
He talked about their forms—the taper limb
The flexile waist, round loin, and budding bosom
Like white twin roses opening to the bloom.
Then came the smiles, the dimples, and the blushes;

139

And these he likened to the dawning beauties
Of summer morn.—All was so wonderful,
So rich, so pure, so made for love and Joy.
That faith Sir John I fairly caught th'infection
And fell in love. Long did I pray against it;
And sob, and weep alone. But straight I came
Back to that flaming Borderer's society,
And all my efforts vanished in his breath.
I listened with devotion—groaned in spirit
And then besought him to describe to me
The dear bewitching beings over again.
    I was in woful plight! But all was nought
Until he came to talk about their eyes.
Good lord Sir John! If you had heard him talk
About their eyes, you must have fallen a victim
As well as I. He called them living mirrors
Deep as the sea—the fountains of the soul
In which one saw pourtrayed all that was lovely
In God's fair universe—the woods, the hills,
The bowers and deep recesses of the forest
So framed for secret love—the clouds, the skies,
And marble pavements of the firmament.
I trembled in amaze! But when he said
That in these heavenly mirrors he could see
The secret workings of the soul within,
The beatings of the heart, and all the motions
Within the fair one's breast, I felt my brain
Turn swifter than a millstone, and my scull
Grew rigid as if scalp'd. Then, worst of all!
He raved about some bright twin gods of love
That smiled within those eyes; fair lovely cherubs
That much resembled him the fair one loved,
Or him that looked into those lovely orbs
With pure, with holy, and with kind affection.
O they were lovely smiling babes, and thrilled
The very hearts of those that looked at them.
I asked if they were naked?—He said "No
But thinking made them so"—O then Sir John
The fatal shaft was flung! my very soul
Had gone out after women—I was a corpse,
A blind automaton that moved alone
To that one spring. I saw nought on the earth,
On the broad sea, among the sailing clouds,
The hosts of heaven, the warring elements
Even to the burning flame; nought could I see

In all but beauteous maids and naked bairns!
So boundless was the measure of my love.

Sir John.—And all this while had'st thou no elect maid
No chosen one on whom that love was centred?

Gabriel.—No—None—I loved the women.
The dear women; the angelic things,
Of whom this Borderer spoke; 'twas those I loved.
I longed to look into their liquid eyes,
Those windows of the soul, and there to scan
Love's most profound and everlasting springs,
But most of all I long'd to see the babes,
Those little images of living joy;
But not one virgin's eye in all the land
Could I see into; for whene'er my nose,
The Antiburgher elder's nose came nigh
Poking to their's, then would they turn away
And scream with laughter. Then I had such dreams!
I dreamed I looked into their deep blue eyes,
And saw those hidden mysteries which the tongue
Of mortal dares not name. Once on a time
I saw a lovely mother with a child
Pressed naked to her breast, and still she wept
And looked to heaven—But the tears she shed
Were liquid fire; upon *my* breast they fell
And seared it to the core. Then I grew sick,
And wished to die outright, for I had been
Mentally dead for days and months and years
To all but love. Longer I could not live
In such lone misery and dark despair.
So I grew *mortal* sick—took to my bed—
Sent for a surgeon—lost some two'r three pounds
Of my worst love-sick blood—and here I am.
But often have I wished that Border wight,
That meteor of the element of love,
And worshipper of woman's eye, might fall
And break his neck over a woman's foot.
This is my tale Sir John.

Sir John—Yes and a very wonderous tale it is.

If e'er I'm thine, the birds of the air,
   The beasts of the field, and fish of the sea,
Shall in our love and happiness share,
   Within their elements fair and free,
And rejoice because I am thine, love.

We'll have no flowers, nor words of love,
   Nor dreams of bliss that never can be;
Our trust shall be in heaven above;
   Our hope to a far futurity
Must arise when I am made thine, love.

And this shall raise our thoughts more high
   Than visions of vanity here below;
For chequer'd thro' life our path must lie;
   'Mid gleams of joy and shades of woe
We must travel when I am thine, love.

THE GREAT MUCKLE VILLAGE
OF BALMAQUHAPPLE

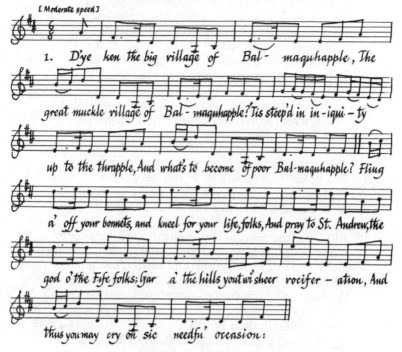

D'ye ken the big village of Balmaquhapple, The
great muckle village of Balmaquhapple? 'Tis steep'd in in-iqui-ty
up to the thrapple, And what's to become of poor Balmaquhapple? Fling
a' off your bonnets, and kneel for your life, folks, And pray to St. Andrew, the
god o' the Fife folks; Gar a' the hills yout wi' sheer vocifer – ation, And
thus you may cry on sic needfu' occasion:

D'YE ken the big village of Balmaquhapple,
The great muckle village of Balmaquhapple?
'Tis steep'd in iniquity up to the thrapple,
And what's to become of poor Balmaquhapple?
Fling a' off your bonnets, and kneel for your life, folks,
And pray to Saint Andrew, the god o' the Fife folks;
Gar a' the hills yout wi' sheer vociferation,
And thus you may cry on sic needfu' occasion:

"O blessed Saint Andrew, if e'er ye could pity folk,
Men folk or women folk, country or city folk,
Come for this aince wi' the auld thief to grapple,
And save the poor village of Balmaquhapple!
Frae drinking, and leeing, and flyting, and swearing,
And sins that ye wad be affrontit at hearing,
And cheating, and stealing, O grant them redemption,
All save and except the few after to mention.

There's Johnny the elder, wha hopes ne'er to need ye,
Sae pawkie, sae holy, sae gruff, and sae greedy,
Wha prays every hour, as the wayfarer passes,
But aye at a hole where he watches the lasses:
He's cheated a thousand, and e'en to this day yet
Can cheat a young lass, or they're leears that say it;
Then gie him his way, he's sae sly and sae civil,
Perhaps in the end he may cheat Mr Devil.

There's Cappie the cobler, and Tammie the tinman,
And Dickie the brewer, and Peter the skinman;
And Geordie, our deacon, for want of a better;
And Bess, that delights in the sins that beset her.
O, worthy Saint Andrew, we canna compel ye,
But ye ken as weel as a body can tell ye,
If these gang to heaven, we'll a' be sae shockit,
Your garrat o' blue will but thinly be stockit.

But for a' the rest, for the women's sake, save them!
Their bodies at least, and their souls, if they have them;
But it puzzles Jock Linton, and small it avails,
If they dwell in their stomachs, their heads, or their tails.
And save, without frown or confession auricular,
The clerk's bonny daughters, and Bell in particular;
For ye ken that their beauty's the pride and the stapple
Of the great wicked village of Balmaquhapple."

144

I DOWNA LAUGH, I DOWNA SING.

Words & Melody
by the
Ettrick Shepherd
Arranged with Symphonies
AND
Accompaniments
— by —
HENRY R. BISHOP.

RATHER SLOW,
and with much
EXPRESSION.

Dol.

Dim. I dow..na laugh, I

mf p

downa sing, Though sweet beseeching looks I see, Though smiles abound, and

of the Ettrick Shepherd, H. L.

wine goes round. And ev'..ry eye is turn'd on me; For there is ane out

o'.... the ring, Wha ne...ver can for...got...ten be! Aye, there's a blank at

Slentando.

my right hand That ne'er can be made up to me!

colla voce. *mf*

'Tis said as wa...ter wears the rock, That

f *rf* *p*

time wears out the deep...est line, It may be true wi' hearts e...new, But
ne...ver shall ap...ply to mine! For I have liv'd to know and feel, Though
losses should for...got...ten be, That still the blank at my right hand, Can
never be made up to me. I blame not Provi...dences sway, For

Slen?

colla voce.

I have many joys beside, And I would fain wi' grateful heart. Es-

teem the same, what e'er be tide. A mortal thing should ne'er repine, But

stoop to the supreme decree; Yet O! the blank at my right hand, Can

never be made up to me.

colla voce. *f* *p* *pp e dim.*

THE LADIES' EVENING SONG

Written by the

ETTRICK SHEPHERD,

Arranged with

Symphonies & Accompaniments,

BY

HENRY R. BISHOP.

SLOW, and with EXPRESSION.

Dol.

Cres.

Original.

O the glass is no for you, Bonny lad...die, O, The glass is no for you, Bonny lad....die, O, The

Songs of the Ettrick Shepherd, R.I.

149

glass is no for you, For it paints your manly brow, An' it fills you roaring

fou, Bonny lad...die, O; Then drive us not a......way wi' your

drinking, O, We like your pre...sence mair Than you're thinking o', How

happy wad you be In our blithsome compa...ny, Taking innocence an' glee For your

Songs of the Ettrick Shepherd. B.1.

150

drinking. O. Now your een are glancing bright, Bonny lad...die, O, Wi' a pure an' joyfu' light, Bonny lad...die, O, But at ten o' clock at night, Take a lady's word in plight, We will see a...no...ther, sight, Bonny lad.....die, O. There's a

Songs of the Ettrick Shepherd. B.4.

151

right path and a wrang, Bonny lad.....die, O, An' you need.na ar.guy

lang, Bonny lad...die, O, For the mair you taste an' see Of our

guileless compa...ny Ay the hap..pier you will be, Bonny lad...die, O.

Orig.

THE p AND THE q
OR
THE ADVENTURES OF JOCK M'PHERSON

"THERE was an auld man, and he had an auld wife,
And they had a son was the plague of their life;"
For even frae the time, when a bairn on the knee,
He was as contrary as callant could be.
He gloom'd and he skirl'd, and, when in hard case,
He whiles gae his mother a yerk on the face;
And nought sae well pleased him, when he could win at her,
As to gar her mild grey een stand in back-water.
They scolded, they drubb'd him, they ruggit his hair,
They stripp'd off his claes, and they skelpit him bare—
But he took every chance baith to scart and to spar,
And instead o' growing better, he rather grew waur.

This old crabbed carle it is hard to make verse on:
His trade was a miller, his name was M'Pherson—
And this wicked callant, the plague o' his stock,
I ne'er heard his name, but I'm sure it was Jock—
For I never yet heard of a stripling of game,
The son of an auld pair, but Jock was his name.
I am sure that my mother had thirty old stories,
And every one of them began as before is;
Or, "there was a man and wife like other folk,
An' they had a son, an' they ca'd him Jock;"
And so it went on—Now this that you're hearing
Was one of these stories—you'll find it a queer ane.—

Jock went to the school—but there rose sic a rumpus!—
The scholars were maul'd, and their noddles grew bumpous;
The pretty wee girls were weel towzled and kiss'd,
In spite of their teeth, ay, and oft ere they wist;
But yet for as ill as the creatures were guided,
In Jock's fiery trials wi' him still they sided.
Good sauf's, how they squeel'd in their feckless resistance!
Good sauf's, how the master ran to their assistance!
He ca'd Jock a heathen, a Turk, and a Nero,
Grinn'd, clench'd his auld teeth, and laid on like a hero;
But no mends could he get—for, despite of his sway,
Jock fought him again twenty times in a day.

Of course, Jock's advancement in learning was slow;
He got with perplexity as far as O;

153

But the p and the q, that sister and brother,
He wish'd at the deil, and he never wan further.

He hated the Dominie's teasing and tattles—
He hated the school, except for the battles—
But he liked the sweet wenches, and kindly caress'd them,
Yet when they would not let him kiss them, he thrash'd them.

There was ae bit shy lassie, ca'd Phemie Carruthers,
Whom he either lo'ed waur or lo'ed better than others;
From morning to e'en you'd have heard or have seen them,
For peace there was never a moment between them;
She couldna bide frae him, he seem'd to bewitch her,
Yet neither would she let him kiss her or touch her,
But squeel'd like a rabbit, and giggled and ran,
Till Jock ran her down, wi' a curse or a ban.
Then many a sair drubbing he gat frae her brothers;—
O dear was his flirting wi' Phemie Carruthers!

The auld miller kendna what way to bestow him,
Or what in the world's wide range to make o' him;
For when at the mill, at the meadow, or mart,
He fought wi' the horses and coupit the cart;
He couldna even gang wi' the horse to the water,
But there was a battle, and gallop full blatter.
To a smith he was enter'd, to yerk at the stiddy,
But he lamed the auld smith, and he fired the smiddy.
Then went to a tailor of high estimation,
To learn to make trousers and breeks in the fashion;
But a' that the tailor could threaten or wheedle,
At every steek Jock gae'm the length of the needle.
Ten times in a day he provoked him or trick'd him,
Then ance for amusement he fought and he lick'd him;
So Snip turn'd him off, and accepted another,
And Jock went once more to his father and mother.

Then they sent him to sea, to efface his reproach,
In fighting the Spaniards, the French, and the Dutch.
Jock fought with them all, for he happen'd to hate them;
Whenever he met them, he fought, and he beat them;
He fought from his childhood, and never thought ill o't:
But then he acknowledged he whiles got his fill o't;
Of all naval heroes, our country had never,
Than this Jock M'Pherson, a truer or braver.
He fought thirty battles, and never retreated,
Round a' the hale world that God has created,

And for twenty long years, for ill or for well o't,
He never saw Britain, and seldom heard tell o't;
Yet never in life such resistance he knew,
Nor retreated, except from the p and the q!

But the sights that Jock saw—O, no man can conceive them!
They're really so grand, folks will hardly believe them.
He cross'd both the circles, which we're rather dark about,
He saw both the poles, which folk make sic a wark about;
And by a most rigid and laboursome scanning,
Not only the poles, but the sockets they ran in;
And also the giants, austere and outlandish,
That wheel'd the world round, like a kirn on its standish;
They were cover'd with ice, and had faces most grievous,
And their forms were mis-shapen and huge as Ben-Nevis;
Yet they stood to their business, though fretting and knarl'd,
With their cans of bear's grease for the poles of the world.
Let Barrow, and Parry, and Franklin, commence
From this as example, and learn to speak sense.

Jock sailed where no Christian ever had been afore,
And found out some countries that never were seen afore;
He came to a land where the language they spoke
Had exactly the sound of the Scottish moor-cock,
With a ick-ick-ick, uck-uck-uck—ne'er was such din heard!
And instead of coming outward, their voices went inward.
He came to another, where young women wore
Their faces behind, and their bottoms before;
Jock tried to embrace these maids once and again,
But the girls were confounded, and giggled amain—
For forward they fled in a moment, and smack
Jock came to the ground on the broad of his back;
Which makes me suspect—though I hate to asperse—
That their forms were like ours, but their clothes the reverse.
Pooh! Franklin's, and Hall's, and the whole, are a mock,
Compared with the voyages and travels of Jock!

Jock sail'd up a branch of the Plate through the Andes;
He visited Lima and Juan Fernandez;
Then spread all his canvass, and westward he ran,
Till he came to the shores of the famous Japan,
And an island beyond it, which Britons ne'er knew,
But Jock thought the natives pronounced it Cookoo;
The half of its wonders no history relates,
For its slates are all gold, and its money is slates!

*　　*　　*　　*　　*　　*

Jock rose from a midshipman up to an admiral,
And now to that island for ever he bade farewell,
And sailed by a coast that had skies very novel,
The sun was an oblong, the moon was an oval;
And from the horizon midway up the skies,
The stars danced outrageously reels and strathspeys;
But none of the stars he remember'd were there,
He missed his old friends of the Serpent and Bear;
But those that they had were of brilliant adorning,
All bright as Dame Venus, the star of the morning;
At midnight there glow'd out a radiance within them,
As the essence of light and its spirit were in them,
Till even the rude sailors with awe looked upon them,
As if a light sacred and heavenly shone on them.

One ship and one crew (a bold and uncanny ane)
At first sailed with Jock from the Mediterranean;
But now every thing was with him *sesquialter*,
As proudly he passed by the bay of Gibraltar.
He returned a commander, accomplished and nautical;
It is true, some suspected his conduct piratical;
But Jock from such chances and charges got well off,
For they happened so distant they ne'er were heard tell of.
He had as much good money—gold, silver, and copper—
As filled to the brim his old father's mill-hopper;
Two ships and a frigate, all trim and untented—
Such feats and such fortune are unprecedented!

Jock bought his old father the lands of Glen-Wharden,
The old wicked Dominie a house and a garden;
And all his school-fellows that thrashed him a-going it,
He gave them large presents, and blessed them for doing it;
Then took for his lady, in preference to others,
The wild little skelpie called Phemie Carruthers.
But he swore, that through life he had never been stopp'd
By Christian or Pagan with whome'er he coped;
By all the wild elements roused to commotion,
The roarings of storm, and the rollings of ocean;
Wild currents and mountains of icicles blue,
Except the two bouncers, and p and the q!!
"And blast my two eyes!" Jack would swear and would say,
"If I do not believe to this here blessed day,
That the trimmers were nothing for all the kick-up just,
Than a b and a d with their bottoms turn'd upmost!"

ST. MARY OF THE LOWS

O LONE St. Mary of the waves,
   In ruin lies thine ancient aisle,
While o'er thy green and lowly graves
   The moorcocks bay and plovers wail;
   But mountain-spirits on the gale
Oft o'er thee sound the requiem dread,
   And warrior shades and spectres pale
Still linger by the quiet dead.

Yes, many a chief of ancient days
   Sleeps in thy cold and hallow'd soil,
Hearts that would thread the forest maze
   Alike for spousal or for spoil,
   That wist not, ween'd not, to recoil
Before the might of mortal foe,
   But thirsted for the border-broil,
The shout, the clang, the overthrow.

Here lie those who, o'er flood and field,
   Were hunted as the osprey's brood,
Who braved the power of man, and seal'd
   Their testimonies with their blood:
   But long as waves that wilder'd flood
Their sacred memory shall be dear,
   And all the virtuous and the good
O'er their low graves shall drop the tear.

Here sleeps the last of all the race
   Of these old heroes of the hill,
Stern as the storm in heart and face;
   Gainsay'd in faith or principle,
   Then would the fire of heaven fill
The orbit of his faded eye,
   Yet all within was kindness still,
Benevolence and simplicity.

GREIVE, thou shalt hold a sacred cell
   In hearts with sin and sorrow tost,
While thousands, with their funeral-knell,
   Roll down the tide of darkness lost;

157

For thou wert Truth's and Honour's boast,
Firm champion of Religion's sway—
    Who knew thee best revered thee most,
Thou emblem of a former day!

Here lie old forest bowmen good;
    Ranger and stalker sleep together,
Who for the red-deer's stately brood
    Watch'd, in despite of want and weather,
    Beneath the hoary hills of heather:
Even Scotts, and Kerrs, and Pringles, blended
    In peaceful slumbers, rest together,
Whose fathers there to death contended!

Here lie the peaceful, simple race,
    The first old tenants of the wild,
Who stored the mountains of the chace
    With flocks and herds—whose manners mild
    Changed the baronial castles, piled
In every glen, into the cot,
    And the rude mountaineer beguiled,
Indignant, to his peaceful lot.

Here rural beauty low reposes,
    The blushing cheek and beaming eye,
The dimpling smile, the lip of roses,
    Attractors of the burning sigh,
    And love's delicious pangs that lie
Enswathed in pleasure's mellow mine:
    Maid, lover, parent, low and high,
Are mingled in thy lonely shrine.

And here lies one—here I must turn
    From all the noble and sublime,
And o'er thy new but sacred urn
    Shed the heath-flower and mountain thyme,
    And floods of sorrow, while I chime
Above thy dust one requiem.
    Love was thine error, not thy crime,
Thou mildest, sweetest, mortal gem!

For ever hallowed be thy bed,
    Beneath the dark and hoary steep;
Thy breast may flowerets overspread,
    And angels of the morning weep

In sighs of heaven above thy sleep,
And tear-drops of embalming dew;
    Thy vesper-hymn be from the deep,
Thy matin from the æther blue!

I dare not of that holy shade
    That's pass'd away one thought allow,
Not even a dream that might degrade
    The mercy before which I bow:
    Eternal God, what is it now?
Thus asks my heart, but the reply
    I aim not, wish not, to foreknow;
'Tis veiled within eternity.

But O, this earthly flesh and heart
    Still cling to the dear form beneath,
As when I saw its soul depart,
    As when I saw it calm in death:
    The dead rose and funereal wreath
Above the breast of virgin snow,
    Far lovelier than in life and breath,
I saw it then and see it now.

That her fair form shall e'er decay
    One thought I may not entertain;
As she was on her dying day,
    To me she ever will remain:
    When Time's last shiver o'er his reign
Shall close this scene of sin and sorrow,
    How calm, how lovely, how serene,
That form shall rise upon the morrow!

Frail man! of all the arrows wounding
    Thy mortal heart, there is but one
Whose poisoned dart is so astounding
    That bear it, cure it, there can none.
    It is the thought of beauty won
To love in most supreme degree,
    And by the hapless flame undone,
Cut off from nature and from thee.

Farewell, dear shade! this heart is broke
    By pang which no allayment knows;
Uprending feelings have awoke
    Which never more can know repose.

O, lone St. Mary of the Lows,
Thou hold'st a treasure in thy breast,
That, where unfading beauty glows,
Must smile in everlasting rest.

THE MINSTREL BOY

TREAD light this haunted grove of pleasure,
And list the fall of that dying measure;
O breathe not, stir not foot or hand—
There are visitants here from the Fairy land!
For such a sweet and melting strain
Was never framed in this world of pain;
It had breathings of ecstasy and bliss—
Of a happier, holier sphere than this!

I see the vision—I see it now—
And the grey hairs creep upon my brow;
For I know full well, from a thrilling smart
And a joy that quivers through my heart,
That this most sweet and comely boy,
With his pipe and his looks of sunny joy,
Is either the prince of the land unseen,
The child of my loved Fairy Queen,
Or cherub sent from a region higher,
The son of Apollo the king of the lyre!

Hail lovely thing! Ah might it be
That I were again such a being as thee,
With my pipe and my plaid in the wild green wood,—
If thou art indeed of flesh and of blood!
But be thou a child of this world of strife,
Or a stranger come from the land of life,
Where the day of glory closes never,
And the harp and the song prevail for ever,
Still, vision fair, I long to be
A thing as holy and pure as thee.

Is it a dream or fairy trance,
This scene of grandeur and wild romance?

That chrystal pool with its sounding linn,
And the lovely vista far within,
The weeping birch and the poplar tall,
And the minstrel boy, the loveliest of all,
Thus singing his lay to the waterfall?

It is no vision of aught to be,
But a wild and splendid reality.
Then here let me linger, enwrapt, alone,
And think of the days that are past and gone—
Days of brightness, but fled as soon
As the bow from the cloud in the afternoon—
Gone like the purpled morning ray—
Gone like the blink of a winter day—
Gone like the strain of ravishing joy,
Late poured from the pipe of the minstrel boy,
That has left no trace in its airy flight,
Though the leaves were dancing with delight;
Gone like the swallow far over the main,
But never like her to return again!

Yes, there was a time with memory twined,
(But time has left it afar behind),
When I, like thee, on a summer day
Would fling my bonnet and plaid away,
And toil at the leap, the race, or the stone,
With none to beat but myself alone.
And then would I raise my tiny lay
And lilt the songs of a former day;
Till I believed that over the fell
The fairies peeped from the heather bell;
That the lamb, so fraught with fond regard,
Had ceased to nibble the flowery sward;
That the plover came nigh with his corslet brown,
And the moorcock showed his scarlet crown;
That I even beheld, with reverence due,
The goss-hawk droop his pinion blue,
And the tear in the eye of the good curlew:
These things I trowed in my ecstasy,
So they were the same as truth to me;
And I decided, with placid brow,
That at the leap, the race, or the throw,
Or tuneful lay of the greenwood glen,
I was the chief of the sons of men.

Well, time flew on; and this conceit,
This high resolve not to be beat,
So urged me on these sports to head,
Though rarely the first, I had no dread
With *all* the first my skill to try,
And little lose in the contest high.
—Without resolve that mocks controul,
A conscious energy of soul
That views no height to human skill,
Man never excelled and never will.
Forgive, dear boy, this barren theme,
But be this phrase thy apothegm—
Better in the first race contend,
Than all that follows to transcend.

But thou shalt rise, full well I know,
If health still beam on thy comely brow;
For thou hast a hand to lead thee on
That stands unequalled and alone,
While thy old monitor had none—
None, save the song of the rural hind,
The bleating flocks, and the wailing wind,
The wildered glen with its gloomy pall,
The cliff, and the cairn, and the waterfall,
The towering clouds of ghastly form,
And the voice that spoke in the thunder storm!

Yes—there was another—a fervid flame,
Dear of remembrance, and dear of name,
With a thousand pains and pleasures blent,
But scarcely a thing of this element;
And thou shalt know it some time hence
To thy sweet and thy hard experience;
And thou shalt heave the burning sigh,
And be its slave as well as I.
Much do I owe to its sacred sway,
For he who sends thee this simple lay,
In his remote and green alcove
Was the pupil of NATURE and of LOVE.
With these and ART, shalt thou excel:
Dear Minstrel Boy! a while farewell.

Second POETIC MIRROR

ANDREW THE PACKMAN
after the manner of Wordsworth

IN vale of Bassenthwaite there once was bred
A man of devious qualities of mind;
Andrew the Packman, known from Workington,
And its dark and uncomely pioneers,
Even unto Geltsdale forest, where the county
Borders on that of Durham, vulgarly
Called Bishoprigg. But still within the bounds
Of ancient Cumberland, his native shire,
Andrew held on his round, higgling with maids
About base copper, vending baser wares.
Not unrespective, but respectively,
As suited several places and relations,
Did he spread forth muslins, and rich brocades
Of tempting aspect; likewise Paisley lace,
Upholden wove in Flanders, very rich
Of braid, inwove with tinsel, as the blossoms
Of golden broom appear in hedgerows, white
With flowers of budding hawthorn. Then his store
Of maidenish nick-nacks greatly overran
My utmost arithmetical operation.

Andrew knew well, better than any man
In all the eighteen towns of Cumberland,
The prime regard that's due to pence and farthings,
The right hand columns of his ledger-book.
This I call native wisdom, and should stand
Example to us of each small concern
That points to an hereafter. For how oft
Is heaven itself lost for a trivial fault!
First we commit one sin—one little sin—
A crime so venial, that we scarcely deem
It can be register'd above. Yet that one
Leads to another, and, perchance, a greater:
Higher and higher on the scale we go,
Till all is lost that the immortal mind
Should hold to estimation or account!

Thus wisdom should be earn'd. But I forgot,
Or rather did omit, at the right place,
To say that Andrew at first sight could know
The nature, temper, habits, and caprices
Of every customer, man, wife, or boy,
Stripling, or blooming maid. Yet none alive
Could Andrew know, for he had qualities
Of eye, as well as mind, inscrutable.
For when he look'd a person in the face,
He look'd three ways at once. Straightforward one,
And one to either side. But so doth he,
That wondrous man, who absolutely deducts,
Arranges, and foretells, even to a day,
Nature's last agony and overthrow.
Presumptuous man! Much would I like to talk
With him but for one hour. So I am told
Looks a great man—a man whose tongue and pen
Hath hope illimitable. One who overrules
A great academy of northern lore.
So look three of our noble peers. And so
Looks one—and I have seen the man myself—
A fluent, zealous holder forth, within
The House of Commons. So look'd Andrew Graham,
That peddling native of fair Bassenthwaite.

Now this same look had something in't, to me
Deeply mysterious. For, if that the eye
Be window of the soul, in which we spy
Its secret workings, here was one whose ray
Was more illegible than darkest cloud
Upon the cheek of heaven; whene'er he look'd
Straight in my face, and I return'd that look,
He seem'd not bent on me, but scatter'd
To either hand, as if his darkling spirit
Scowl'd in the elements. Yet there was none
Could put him down when loudly sceptical,
But I myself. A hard and strenuous task!
For he was eloquence personified.

Now it must be acknowledged, to my grief,
That this same pedlar—this dark man of shawls,
Ribbons, and pocket napkins—he, I say,
Denied that primal fundamental truth,
The Fall of man! Yea, the validity
Of the old serpent's speech, the tree, the fruit,
The every thing concerning that great fall,

In which fell human kind! The man went on,
Selecting and refusing what he chose
Of all the sacred book. Samson's bold acts,
(The wonders of that age, the works of God!)
The jaw-bone of the ass,—the gates of Gaza,—
Even the three hundred foxes, he denied—
Terming them fables most impossible!
But what was worse,—proceeding, he denied
Atonement by the sacrifice of life,
Either in type or antitype, in words
Most dangerously soothing and persuasive.

　　Roused into opposition at this mode
Of speech, so full of oleaginiousness,
Yet sapping the foundation of the structure
On which so many human hopes are hung,
It did remind me even of a pillar
Of pyramidal form, which I had seen
Within the lobby of that noble peer,
The Earl of Lonsdale. On the right hand side,
As entering from the door, there doth it stand
For hanging hats upon. Not unapplausive
Have I beheld it cover'd o'er with hats.
Apt simile in dissimilitude
Of that most noble fabric, which I have
In majesty of matter and of voice
Aroused me to defend. "Sir, hear me speak,"
(Now at that time my cheek was gently lean'd
On palm of my left hand; my right one moving
Backwards and forwards with decisive motion,)—
"Sir, hear me speak. Will you unblushingly
Stretch your weak hand to sap the mighty fabric,
On which hang millions all proleptical
Of everlasting life? That glorious structure,
Rear'd at the fount of Mercy, by degrees
From the first moment that old Time began
His random, erring, and oblivious course?
Forbid it, Heaven! Forbid it Thou who framed
The universe and all that it contains,
As well as soul of this insidious pedlar,
Aberrant as his vision! O, forbid
That one stone—one small pin—the most minute,
Should from that sacred structure e'er be taken,
Else then 'tis no more perfect. Once begun
The guilty spoliation, then each knave
May filch a part till that immortal tower

Of refuge and of strength,—our polar star,
Our beacon of Eternity, shall fall
And crumble into rubbish. Better were it
That thou defaced the rainbow, that bright pledge
Of God's forbearance. Rather go thou forth,
Unhinge this world, and toss her on the sun
A rolling, burning meteor. Blot the stars
From their celestial tenements, where they
Burn in their lambent glory. Stay the moon
Upon the verge of heaven, and muffle her
In hideous darkness. Nay, thou better hadst
Quench the sun's light, and rend existence up,
By throwing all the elements of God
In one occursion, one fermenting mass,
Than touch with hand unhallow'd, that strong tower,
Founded and rear'd upon the Holy Scriptures.
Wrest from us all we have—but leave us that!"

    The spirit of the man was overcome,
It sunk before me like a mould of snow
Before the burning flame incipient.
He look'd three ways at once, then other three,
Which did make six; and three, and three, and three,
(Which, as I reckon, made fifteen in all,)
So many ways did that o'er-master'd pedlar
Look in one moment's space. Then did he give
Three hems most audible, which, to mine ear
As plainly said as English tongue could say,
"I'm conquer'd! I'm defeated! and I yield,
And bow before the majesty of Truth!"

    He went away—he gave his pack one hitch
Up on his stooping shoulders; then with gait
Of peddling uniformity, and ell
In both his hands held firm across that part
Of man's elongated and stately form
In horses call'd the rump, he trudged him on,
Whistling a measure most iniquitous.
I was amaz'd; yet could not choose but smile
At this defeated pedlar's consecution;
And thus said to myself, my left cheek still
Leaning upon my palm, mine eye the while
Following that wayward and noctiferous man:

    "Ay, go thy ways! Enjoy thy perverse creed,
If any joy its latitude contains!

How happy mightst thou be through these thy rounds
Of nature's varied beauties, wouldst thou view
Them with rejoicing and unjaundiced eye!
The beauteous, the sublime, lie all before thee;
Luxuriant valleys, lakes, and flowing streams,
And mountains that wage everlasting war
With heaven's own elemental hosts, array'd
In hoary vapours and majestic storms.
What lovely contrasts! From the verdant banks
Of Derwent, and the depths of Borrowdale,
Loweswater, Ennerdale, with Buttermere
And Skiddaw's grisly cliffs. Yet, what to thee
Are all these glimpses of divinity
Shining on Nature's breast?—Nay, what to thee
The human form divine? The form of man,
Commanding, yet benign? Or, what the bloom
Of maiden in her prime, the rosy cheek,
The bright blue laughing eye of Cumberland,
Lovliest of England's maids? What all to thee,
Who, through thy darkling and dissociate creed,
And triple vision, with distorted view,
Look'st on thy Maker's glorious handywork,
And moral dignity of human kind!
—Even go thy ways! But, when thou com'st at last,
To look across that dark and gloomy vale
Where brood the shadows and the hues of death,
And see'st no light but that aberrant meteor
Glimmering like glow-worm's unsubstantial light
From thy good works, in which thou put'st thy trust,
Unhappy man! then, woe's my heart for thee!"

A COMMON LOT
Montgomery

PAST what our parish record scans,
    There lived a man, and *who* was he?
Mortal! if bred to mending pans,
    That youth resembled thee!

Unknown the hovel of his birth,
   The dykeside where he died unknown;
His name hath perish'd from the earth,
   This truth survives alone:

That ducks and hens, when he was near,
   Alternate vanish'd from the loans;
His bliss and woe, roast fowl, small beer!
   Oblivion hid the bones.

The tatter'd coat, the old straw hat,
   The breeches pepper'd at the knees;
They say that he was round and fat,
   His eyes were hid in grease.

He stole—but now his art is done;
   Loved ducks—his taste for fowls is dead;
Had friends—each ragged soul is gone;
   Had foes—the horde has fled.

He loved—but her he loved, a scamp
   One evening bore from his embrace;
Oh! she was fair, but prone to tramp
   With every taking face.

The rolling seasons, day and night,
   Sun, moon, and stars, and wind and rain,
Tann'd, blighted, batter'd, pour'd downright
   On him, but all in vain!

Each gift turn'd up as gipsies find,
   Where blear-eyed Sawney found the tongs;
He toy'd when tawny dames were kind,
   And sang when they loved songs.

The coat and breeches which he wore,
   The brimless hat that bound his brow,
Search ye the Cowgate o'er and o'er,
   There hangs no vestige now!

The annals of the gipsy race
   Bears not this friend to pot and pan;
Than this, you'll find no other trace—
   Once lived poor tinkler Dan.

A GRAND NEW BLACKING SONG

Black-makers now their shops may seal
Warren may gang an' black the deil
For a' their whuds an' a' their wiles
They'll ne'er compare wi' Jamie Kyle's.
I've tried them all with burnished gold
And Kyles is best a thousand fold!
But Gude preserve my glancing cloots
The cocks came feechtin wi' my boots
The dogs sit gurrin at their shadows
An' a tom cat completely mad is.
The birds come hanging wing an' feather
To woo upon my upper leather
An' the bull trout the warst of a'
Whene'er my glancing limb he saw
Came splashin out frae mang the segs
An' bobb'd an' swattered round my legs
For in those mirrors polish'd gleaming
He saw a mate in chrystal swimming.
Now this is (joking all apart)
Complete perfection o' the art

Sae a' the bloustin blacking-makers
May claw their paws an' turn street-rakers
Or gang wi' ane that's right auld farren
The sly redoubted Robin Warren
To hunt the otter and the beaver
By sources of Missoury river
Or fly to Afric's sultry shores
An' try to black the blackimores
For business here they can have none
Othello's occupation's gone
While Kyles the sprightly Kyles shall stand
The hero of his native land.
A blacking-maker all uncommon
Is equalled or excelled by no man
The first that e'er was born of woman!
N.B. Pray call before tis over late
At Hunder an' twall the Canongate

THE FIRST SERMON

Once on a lovely day—it was in spring
I went to hear a splendid young divine
Preach his first sermon. I had known the youth
In a society of some renown, but liked him not
Because he held his head too high for me
And ever and anon would sneer and poogh!
And cast his head all to one side as if
In perfect agony of low contempt
At every thing he heard. I liked not this

Besides there are some outward marks of men
One scarcely can approve. His hair was red
Almost as red as German sealing wax
And then 'twas curled—Mercy how it was curled
'Twas like a tower of strength. O what a head
For Combe or Dr Spurziem to dissect
After 'twas polled. His shoulders rather narrow
And pointed like two pins. And then there was
A primming round the mouth of odious cast
Bespeaking the proud vacancy within

Well—to the old Greyfriars church I went
And many more with me. The church was crowded.
In came the beadle; then our hero followed
With gown blown like a main-sail flowing on
To right and left alternate. Such a sight
Of graceful elegance and dignity
Never astounded heart of youthful dame
But I bethought me what a messenger
From the world's pattern of humility

The psalm was read with beauteous energy
And sung And then the prayers! Such a face
Of simpering seriousness and mockery
Of all things sacred many men have seen.
I never. Eyes close shut, one cheek turned up,
The mouth quite long and narrow like a seam
Holding no fit proportion of a mouth
Ever by man beheld. The high curled hair
With quiver and with shake announced supreme
The heart's devotion. Unto whom? Ask not.
It is unfair! Suppose it to high heaven
Unfair to ask? Unto the comely dames

Around the gallery. Glad was I at last
To hear the soft and graceful long AY-MAIN!

Then came the sermon O ye mighty powers
Of poesy sublime give me to sing
The splendors of that sermon. The bold *hem*!
The look sublime and confident withal
The three wipes with the cambrick handkerchief
The strut, the bob, and the important blow
Upon the holy book. No notes were there!
No not a scrap! all was intuitive
Flowing like water from a sacred fountain
Gleamed the grey eye with fervor the red hair
Shook like the withered juniper in wind.
Twas grand! O'erpowering! Such an exhibition
Is not to be seen every day. The sermon?
Aha! There comes the rub. For I'll defy
That man on earth to say what was the sermon
Twas all made up of scraps. from Johnson some
And some from Joseph Addison, John Logan,
Blair, William Shakespeare, Young's *Night Thoughts*,
Gillespie on the Seasons. Even the plain
Bold energy of Andrew Thomson there
Was pressed into the jungle. Plan or system
In it was none; connectionless. A thing
Made up of shreds and patches; but the blare
Went on for fifteen minutes haply more.
The *hems* and *haws* began to come more close.
Three at a time! The scented handkerchief
Came greatly in request—The burly head
Gave over tossing, and the cheeks grew red
Then pale, then blue. Then crimson turned again.
The beauteous ladies in the galleries
Began to look dismayed.Their rosy lips
Wide opened, and their bosoms heaving so
One might have weened a rolling sea within
The preacher sat him down—opened the bible
Got up again, gave half a dozen *hems*!
It would not do! His countenance bespoke
The loss of reccollection. All within
Became a blank, a chaos of confusion
Producing naht but agony of soul
The agony within. He seized his hat
And stooping floundering plaitting at the knees
Made his escape. But O how I admired
The Scottish audience. There was neither laugh

171

Nor titter but a softened sorrow
Pourtrayed in every face. As for myself
I laughed till I was sick Went home to dinner
Drank the poor preacher's health and laughed again
Till I could laugh no longer. But alas
Far otherwise it fared with him for he
Went home to his own native kingdom—Fife,
Passed to his father's stable where he seized
A pair of strong plough-reigns and hanged himself!
His pride could not o'ercome it—He is gone!

THE LASS O' CARLISLE

I'LL sing you a wee bit sang,
    A sang in the aulden style;
It is of a bonny young lass,
    Wha lived in merry Carlisle.
An' O, but this lass was bonny,
    An' O, but the lass was braw;
An' she had goud in her coffers
    An' that was the best of a'.

Sing hey, hickerty, dickerty,
    Hickerty, dickerty, dear,
The lass that has goud and beauty,
    Has naething on earth to fear.

This lassie had routh o' wooers,
    As beauty an' wealth should hae:
This lassie she took her a man,
    An' then she could get nae mae.
This lassie had bairns galore,
    That keepit her han's astir,
An' then she dee'd an' was buried,
    An' there was an end o' her.

Sing hey, hickerty, dickerty,
    Hickerty, dickerty, dan,
The best thing in life is to mak
    The maist o't that we can.

THE CUTTING O' MY HAIR

Frae royal Wull that wears the crown
To Yarrow's lowliest shepherd-clown,
Time wears unchancy mortals doun,
      I've mark'd it late and air.
The souplest knee at length will crack,
The lythest arm, the sturdiest back—
And little siller Sampson lack
      For cuttin' o' his hair.

Mysell for speed had not my marrow
Thro' Teviot, Ettrick, Tweed, and Yarrow,
Strang, straight, and swift like winged arrow,
      At market, tryst, or fair.
But now I'm turn'd a hirplin' carle,
My back it's ta'en the cobbler's swirl,
And deil a bodle I need birl
      For cuttin' o' my hair.

On Boswell's green was nane like me,
My hough was firm, my foot was free,
The locks that cluster'd owre my bree
      Cost many a hizzie sair.
The days are come I'm no sae crouse—
An ingle cheek—a cogie douce,
An' fash nae shears about the house
      Wi' cuttin' o' my hair.

It was an awfu' head I trow,
It waur'd baith young and auld to cow,
An' burnin' red as heather-lowe,
      Gar'd neeboors start and stare.
The mair ye cut the mair it grew
An' ay the fiercer flamed its hue—
I in my time hae paid enew
      For cuttin' o' my hair.

But now there's scarce aneuch to grip—
When last I brought it to the clip,
It gied the shaver's skill the slip
      On haffets lank and bare.

Henceforth to this resolve I'll cling,
Whate'er its shape to let it hing,
And keep the cash for ither thing
        Than cuttin' o' my hair.

LINES FOR THE EYE
OF THE BEAUTIFUL MISS E.B.

O BESSIE, dinna smirk sae sweetly,
An' turn sae naturally an' featly,
Where that bit weary mirror hings,
That up a lovely image brings,
Wha's very glance is sae unbrooking,
I wonder how ye can be looking;
Ah, Bessie, ye're but decking gay
A flower that soon maun fade away.

My bonny woman, wad ye think,
How soon that bright an' glossy blink
Maun tine its tint of vernal gladness,
An' change its cheer for hue o' sadness;
Ye wad think mair wi' little din,
About the spark that burns within.

Just now ye think but o' flirtation,
Of love an' dear, dear admiration,
Of laces, ribbans, an' of rings,
Of flounces, flirds, and kippling strings;
Of leading down the envied dance,
Or grand quadrille brent new frae France.
But dear—dear Bessie take a view
O' future years a very few:
Mark the wide difference an' apply it,
You canna do't!—sae I maun try it.

Married, of course you needs must be;
If not, nae blame will rest wi' thee;

Which in that mirror I can spy,
From brightness of a liquid eye.
Alas! a year hath scarce gone round,
Scarce half, on that enchanted ground,
When—what a form is yon I see,
With face of languor sipping tea!
Wi' hoffats rather bleached an' thin,
An' cheekbanes blue out through the skin.
'Tis really waesome like to look at
The very toast she's like to puke at;
While sickness glittens on the mien,
Like schoolboy's at his medicine.

I must go on frae age to age,
Through all your lady pilgrimage;
An' next I mark you pale an' weeping,
Above a sickly baby sleeping;
Whose face of clay and panting breath
Announce the near approach of death;
Yet hope still holds a vital part
Around the mother's aching heart.
The tear that rolls within the eye,
The cheek of sorrow never dry,
In moving eloquence reveal
What nought but parent's heart can feel.

What see I next?—The sable weed!
And flowing crape, where I can read
The heart's bereavement throbbing under
Nature's strong ties all rent asunder;
No farther earthly hope to crave,
No mansion but the silent grave;
But onward joys a glorious sum,
Of meeting in a world to come.

A glance beyond—And what remains!
Old, tottering, frailty, fears and pains;
Of maiden beauty, pride, and glory,
A woeful, sad *memento mori*.
The vein weak, quavering, and opprest,
Like infant's puling to its rest;
The memory vanished, past regaining,
The days of youth alone remaining;
The silly tale, like Sunday chimes,
Repeated o'er a thousand times;
The shaking head, the eye of rheum,

The S's whistled on the gum,
Announce each energy inurned,
And childhood of the soul returned;
Making poor Nature's last retreat,
The grave, appear a dwelling meet.

Then dear—dear Bessie think a wee,
On what has been, and what maun be;
An' when you to your mirror turn,
Think of a future day, an' mourn;
An' rather than, in maiden glory,
Smile at the ripening form before ye,
Say, with a humble heart but human,
"Ah, who would wish to be a woman!
The first that sinned in virgin prime,
Ay—doomed to suffer for the crime!
While this young flush, our sex's boast,
Is all we have for glory lost."
These things, dear Bessie, call to mind,
Whene'er you feel your heart inclin'd
To vanity of beauty's bloom,
That flower that hastens to the tomb.

A BARD'S ADDRESS
TO HIS YOUNGEST DAUGHTER

Come to my arms my wee wee pet
My mild my blithesome Harriet
The sweetest babe art thou to me
That ever sat on parent's knee.
Thou hast that eye was mine erewhile
Thy mother's blithe and grateful smile
And such a playful merry vein
That greybeards smile at pranks of thine

And if aright I read thy mind
The child of nature thou'rt designed
For even while yet upon the breast
Thou mimic'st child and bird and beast
Can'st cry like Moggy o'er her book
And crow like cock and caw like rook
Boo like a bull and blare like ram
And bark like dog and bleat like lamb
And when abroad in pleasant weather
Thou minglest all these sounds together

Then who can say, thou happy creature,
Thou'rt not the very child of nature

Child of my age and dearest love
As precious gift from God above
I take thy pure and gentle frame
And tiny mind of mounting flame
And hope that through life's chequered glade
That weary path which all must tread
Some credit from thy name will flow
To the old bard who loved thee so.
At least thou shalt not lack as meed
His blessing on thy beauteous head
And praying to him whose sacred breath
Lightened the shades of life and death
And said with sweet benignity
"Let little children come to me."

'Tis very strange my little dove
That all I ever loved or love
Come o'er my mind in visions bright
While gazing on thee with delight
Thy very name brings to my mind
One whose high birth and soul refined
Withheld her not from naming me
Even in life's last extremitye.
Sweet babe thou art memorial dear
Of all I honour and revere

Come look not sad—though sorrow now
Broods on thy father's cloudy brow
Thy prattle soon will that remove
Although the sorrow's sweet to prove.
One kiss I crave for grandam's sake
Who never saw thy tiny make
And one for her who left thee late
Laid low but not forgotten yet
One for thy sweet mamma's dear claims
And one for Jessy and for James
One for wee Moggy next and dearest
And one for her whose name thou bearest
And now again I say thou art
A strange memorial to my heart

How dar'st thou frown, thou freakish fay,
And pout and look another way?

177

Why turn thy chubby cheeks athraw
And skelp the beard of thy papa?
I know full well thy deep design
'Tis to turn back thine eye on mine
With triple burst of joyful glee
And fifty strains at mimicry
What wealth from nature may'st thou won
With pupilage so soon begun.
Well, hope is all; thou art unproved,
The bard's and nature's best beloved.
And now above thy brow so fair
And flowing films of flaxen hair
I lay my hand once more and frame
A blessing in the holy name
Of that supreme divinity
Who breathed a living soul in thee

A TRUE STORY OF
A GLASGOW TAILOR

   I sing the deeds of Francis Anderson
Tailor in Glasgow. One who had his name
Conferred in perilous times when rev^d pastors
Driven to the wilds were glad at dead of night
Their sacred duties to perform. Even then
In a deep dell somewhere about the source
Of Douglas water was this Frank baptized
About the cock-crow of a winter morning.
And there too was he blessed most fervently
With prayer and praise and parent's vow sincere
Breathed through the hour of wretchedness and dread
For the last suffering remnant of the land

   Frank was a tailor—True he was a tailor
But that was not his choice. One he revered
And loved chose for him; then it him behoved
To make the most of that his honest craft
And so he did. With good grey-paper tape
He took the measure of a man or boy
Stretched here and there he took the measurement
Of man or boy with infinite adroitness

178

Or round Salt Market grocer men that had
No shape at all save of a dumplin. Frank
Could take their huge dimensions most acutely
With much of pleasant wit and hem! and heh!
As viewing the clip upon his paper tape
Hard at the end thereof. Then went the scissors
Alongst the board rap rap with fearless sweep
In such a way that customers grew pale
At the deray wrought in the precious web
Where all the carding spinning weaving glossing
And dying of its rich and curious texture
Went smash before this ruthless tailor's sheers
While prospect was there none that all these shreds
Squares ovals triangles and semi-circles
Swept from the board like rubbish ever more
Should rise in likeness of a Sunday coat
Vest spatterdash or inexpressible

There lay our hero's art! The things came forth
Handsome and elegant, in every part
Most suitable; and good men's hearts rejoiced
In full proportion with their dread before.
Twas thus Frank rose to fame, and what was better
To very fair won and abundant wealth

But I must hurry on though loth I am
The courtship to pass over—the fond sighs
And ardent longings of a tailor's heart;
And the blithe quips and quibbles that so well
Became his flippant tongue. But most of all
The suit rejected. Think but of his pangs
When she he loved so well, of whom he spoke
Early and late with raptures of delight;
Of whom he dreamed, of whom he mention made
In all his prayers. With a saucy leer
Said "Who would wed a Tailor?"—Out upon
The Paisley jilt I have no patience with her!
A Tailor? What's a Tailor? On my word
I see no business in our bustling land
By half so clearly useful and genteel.
Nor one to which the half of all mankind
So deeply are indebted for their shapes
And graces of the person. This I mean
Exclusive of the dandies, for in truth
Tailors are their creators. Take that away
Which these impart—Lord what have we behind!

A soulless shred! a mere nonentity!

These and a thousand other trivial things
That would tell prettily in verse like mine
I must pass over simply to relate
One great event that marked our hero's life

The fashions changed and business by degrees
Stole from his grasp. Idle he could not be
He made clothes without end and these he sold
Or changed with others—haply some half worn
Some more than half some scarcely touched
With the full gloss upon them—clothes he had
For all ranks and degrees of men—for hind
For meagre student—drover—poet—clerk
Or country parson—Never in Frank's days
Did business pay so well! But having noted
That most of his were country customers
And his house overflowing with the goods
So precious in their eyes, he took a jaunt
Among the villages with a horse load
Or two of clothes all trim and clean and cheap
Beyond conception! Then there was such stripping
Pricing and trying on; with buttoning
And turning round. Frank found the villagers
A herd of boors—He left them gentlemen!
Hoard after hoard load after load he sold
Through all the links of Irvine air and Clyde
And every servant ready credit had
Till the next term—others he trusted not.

Of course when term-time came Frank's pockets were
Well stored with money. Still he was a man
That held his trust in heaven and never [took]
Offensive weapon till one night he dreamed
He saw his martyred father in a shroud
Which well Frank knew was not bestowed on him
At his unhousseled death and kythless tomb
Frank joyed at sight of his beloved sire
Forgetful that the grave divided them
And made great efforts to express delight
But a strange stiffness of the vocal member
That filled his mouth as with a huge potato
Void of all elasticity in nature
Prevented him at which he shed hot tears
And whined most piteously in nasal strains

The spectre beckoned silence and began
"My son thou knowest the evils that we bore
From the accursed red-coats. O my son
Beware of that dire race for they are men
That have no fear of God before their eyes
Nor man nor devil! Seest thou yon tall ruffian
Swigging his glass and cursing boastfully?
Of all men in the world I pray my son
Beware of yon. He's going straight to hell;
At least he looks for nothing else. And yet
See how he quaffs and swears and raps the board
And talks of wars of women and of blood
As if the world were made for him alone
Beware of him, if death thou wouldst avert
And loss of riches which thou valuest more
Than well behoves a Christian's estimate."

Frank shuddered to the very core at thought
Of such a headlong and confounded rascal
But word he could not fathom. Then the spirit
Withdrew shaking its head and lifted hands
And left our tailor bathed in a cold sweat
At sight of such a ruthless reprobate

Some time thereafter, Months or days or years
I cannot tell, as Frank was homeward bound
Loaden with riches at a hostel famed
[He] lighted on this very officer
[His] father's spirit pointed out to him
[Sit]ting in the same guise quaffing his cups
And swearing the same oaths which Frank had heard
[Sw]orn in his dream   Gads how the tailor's heart
Began to quake! Was this same night to be
His last on earth! He felt as if the edge
Of that portentuous weapon were already
A quivering at his heart! It had a curve
[Of] such a dangerous cast that at one stroke
[The] gigantic ruffian who bore it
[Could] sever a tailor into equal halves
[As] easily as a tailor's sheers divide
A soldier's sleeve   "Good e'en sir" said the soldier
"How far to night?" "I mean for Hamilton"
The good man said unused to tell a lie
"Well we shall go together. Thither I
am likewise bound express"   Frank's heart grew cold

181

He prayed an inward prayer but thankful word
He uttered not to such a kindly proffer

"The words must come to pass! My father's words
Spoke from a world of spirits. Still it is
My duty to preserve this humble life
While in my power." This Frank said to himself
The glass went round the soldier laughed and swore
And talked of wars of women and of blood
As if the world were made for him alone
At length he drained a mighty cup and said
"Why friend then shall we ride?" Frank's mouth grew dry
His tongue unwieldy like a boiled potato
At length he lisped forth. "Tis wearing late
And we are comfortable here—I think
I'll rather stay"—"Well, be it so good sir
Then I'll stay with you. D—n it let us have
Some jollification I approve the man
That sticks hard to his liquor and his friend
Come lay aside these cursed whiggish looks
And let's be merry. I perceive your doublet
Is better lined with this world's gear than mine
No matter—Mine will last me over night
Then pledge me neighbour" "Thank you honoured sir
I've a poor stamach drink oersets it quite"

The soldier swore and to the landlord turned
With swinging boisterous tale   Frank slip'd away
Payed all the liquor ordered out his horse
But as he mounted the good ostler said
(These hostel men are cunning honest folks)
"Sir there was twae men here an' them was axing
In maist partikler way for you—I think
You best had be content an' stay a' night"

Frank saw his drift! He saw the combination
To have his life and money. Yet he gave
The man a groat a mighty guerdon then
Thanked him mounted his horse and took the road
Faster than ever tailor rode before
Even not excepting him that rode to Brentford

He galloped on for miles but O his steed
Was jaded and could not keep pace by half
With his desires Till in a lonely dell
He heard a voice behind him a hilloa!

That sounded to him like the knell of death
He threshed upon his horse with might and main
But all was vain—tramp tramp and plash for plash
The Officer's huge horse came on behind
Along side soon he came his sword was drawn
And heaved above his shoulder while his wrath
Roared like a torrent—loud he cursed the tailor
By every epitaph he could invent
Of base and horrid import. As for Frank
His heart was turned to lead his soul had sunk
Into his stocking boots   He spoke no word
Or if he did he knew not what he said
Expecting every breath to be his last

    The soldier whistled on and whiles he sung
And whiles he swore   Then would he d—n the tailor
And eke the tailor's horse. Then canter on
To make the tailor follow. He had more sense!
Whene'er the soldier spurred the tailor paused
Glad to be quit of him on any terms
At length upon a wild and lonely height
He quite lost sight of him and had no guess
Which way he vanished   Then the tailor paused
And let his horse eat grass. Some hope he had
Of being freed from this his destined murderer

    Alas who can his destiny forego!
For in one moment ere he was aware
An unseen hand had griped him by the throat
And pulled him down. He offered no resistance
But MURDER called out with vociferous breath
Two villains held him down—one throttled him
The other had begun from pockets crammed
To extract his well earned store   another squeak
Of murder issued from the tailor's mouth
When lo a well known and much dreaded voice
Brayed out "Murder you cowardly whelp!
And who the devil dares to murder you
And Captain Morris here"   And at a stroke
He clove one robber's skull. The other fired
Wounding the captain's horse. But the next moment
The villain spurred in death   The soldier then
Seizing the tailor by the throat exclaimed
Shout MURDER sir Cry MURDER MURDER MURDER
If you would shun the fate of those you see"
The tailor roared out MURDER till the rocks

And every hill and every tree on Clyde
Shreiked as if in the very throes of death

   Anon there came two horsemen at full speed
Crying "Have you down the tailor? Have you all"
"Yes All" the soldier said but still kept hid
Between the horses. Quick the robbers lighted
Pop went the one and then the other sooner
Than one could say Jock Robson   Frank the tailor
Turned to a statue! Such a reckless waste
Of human life he ne'er had witnessed
He prayed to heaven inwardly   His lips
Moved quick although his tongue no utterance had

   "Come sir now" said the soldier "let us see
How these d——d villains have come on of late
Upon your Scottish roads"   "O gallant Captain!"
Frank cried with clasped hands "If you have value
For your own life or mine touch not these bodies
Else both of us will die upon the gallows
We turn the robbers these the murdered men"

   "Tuts!" said the captain and began forthwith
The scrutiny and from the four he took
Ten silver watches two of gold and three
Of some base metal covered o'er with shells
With gold and silver more than he could count
In sixteen purses which these highwaymen
Seemed never to have opened. Then he mounted
The tailor on the best of all the steeds
And bade him ride with him for life or death

   Gads how they scoured the strath   The tailor now
Always the foremost man   At Hamilton
They're safely housed at last right sore fatigued
And covered o'er with blood   They tried to count
Their booty but in vain it was so huge
And there were coins of England France and Spain
Of Scotland Ireland and the Isle of Man
The Captain kept the watches cased in gold
And some broad pieces of that precious metal
And spite of all the tailor's warm intreaties
He hurled the rest into the tailor's bags
Thirteen good watches, silver, gold and copper
And other coins of metal non-descript
A perfect hoard of treasure. The tailor said not

How that his father's spirit had misled him
But frankly did confess that all his dread
Was of the Captain and the cunning ostler

   "Why sir" the captain said "You paid my drink
I like a man that pays his shot. And though
You seemed somewhat ungracious yet I loved you
So did the ostler. How you caught his favour
I know not but straight he came to me
And says "Sir onest Anderson is gone
An' fer ower muckle siller in his pouch
For sic a night
There's robbers on the road for twa men came
An' axed about him maist partiklerly
And then twa horsemen came an' axed for them
If nane proteck him he'll ne'er see the morn"
That moment did I mount my horse and follow
And saved your property if not your life
I have dispatches from our gracious king
Unto the Marquis   All is safe with us
I answer for the whole meantime farewell
But never again suspect an English Officer!
We love the plunder of an enemy's camp
But not one of our own dear countryman
The thing's impossible! Honour's our badge
And for an honest simple man like you
There is not one of us who would not risk
His life at any hour. Again farewell
And think of Captain Morris as a friend

   The tailor did so all his life thereafter
And boasted of the English officer
As the first hero ever born of woman
So brave disinterested and downright
But still the revelation made to him
By his loved father's spirit in his dream
Remained a puzzle. Till his dying day
He ne'er could fathom it nor solve the mystery
Except by this *That dreams are ay contrary*

THE DOMINIE

A Dominie!—once when I heard the term
The title, appellation—What you will;
I saw him full before me. There he sat,
Or stood, or walked, or leaned with threatening frown,
The real epitome of domination!
The noun, the proposition to conceit;
The pourtrayed hyperbole of despotism;
Dogmatick, cruel, heartless and severe,
The very *ne plus ultra* of abhorrence!!

And then how callous his thin shrivelled cheek
And grey eye of intolerant tyranny!
His wig of dirty brown, that scantly reached
Half way unto his ear, all frizzled round
With fringe of thin grey hair. His coat thread bare,
Long backed, and shapeless, with the pocket holes
A weary width between. Yet what a shake
Of majesty was there—I see him still!
Pray view the man in your mind's eye, and say
If e'er you saw aught in this graceless world
So much to be detested, dreaded, shunned,
Despised and persecuted to the death?

So thought I once; and many a thousand time
Have cherished the prospective sweet resolve
Of ample, hideous, and most dire revenge
For youthful degradation. Base desire!
But long ere manhood had my flagrant brain
Tempered with wisdom, I could have fall'n down
At the good old man's feet and worshipp'd him

Oh when I thought of all his sufferance
Contending with the obstinate, the stupid,
The petulent, the lazy; every one
His mortal enemy. Like old Ismael
His hand against a whole obstreporous host
And every urchin's heart and hand 'gainst him,
I marvelled at his patience. Then I thought
Of all his virtuous precepts. Of his care
His watchful vigilance o'er rectitude
In every moral duty. Then each morn
Of the loud fervent prayer poured out to heaven
For grace and favour on each stripling's head
And success on his own painful endeavours

Then of his poverty, and endless task
Of duty and necessity—the sigh
The smile oft ill concealed, in haughty dread
Of aught approaching to familiarity.
A face of brass to hide a heart of love.
For when obliged to punish rigorously
Then with majestic swagger would he turn
That none might see him wipe the falling tear
From off the withered cheek. O good old man
Remembrance now weeps o'er thy narrow house
And sore neglected precepts learned from thee

It was my pride my joy in after life
To take him home with me weekly or so
Or by ourselves we went to the snug alehouse
As I required some most profound advice.
Then I oft think with tears, how his kind heart
Would lighten up; and he would talk of Homer,
Of Eschylus, and even of Zoroaster!
In language most intense and dignified.
Burns he liked not. On hearing him extolled
He shook his head, and bade me rather take
A model from Isaiah; or adapt
The stile of one John Milton. Then his eye
Would gleam with joy at each goodnatured sally
Of his, or mine; and he would slap his hand
Upon his knee and say with loud Ha ha!
"Daft poet! Foolish poet! Ah! what whims
Revel in your crazed head! Give me your hand
I must confess my old heart warms to you
For all your fictions and extravagance."

My old preceptor, if thy spirit knew
How thy once wayward pupil mourns for thee,
And broods upon thy memory, it might add
Unto the joys which now thy grateful heart
Reap'st in thy father's house. The sure reward
Of sterling rectitude and moral worth,
Long suffering, patience, holiness of life,
Contentment, charity and Christian love.

DISAGREEABLES

"For four things the earth is disquieted, and five which it cannot
    bear."—AGUR.

THIS world is a delightful place to dwell in,
And many sweet and lovely things are in it;
Yet there are sundry, at the which I have
A natural dislike, against all reason.
I never like A TAILOR. Yet no man
Likes a new coat or inexpressibles
Better than I do—few, I think, so well:
I can't account for this. The tailor is,
A far more useful member of society,
Than is a poet.—Then his sprightly wit,
His glee, his humour, and his happy mind
Entitle him to fair esteem. Allowed.
But then, his self-sufficiency.—His shape
So like a frame, whereon to hang a suit
Of dandy clothes. His small straight back and arms,
His thick bluff ankles, and his supple knees,
Plague on't!—'Tis wrong—I do not like a tailor.

    AN OLD BLUE-STOCKING MAID! Oh! that's a being,
That's hardly to be borne! Her saffron hue,
Her thinnish lips, close primmed as they were sewn
Up by a milliner, and made water-proof,
To guard the fount of wisdom that's within.
Her borrowed locks, of dry and withered hue,
Her straggling beard of ill-condition'd hairs,
And then her jaws of wise and formal cast;
Chat-chat! chat-chat! Grand shrewd remarks!—
That may have meaning—may have none for me.
I like the creature so supremely ill,
I never listen, never calculate:
I know this is ungenerous and unjust:
I cannot help it; for I do dislike
An old blue-stocking maid, even to extremity.
I do protest I'd rather kiss a tailor!

    A GREEDY EATER! He is worst of all.
The gormand bolts, and bolts, and smacks his chops:
Eyes every dish that enters, with a stare
Of greed and terror, lest one thing go by him.
The glances that he casts along the board,
At every slice that's carved, have that in them,

Beyond description. I would rather dine
Beside an ox, yea, share his cog of draff;
Or with a dog, if he'd keep his own side;
Than with a glutton on the rarest food.

A thousand times I've dined upon the waste,
On dry-pease bannock, by the silver spring.
O, it was sweet—was healthful—had a zest;
Which at the paste, my palate ne'er enjoyed!
My bonnet laid aside, I turned mine eyes
With reverence and humility to heaven,
Craving a blessing from the bounteous Giver;
Then grateful thanks returned. There was a joy
In these lone meals, shared by my faithful dog,
Which I remind with pleasure, and has given
A verdure to my spirit's age. Then think
Of such a man, beside a guzzler set;
And how his stomach nauseates the repast.

"When he thinks of days he shall never more see,
Of his cake and his cheese, and his lair on the lea,
His laverock that hung on the heaven's ee-bree,
    His prayer and his clear mountain rill."
I cannot eat one morsel. There is that,
Somewhere within, that baulks each bold attempt;
A loathing—a disgust—a something worse:
I know not what it is.—A strong desire
To drink, but not for thirst. 'Tis from a wish
To wash down that enormous eater's food—
A sympathetic feeling. Not of love!
And be there ale, or wine, or potent draught
Superior to them both, to that I fly,
And glory in the certainty that mine
Is the etherial soul of food, while his
Is but the rank corporeal—the vile husks,
Best suited to his crude voracity.
And far as the bright spirit may transcend
Its mortal frame, my food transcendeth his.

A CREDITOR! Good heaven, is there beneath
Thy glorious concave of cerulean blue,
A being formed so thoroughly for dislike,
As is a creditor? No, he's supreme,
The devil's a joke to him! Whoe'er has seen
An adder's head upraised, with gleaming eyes,

About to make a spring, may form a shade
Of mild resemblance to a creditor.

I do remember once.—'Tis long agone,
Of stripping to the waist to wade the Tyne—
The English Tyne, dark, sluggish, broad, and deep;
And just when middle-way, there caught mine eye,
A lamprey of enormous size pursuing me!
L—— what a fright! I bobb'd, I splashed, I flew!
He had a creditor's keen ominous look,
I never saw an uglier—but a real one.

This is implanted in man's very nature,
It cannot be denied. And once I deemed it
The most degrading stain our nature bore:
Wearing a shade of every hateful vice,
Ingratitude, injustice, selfishness.
But I was wrong, for I have traced the stream
Back to its fountain in the inmost cave,
And found in postulate of purest grain,
Its first beginning.—It is not the man,
The friend who has obliged us, we would shun,
But the conviction which his presence brings,
That we have done him wrong. A sense of grief
And shame at our own rash improvidence:
The heart bleeds for it, and we love the man
Whom we would shun.—The feeling's hard to bear!

A BLUSTERING FELLOW! There's a deadly bore,
Placed in a good man's way, who only yearns
For happiness and joy. But day by day,
This blusterer meets me, and the hope's defaced!
I cannot say a word—make one remark,
That meets not flat and absolute contradiction—
I nothing know on earth—am misinformed
On every circumstance. The very terms,
Scope, rate, and merits of my own transactions
Are all to me unknown, or falsified,
Of which most potent proof can be adduced.
Then the important thump upon the board,
Snap with the thumb, and the disdainful 'whew!'
Sets me and all I say at less than naught.

What can a person do?—To knock him down
Suggests itself, but then it breeds a row

In a friend's house, or haply in your own,
Which is much worse; for glasses go like cinders;
The wine is spilled—the toddy.—The chair-backs
Go, crash! No, no, there's nothing but forbearance,
And marked contempt. If that won't bring him down,
There's nothing will. Ah! can the leopard change
His spots, or the grim Ethiop his hue?
Sooner they may and nature change her course,
Than can a blusterer to a modest man:
He still will stand a beacon of dislike.
A fool—I wish all blustering chaps were dead,
That's the true bathos to have done with them.

THE SUMMER MIDNIGHT

The breeze of night has sunk to rest,
Upon the river's tranquil breast,
And every bird has sought her rest,
    Where silent is her minstrelsy.
The queen of heaven is sailing high,
A pale bark on the azure sky,
Where not a breath is heard to sigh—
    So deep the soft tranquility.

Forgotten now the heat of day
That on the burning waters lay,
The noon of night her mantle gray,
    Spreads, from the sun's high blazonry:
But glittering in that gentle night
There gleams a line of silvery light,
As tremulous on the shores of white
    It hovers sweet and playfully.

At peace the distant shallop rides,
Not as when dashing o'er her skies
The roaring bay's unruly tides
    Were beating round her gloriously.
But every sail is furl'd and still,
Silent the seaman's whistle shrill,
While dreamy slumbers seem to thrill
    With parted hours of extacy.

Stars of the many spangled heaven!
Faintly this night your beams are given,

Though proudly where your hosts are driven
    Ye rear your dazzling galaxy:
Since far and wide a softer hue
Is spread across the plains of blue,
Where in bright chorus ever true
    For ever swells your harmony.

O for some sadly dying note
Upon this silent hour to float,
Where, from the headlong world remote,
    The lyre might wake its melody:
One feeble strain is all can swell
From mine almost deserted shell,
In mournful accents yet to tell
    That slumbers not its minstrelsy.

There is an hour of deep repose
That yet upon my heart shall close,
When all that nature dreads and knows
    Shall burst upon me wond'rously:
O may I then awake for ever,
My harp to rapture's high endeavour,
And as from earth's vain scene I sever,
    Be lost in immortality.

THE MONITORS

The lift looks cauldrife i' the west,
    The wan leaf wavers frae the tree,
The wind touts on the mountain's breast
    A dirge o' waesome note to me.
    It tells me that the days o' glee,
When summer's thrilling sweets entwined,
    An' love was blinkin' in the ee,
Are a' gane by an' far behind;

That winter wi' his joyless air,
    An' grizzly hue, is hasting nigh,
An' that auld age, an' carkin' care,
    In my last stage afore me lie.

192

Yon chill and cheerless winter sky,
Troth but 'tis eeriesome to see,
   For ah! it points me to descry
The downfa's o' futuritye.

I daurna look unto the east,
   For there my morning shone sae sweet;
An' when I turn me to the west,
   The gloaming's like to gar me greet;
   The deadly hues o' snaw and sleet
Tell of a dreary onward path;
   Yon new moon on her cradle sheet,
Looks like the Hainault scythe of death.

Kind Monitors! ye tell a tale
   That oft has been my daily thought;
Yet, when it came, could nought avail,
   For sad experience, dearly bought,
   Tells me it was not what I ought,
But what was in my power to do,
   That me behoved. An' I hae fought
Against a world wi' courage true.

Yes—I hae fought an' won the day,
   Come weal, come woe, I carena by,
I am a king! My regal sway
   Stretches o'er Scotia's mountains high,
   And o'er the fairy vales that lie
Beneath the glimpses o' the moon,
   Or round the ledges of the sky,
In twilight's everlasting noon.

Who would not choose the high renown,
   'Mang Scotia's swains the chief to be,
Than be a king, an' wear a crown,
   'Mid perils, pain, an' treacherye?
   Hurra! The day's my own—I'm free
Of statemen's guile, an' flattery's train;
   I'll blaw my reed of game an' glee,
The Shepherd is himself again!

"But, Bard—ye dinna mind your life
   Is waning down to winter snell—
That round your hearth young sprouts are rife,
   An' mae to care for than yoursell."

Yes, that I do—that hearth could tell
How aft the tear-drap blinds my ee;
    What can I do, by spur or spell,
An' by my faith it done shall be.

And think—through poortith's eiry breach,
    Should Want approach wi' threatening brand,
I'll leave them canty sangs will reach
    From John o' Groats to Solway strand.
    Then what are houses, goud, or land,
To sic an heirship left in fee?
    An' I think mair o' auld Scotland,
Than to be fear'd for mine or me.

True, she has been a stepdame dour,
    Grudging the hard-earn'd sma' propine,
On a' my efforts looking sour,
    An' seem'd in secret to repine.
    Blest be Buccleuch an' a' his line,
For ever blessed may they be;
    A little hame I can ca' mine
He rear'd amid the wild for me.

Goodwife—without a' sturt or strife,
    Bring ben the siller bowl wi' care;
Ye are the best an' bonniest wife,
    That ever fell to poet's share;
    An' I'll send o'er for Frank—a pair
O' right good-heartit chiels are we—
    We'll drink your health—an' what is mair,
We'll drink our Laird's wi' three times three.

To the young Shepherd, too, we'll take
    A rousing glass wi' right good-will;
An' the young ladies o' the Lake,
    We'll drink in ane—an awfu' swill!
    Then a' the tints o' this warld's ill
Will vanish like the morning dew,
    An' we'll be blithe an' blither still—
Kind winter Monitors, adieu!

This warld has mony ups an' downs,
    Atween the cradle an' the grave,
O' blithsome haun's an' broken crowns,
An' douks in chill misfortune's wave;

194

All these determined to outbrave,
O'er fancy's wilds I'll wing anew,
    As lang as I can lilt a stave,—
Kind winter Monitors, adieu!

A BOY'S SONG

Where the pools are bright and deep
Where the grey trout lies asleep
Up the river and o'er the lea
That's the way for Billy and me

Where the blackbird sings the latest
Where the hawthorn blooms the sweetest
Where the nestlings plentiest be
That's the way for Billy and me

Where the mowers mow the cleanest
Where the hay lies thick and greenest
There to trace the homeward bee
That's the way for Billy and me

Where the poplar grows the smallest
Where the old pine waves the tallest
Pies and rooks know who are we
That's the way for Billy and me

Where the hazel bank is steepest
Where the shadow falls the deepest
There the clustering nuts fall free
That's the way for Billy and me

Why the boys should drive away
Little sweet maidens from the play
Or love to tear and fight so well
That's the thing I never could tell

But this I know I love to play
Through the meadow among the hay
Up the water and o'er the lea
That's the way for Billy and me

MY EMMA MY DARLING

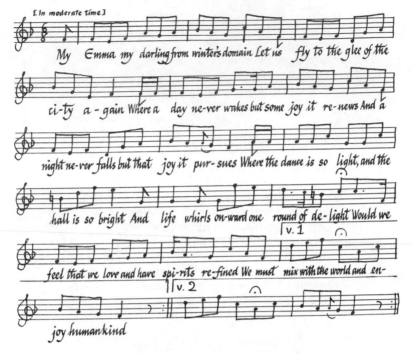

My Emma my darling from winter's domain
Let us fly to the glee of the city again
Where a day never wakes but some joy it renews
And a night never falls but that joy it pursues
Where the dance is so light, and the hall is so bright
And life whirls onward one round of delight
Would we feel that we love and have spirits refined
We must mix with the world and enjoy humankind

Mute nature is lovely in earth and in sky
It cheers the lone heart and enlivens the eye
But nowhere can beauty and dignity shine
So as in the human face fair and divine
Mong'st these could I love thee and that love enjoy
But oh! in the wilderness fond love would cloy
To the homes of our kindred our spirits must cling
And away from their bosoms at last take their wing

THIS WARLD'S AN UNCO BONNY PLACE

This warld's an unco bonny place
  When summer woos the southlan' breeze
With mellow breath our dales to trace
  And wave the tresses of the trees
  And when the corn waves o'er the leas
Like gouden seas on Autumn day
  O really 'tis a bonny place
Whate'er the dour divines may say

They ca't a dark an' dreary path
  Where sin and sorrow set their seal
And us poor serfs of heaven's wrath
  Condemned in prenticeship to speel
  To that great chimney-sweep the deil
Really the picture's past enduring
  When every honest heart must feel
That bliss lies in his own procuring

Sure every humble holy man
  Will say "I'm here as God hath made me
I'll make the most o't that I can
  A gratefu' heart shall ne'er upbraid me
  Nor gnawing jealousy perswade me
To grovel at those I'm bound to serve
  My lot whatever may betide me
Is better far than I deserve

"He might have placed me wo-begone
  'Mong blackamoors a hideous clan
In climes beneath the burning zone
  With snubby nose—as I should ban
  And lips like puddings in a pan
Scotched with the sand and parching heat
  A ruffian seared barbarian
Who nothing knew but kill and eat

Or far in eastern climes away
  He might have laid my dreary lot
Beneath the morning's cloudless ray
  To kneel to hideous Juggernaut

Then with their blood the soil they bloat
Beneath his chariot crunching o'er them
   And to their wooden god devote
Their silly souls—woe's me for them

But every kind to every clime
   Is fitted well as we may see
The angels to their walks sublime
   The mean of soul to low degree
But all may happy happy be
   Of every climate every race
To savage saint or devotee
   This world I say's a lovely place

I am not quizzing; for I think
   (Though Burns says man was made to mourn)
That every pleasure man may drink
   From seas of bliss without a bourn
   Even winter with her christal horn
And polar sheet of rimy hue
   I love as dear as summer morn
With all her buds and bells of dew

But now I've reached where I set out
   For I've a most confounded way
Of swithering round and round about
   For want of something meet to say
   Or rather rhymes burst forth away
So fast I have not power to stay them
   But I'll be brief if once I may
To search for proper things and say them

I say this world's a bonny place
   I say that winter's hues beseem her
The Summer's flush the Autumn's grace
   But lovelier sweeter and supremer
   Is gentle SPRING with radiant streamer
Of rainbow and of sunny ray
   Of gloaming grey and dawning glimmer
Sweet morning of the solar day!

O she has mildness in her mien
   And joy enkindling in her eye
A brow with heaven's own beauty sheen
   And cheek of morning's orient dye

Disdaining times and tides gone by
Love's dear delight her only theme
Her very breezes sing and sigh
Of onward bliss and joy supreme

And here I have an emblem meet
Which I have toiled to reach and say
An opening spring so lovely sweet
My strain in softness sinks away.
What is the dawn of summer day
What is the spring of solar year
Compared with youth of virgin gay
Nature's one flower without compeer

The flexile form the gliding tread
Of blooming maiden beauty's queen
Too light to bend the gowan's head
Her air and motion cherubin
A meteor of the morning sheen
A gleesome elfin coy and wild
Just dancing on the verge between
The blushing virgin and the child

Too light to mark the mystic bound
When childhood's toys and trifles o'er
Are left upon forgotten ground
And maidhood's glories all before
With love's delights a mighty store
Which sweeten but not break her rest
For such there is no metaphor
This, this is Nature's flower confest

An eaglet o'er her eiry riven
A streamer in the ether blue
A cygnet on the skirts of heaven
A rainbow on the morning dew
More bright than fancy ever knew
A thing to place on fairy throne
To dazzle lover's tranced view
And bloom in nature's fields alone

An angel—no that will not do
My metaphors are mere novators
'Tis said and I believe it too
That angels are most lovely creatures

But flesh and blood and female natures
That love so dear and smile so sweetly
   There's nought in human nomenclatures
That can convey their beauties meetly

This world's a lovely place and dear
   I've said it thrice and say't again
The hills are green the rivers clear
   And sweet's the sunbeam after rain
   The flowers of mountain and of plain
Are sweet as flowrets wild can be
   But virgin's form and virgin's mein
Are sweeter than them all to me

For me I'm woman's slave confest
   She is the prize of my avail
Without her hopeless and unblest
   A ship deserted in the gale
   Without a rudder or a sail
A star or beacon-light before
   No blink of heaven to countervail
Nor hope of haven evermore

THE CHICKENS IN THE CORN

JENNY GILL went out in a May morning,
   An' syndit her bonny brent brow;
An' she wash'd her arms to the elbow noops,
   Her craig an' her rosy mou:

An' she wash'd her cheeks wi' the new won milk,
   As shinin' as they could be,
Till her very breath was like to cut,
   An' the tear stood in her ee.

An' as she look'd in her keeking-glass,
   An' said fu' daintilye,
"Troth, my goodman has sorry skeel
   When he gaiks sae sair at me.

For Johnny will kiss an' toy wi' me
  Where there's nae skaithe nor scorn;
But if there's ane bonny lass in the land,
  He will have her before the morn.

I wonder what can him provoke
  To skyre his mate sae sair:
He's nae better than ane barn-door cock
  With twenty hens an' mair."

Then Jenny rose up to her keeking-glass,
  An' close unto it she came,
And she saw what she wish'd she had not seen;
  An' wha would not wish the same?

For she saw her hair of the raven black
  All mix'd wi' the siller grey;
And the wrinkles ray'd out frae her een;
  An' O Jenny Gill was wae!

But then, good Lord, as she did rave
  And shake her grizzly powe;
For jealousy, lang by her beauty smoor'd,
  Now burst into a lowe.

She lookit through her window blind—
  Her heart loup to her chin;
For she saw ane lass at the stable-door,
  That lithely glidit in.

"By the faith o' my body!" said bauld Jenny Gill,
  "But their haffits I shall claw;
For I see by the limmer's flisky stride
  There's a tryst in the stable sta'."

She kickit her stockings an' syne her shoon,
  Gart a' her body-claes flee;
But her petticoat she hastit on,
  Though it hardly reach'd her knee.

An' she's away to the stable sta'—
  Gramercy as she ran;
An' she gart the door clash to the wa',
  Wi' rage at her goodman.

"Wha have we here?" cried bauld Jenny Gill,
    An' ran through the sta's wi' speed;
"Wha have we here?" cried the jealous jad,
    In a voice wad hae waken'd the dead.

The lass she answer'd frae the loft,
    Since better might not be;
But she was sae fuffled wi' affright,
    That she only cried " 'Tis me!"

"What seek you there, you limmer quean,
    In the stable-bed your lane?"
"I was looking for eggs," quo' the frighten'd lass;
    "But eggs I can get nane.

I think our chickens lay in the corn,
    Or never will lay again;
I heard ane cackling in this loft—
    But eggs I can get nane."

"Are ye sure it was not the auld grey cock?"
    Quo' the wife, wi' girnin' leer;
"For he sometimes cackles in the loft
    When he wants the hens to hear."

Then the lass she shook for very dread,
    Her mistress was sae snell:
"Let down the ladder, you limmer loon!
    I will look for the eggs mysel'."

"There is no ladder," the lass replied;
    "We climb up by the wa'."
Then the wife she rampit as she'd been mad,
    And flew at the stable sta'.

She set her foot on the manger-tree,
    And claught at the loft amain;
But she miss'd her foot, an' down she fell,
    An' snappit her left leg bane.

An' there she lay, and sair she cried,
    An' near fell in ane swoon;
But never a foot would she be moved
    Till the auld grey cock came down.

But the lass she heav'd her up an' ran
　　As fast as she could dree,
An' she never lan'd till she had the wife
　　Where she neither could hear nor see.

An' O she lay in grievous plight!
　　An' sair she made her maen!
But it was not for her bloody snout,
　　Nor yet her left leg bane:

But it was for the bonny young hens
　　That lay'd amang the corn;
An' maist of all for the auld grey cock
　　That cackled so bold at morn.

O wha hasna heard o' the merry merry tale
　　O' the bonny lass that clamb the wa',
An' the chickens in the corn, an' the jealous wife
　　That fell in the stable sta'?

May every auld wife of jealous heart
　　Of the comely an' the young
Get sickan a cast as bauld Jenny Gill,
　　An' gang hirpling o'er ane rung.

TO MISS M. A. C——E

Maid of my worship thou shalt see
Though long I strove to pleasure thee
That now I've changed my timid tone
And sing to please myself alone
And thou wilt read when well I wot
I care not whether you do or not

　Yes I'll be querulous or boon
Flow with the tide change with the moon
For what am I or what art thou
Or what the cloud and radiant bow
Or what are waters winds and seas
But elemental energies?
The sea must flow the cloud descend
The thunder burst the rainbow bend
Not when they would, but when they can
Fit emblems of the soul of man!

Then let me frolic while I may
The sportive vagrant of a day
Yield to the impulse of the time
Be it a toy or shrine sublime
Wing the thin air or starry sheen
Sport with the child upon the green
Dive to the sea-maid's coral dome
Or fairy's visionary home
Sail on the whirlwind or the storm
Or trifle with the maiden's form
Or raise up spirits of the hill
But only if and when I will

Say may the meteor of the wild
Nature's unstaid erratic child
That glimmers o'er the forest fen
Or twinkles in the darksome glen
Can that be bound? Can that be rein'd
By cold ungenial rules restrained?
No! leave it o'er its ample home
The boundless wilderness to roam
To gleam to tremble and to die
'Tis Nature's error—so am I
Then leave to all his fancies wild
Nature's own rude untutored child
And should he forfeit his fond claim
Pity his loss—but do not blame

Let those who list the garden choose
Where flowers are regular and profuse
Come thou to dell and lonely lea
And cull the mountain gems with me
And sweeter blooms may be thine own
By nature's hand at random sown
And sweeter strains may touch thy heart
Than are producible by art
The nightingale may give delight
A while 'mid silence of the night
But the lark lost in the heavens blue
O her wild strain is ever new!

LOVE CAME TO THE DOOR O' MY HEART.

Written by the Ettrick Shepherd.

Love came to the door o' my heart ae night, And he call'd wi' a whin _ _ ing din, "Oh, o _ _ pen the door, for it is but thy part To

205

let an old cro_ny come in." I o __pen'd the

door, though I ween'd it a sin, To the sweet lit_tle

whim_per_ing fay; But he rais'd sic a buzz the

cove with _ in, That he fill'd me with wild dis_may.

"Gae a—way, gae a—way, thou wick——ed wean!" I cried wi' the tear in my e'e; "Ay! sae ye may say!" quo' he, "but I ken Ye'll be laith now to part wi' me." And

what do you think?— by day and by night For these ten lang

years and twain. I have cherish'd the urch_in with

fond_est de_light, And we'll nev_er mair part a_

gain.

COMMENTARY

For a discussion of the texts followed in the present selection, see the Introduction (p. xxxi above). Unless otherwise stated, all poems and songs are reprinted from the first editions.

THE MISTAKES OF A NIGHT is here reprinted from *The Scots Magazine* for October 1794, where it appeared anonymously with the following editorial note:

> We are disposed to give the above a place to encourage a young poet. We hope he will improve, for which end we advise him to be at more pains to make his rhymes answer, and to attend more to grammatical accuracy.

Edith Batho (*The Ettrick Shepherd* (Cambridge, 1927)), and subsequent critics, have accepted this as James Hogg's first published poem. In early versions of his 'Memoir of the Author's Life', the poet writes, 'The first time that I attempted to write verses was in the spring of the year 1793' (see 1972 edition, ed. D. S. Mack, p. 10 and 10n.). A friend of the young poet states that in 1794 Hogg 'had the satisfaction of seeing, for the first time, one of his pieces appear in print. It was called *the mistakes of a night*' (Z., 'Further Particulars of the Life of James Hogg', *Scots Magazine*, Nov. 1805, p. 503). The title of the poem derives from the comedy *She Stoops to Conquer, or The Mistakes of a Night* by Oliver Goldsmith, whom Hogg admired and mentions with respect in his autobiographical 'Love Adventures of Mr George Cochrane' (1820).

(*p. 1*) *o'er the hill frae Yarrow:* the village of Yarrow is situated by Yarrow Water, in the Parish of Yarrow, which is adjacent to the parish of Ettrick, with both parishes making up the greater part of Ettrick Forest, or the sheriffdom of Selkirkshire.

(*p. 1*) *Out-o'er the muir to Maggy:* 'O'er the Muir to Maggie' is an old folk tune which may be found in McLean's *Collection of Favourite Scots Tunes with Variations for the Violin* (Edinburgh, 1772). It seems possible that Hogg wanted his poem to be sung to 'O'er the Muir to Maggie'.

(*p. 1*) *neither warm nor dry:* the original reads, 'not dry'.

(*p. 1*) *He kiss't her o'er and o'er again:* the original reads, 'oe'r and oe'r'.

(*p. 2*) *To rev'rend Doctor C——d:* In his 'Statistics of Selkirkshire' Hogg praises Dr Robert Cramond as an 'energetic preacher' who served at Yarrow until 1791 (*Prize-Essays and Transactions of the Highland and Agricultural Society of Scotland* (Edinburgh, 1832), p. 304).

(*p. 3*) *Now here's a health:* the original reads, 'Now her's'.

THE FOREST MINSTREL (Edinburgh and London, 1810) was described on its title-page as 'a Selection of Songs, adapted to the most favourite Scottish Airs: few of them ever before published', 'by James Hogg, the Ettrick Shepherd, and Others'.

Of the six songs reprinted here from *The Forest Minstrel*, 'The Drinkin', O' had previously appeared with the sub-title 'A Sang for the Edinburgh Ladies' in *The Scots Magazine*, November 1805, and the sub-title 'A Sang for the

Greenock Ladies' in *The Greenock Advertiser*, 13 December 1805. Hogg's contributions to his *Forest Minstrel* were later revised extensively by him and re-published in *Songs, by the Ettrick Shepherd* (Edinburgh and London, 1831).

The Forest Minstrel simply lists the titles of the 'favourite Scottish Airs' to which the lyrics are are to be sung. In the present edition the music for 'How Foolish are Mankind' is adapted from 'The Lone Vale' as printed in Maver's *Collection of Genuine Scottish Melodies* (Glasgow, 1865); for 'Doctor Monro' is 'Humours o' Glen', adapted from the Sharpe Fiddle MS (NLS Ing. 153; c. 1790); for 'The Drinkin', O' is 'Dumbarton's Drums' adapted from Johnson's *Scots Musical Museum* (Edinbugh, 1788); for 'Birniebouzle is 'The Braes of Tullymet' adapted from MacGlashan's *Collection of Strathspey Reels* (Edinburgh, c.1790); and for 'Life is a Weary Cobble o' Care' is 'The Bob of Dunblane' adapted from Thomson's *Orpheus Caledonius* (Edinburgh, 1726).

It is hoped that performers will be inventive and ingenious in adapting, up-dating and accompanying the given tunes of Hogg's songs. I have not been able to locate 'Paddy's Wedding' (the tune for 'Love's Like a Dizziness'); singers will therefore have to find or invent an appropriate score.

(p. 4): 'Doctor Monro' was the name of a respectable surgeon and medical lecturer, and the latest in Edinburgh's long line of Doctors Monro. In a performance, singers may wish to use the variations on the tune to distinguish between the two main speakers of this operatic piece.

(p. 6): In any poor changeling: the original reads 'changling'.

(p. 8): Corryvrekin is a treacherous whirlpool between the islands of Jura and Scarba.

(p. 8) Mungo Park: this 'celebrated African traveller' was a native of Ettrick Forest and a neighbour of James Hogg, who 'knew him partially both before he went first to Africa and after his return' ('Statistics of Selkirkshire', p. 304). It was not yet known at the time of *The Forest Minstrel* that Mungo Park had actually died during his expedition to the Niger River in 1806.

(p. 9) For the rattlin' o' guns: Britain was at war with France for most of the period between 1793 and 1815.

(p. 9) the little footy boy: Cupid, with his arrows.

(p. 10): Burnieboozle is now an area in Aberdeen.

THE QUEEN'S WAKE is described on the title-pages of the early editions as 'a Legendary Poem, by James Hogg' (Edinburgh and London, 1813; 3rd ed. revised, 1814).

'The Witch of Fife' and 'Kilmeny' are the third and eighth of twelve ballads in *The Queen's Wake*, Hogg's most popular long poem and the work which established him as a respected poet in his day. The present selection includes the first edition of 'The Witch of Fife', together with the revised (1814) ending to that ballad, and the 1814 text of 'Kilmeny'. The first edition of 'Kilmeny' is in Hogg's approximation of medieval Scots.

THE WITCH OF FIFE
(pp. 13-14): 'Kilmerrin', 'Lommond height' and 'Loch Leven' are all located in Fife.

(p. 16) the Doffrinis steep: the Dovre Fjell mountain range in Norway.

(p. 17): Ettrick Pen is a mountain in the Scottish Borders near Moffat.

(p. 17): the Braid Hills lie just south of Edinburgh.

(p. 17) gurly James: James IV was King of Scotland from 1488 to 1513. During his reign 'fairies, brownies, and witches, were at the rifest in Scotland' ('Mary Burnet', in *James Hogg: Selected Stories and Sketches*, ed. Douglas S. Mack (Edinburgh, 1982), p. 83).

(p. 20): Hogg re-wrote the conclusion of 'The Witch of Fife' at the suggestion of Walter Scott.

KILMENY

(p. 22) Duneira: the hamlet of Dunira is near Loch Earn, to the west of Perth.

(p. 27) She saw a lady sit on a throne: Kilmeny, in heaven, sees a pageant representing the future history of Scotland, beginning with the crowning of Mary Queen of Scots in 1561. In this allegory the lion represents Scotland, while the bedeman corresponds to John Knox and the early Presbyterian Church. It should be remembered that all the ballads of *The Queen's Wake* are supposedly recited in the presence of Queen Mary at the Palace in Edinburgh.

(p. 28) When crowned with the rose and clover leaf: with the union of the crowns in 1603, Mary's son King James VI became also the monarch of England ('crowned with the rose') and of Ireland (the 'clover leaf').

(p. 28) He gowled at the carle and chased him away, | To feed wi' the deer on the mountain gray: In their campaign against Presbyterianism, Mary's grandsons (Charles II and James VII and II) outlawed and persecuted the Scottish Covenanters. King James received his 'arles', however, in the Revolution of 1688.

(p. 28) Kilmeny a while her een withdrew: on this occasion Hogg prudently avoids mentioning or expressing an opinion about the Jacobite Rebellions that dominated Scottish history from 1703 to 1745 and after.

(p. 28) She saw a people, fierce and fell, | Burst frae their bounds like fiends of hell: Kilmeny sees the horrible results of the French Revolution, followed by the rise of Napoleon (a ravaging eagle) who 'threatned an end to the race of man' until brought down 'by the lion's [i.e. either Scotland's, or Britain's] deadly paw'. The 'campaigns of Buonaparte', Hogg declared in 1834, 'ended so completely in smoke', with the only result being 'the slaughter of so many millions'; 'Look at all the wars of Europe for hundreds of years, and you will see, that, after millions of human beings had been sacrificed, at the end all things were settled the same as when the war began' (*Lay Sermons*, p. 106).

MIDSUMMER NIGHT DREAMS has previously been published as a whole only once, in the 1822 *Poetical Works of James Hogg*, where the Shepherd explains that his poems 'The Pilgrims of the Sun', 'Connel of Dee' and 'Superstition' were

> originally written with the intention of their forming part of a volume to be entitled MIDSUMMER NIGHT DREAMS; but having submitted ['Pilgrims of the Sun'] to the perusal of the late James Park, Esq. of Greenock, a friend in whose good taste and discernment I had the most perfect confidence, he chanced to think so highly of it that he persuaded me, against my own inclination, to publish it as a poem by itself, assuring me of its success. The approbation which the ballad of 'Kilmeny' had received,

probably influenced him in this opinion; but the poem was no sooner issued to the public, than I perceived a sort of wild unearthly nakedness about it, that rendered it unfit to appear by itself, and I repented of what I had done. It is therefore given in this edition as at first intended, namely, one of a series of *Midsummer Night Dreams*; it being literally so,—the visions of one in a trance, or the wanderings of her disembodied spirit during that oblivious cessation of mortal life. (II, 343-44)

This might seem to indicate that at first Hogg wanted to include additional poems in his *Midsummer Night Dreams*. However, the published version of 1822 includes the Dedication, 'Pilgrims', 'Connel of Dee', and 'Superstition', followed by two pieces (an extract from *Mador of the Moor* and a short drama) which had both been published elsewhere and could not have been intended for the series.

The text of the present edition of *Midsummer Night Dreams* is taken from Hogg's manuscript 'Connel of Dee' (Turnbull Library MS Papers 42, Item 16), together with the first edition of *Pilgrims of the Sun* (Edinburgh and London, 1815), which included both 'Superstition' and the Dedication to Byron. The first publication of 'Connel of Dee' was in Hogg's collection of *Winter Evening Tales* (Edinburgh and London, 1820); all subsequent printings followed this edition in omitting certain lines which seemed irregular from a moral, grammatical, or metrical point-of-view.

Midsummer Night is traditionally a celebration for lovers, and a time when supernatural beings of all kinds, both good and bad, are to be encountered. In his note to the 1822 trilogy, Hogg explains that 'Pilgrims of the Sun' has its roots in Scottish folklore and ancient Scottish beliefs:

> The poem is founded on a traditionary tale well known over all Scotland, and affirmed to have happened, not only at old Lindeen, but in some lonely and eiry churchyard here and there over the whole country. From these circumstances it appears probable, that the tale has had, at first, some foundation in reality, and that it is exceedingly old. It is sometimes related as having happened to a parish minister's wife,—sometimes to such and such a great man's lady, but most frequently, as in the poem, to a saintly virgin, who was an heiress, but totally disregardful of worldly concerns. The erratic pilgrimage is given merely as a dream or vision of a person in a long trance, while the soul's short oblivious state, as described in p. (84), is supposed to correspond with the symptoms of re-animation, and the 'gentle shivering of the chin', noted in the corse at Carelha'. (II, 344)

(p. 31) A Pupil in the many chambered school, | Where Superstition weaves her airy dreams: the quotation is taken from Book IV ('Despondency Corrected') of Wordsworth's *Excursion*.

THE PILGRIMS OF THE SUN

(p. 32) Carelha': now called Carterhaugh, a small settlement near Selkirk.
(p. 33): The Hill of *Blackandro* is a high summit overlooking *Bowhill*, which was the residence of Hogg's patrons the Duke and Duchess of Buccleuch.
(p. 34) When she had donned: the original reads, 'doned'.

212

(p. 34) the Eildon green: the Eildon Hills are to the north of Selkirk, towards Melrose. 'No situation can be more beautiful and commanding than that of Selkirk, ... with an extensive view of the Forest hills to the westward, and those of Roxburghshire eastward, many rich vistas being interspersed among them' (Hogg, 'Statistics of Selkirkshire', p. 299).

(p. 37) Harlaw cairn: the upland farm of Harelaw, located near Currie, had a large cairn near the farmhouse.

(p. 42)   where Tweed from distant moors
Far travelled flows in murmuring majesty;
And Yarrow rushing from her bosky banks,
Hurries with headlong haste to the embrace
Of her more stately sister of the hills.

Two rivers, Yarrow Water and Ettrick Water, join before flowing into the River Tweed near Selkirk.

(p. 43) the lone St Mary: St Mary's Loch, at the head of Yarrow Water.

(p. 52) By peer, by pastor, and by bard forlorn: the poets referred to in this line are, perhaps, Lord Byron, George Crabbe, and William Cowper.

(p. 52) By every grub that harps for venal ore: London's Grub Street was famous as the residence of many hack writers.

(p. 52) And crabbe that grovels on the sandy shore: the satirical poet George Crabbe grew up in the sea-side town of Aldeburgh, England.

(p. 52) Come, leave these lanes and sinks beside the sea: the poet bids the muse of English poetry to leave England's depraved cities and towns, and to visit instead 'the silent moorland dale' of Scotland.

(p. 55) the Evening and the Morning star: the planet Venus.

(p. 55) the holy spires of old Lindeen: an ancient church (now in ruins) near Selkirk.

(p. 55): The crimson sphere is the planet Mars, named for the god of war.

(p. 58) A fiend, that in Tartarian gulf was tossed: evidently Hogg was composing these lines at the time of Napoleon's defeat in 1814.

(p. 62) Phillip plain: Philiphaugh is a small settlement on Yarrow Water near Selkirk.

(p. 65) For once the lykewake maidens saw: the first edition reads, 'maiden's'.

(p. 72) Hugo of Norroway: Hogg himself was partly of Scandinavian descent. His family name, he claimed, was 'formerly pronounced Houg ... and had its derivation in an old Danish word, Hecco, meaning an eagle' (G., 'Some Particulars Relative to the Ettrick Shepherd', *New Monthly Magazine*, February 1836, p. 195). The poet implies that he is a descendant of the mythical Mary Lee and Hugo:

For though her name no more remains,
Her blood yet runs in Minstrel veins. (p. 70)

(p. 72) Melrose fane: Melrose Abbey, founded in 1136, was a Cistercian monastery until the Reformation.

(p. 75) 'Mid real instead of fancied woes: the Duchess of Buccleuch died in 1814.

CONNEL OF DEE

The title on the manuscript reads, 'Country Dreams and Apparitions / No 2 Connel of Dee', together with a note, also in Hogg's handwriting, 'This tale to be inserted in the second vol. after the Shepherd's Callander and proofs put to me J. H.' As this implies, the MS was used as a printer's copy for volume two of

213

the *Winter Evening Tales*, where a bowdlerised version of the poem appears as the second of the series 'Country Dreams and Apparitions', and follows 'The Shepherd's Calendar'.

The stanzas are numbered in the original. I have added closed quotation marks in the ninth, twenty-third, and twenty-fifth verses.

(p. 84) At length he stood lone by the side of the Dee: the River Dee flows through the Grampians to Aberdeen.

(p. 87) And when within view of his bowrak they came: the original reads, 'the came'.

SUPERSTITION

(p. 89) A Sovereign of supreme unearthly eye: In this poem Hogg defends various forms of pre-Christian belief including witchcraft and pantheism. He argues that Christianity cannot survive if it is entirely divorced from its roots in primitive thought and emotion.

(p. 91) While o'er our hills has dawned a cold saturnine morn: The modern spirit of rationalism has unfortunately destroyed the 'holiness', 'frame', 'mystic flame', and 'delirious dreams' of earlier, primitive people.

(p. 94) I wish for these old times and Stuarts back again: At times the poet is so disgusted by the rationalism and narrow morality of his age, that he wishes for a restoration of the Stuart kings (even though in other works, such as 'Kilmeny' and his novel *The Brownie of Bodsbeck*, Hogg stresses the disastrous effects in Scotland of the seventeenth-century Stuarts).

THE POETIC MIRROR, *or, The Living Bards of Britain*, anonymous

(London and Edinburgh, 1816). Hogg met Wordsworth in Edinburgh in 1814. At that time the Ettrick Shepherd 'admired many of his pieces exceedingly, though I had not then seen his ponderous "Excursion" '. Wordsworth's 'sentiments seemed just, and his language, though perhaps a little pompous, was pure, sentient, and expressive' ('Memoir of the Author's Life', p. 69). James Hogg then rode down to the Lake District in 1815, where he visited both Wordsworth and Southey. In his 'Memoir' he recalls meeting Robert Southey at a pub in Keswick for

> about an hour and a half. But I was a grieved as well as an astonished man, when I found that he refused all participation in my beverage of rum punch. For a poet to refuse his glass was to me a phenomenon; and I confess I doubted in my own mind, and doubt to this day, if perfect sobriety and transcendent poetical genius can exist together. In Scotland I am sure they cannot. With regard to the English, I shall leave them to settle that among themselves, as they have little that is worth drinking. (p. 67)

(p. 96): 'James Rigg' is one of three parodies of Wordsworth in *The Poetic Mirror*. Above the title in the first edition are the words: 'Still Further Extract from "The Recluse," a Poem'. Wordsworth's *Excursion*, published in 1814, was intended as the middle part of a long philosophical work 'on Man, on Nature and on Human Life', which would have borne the title *The Recluse*, if it had ever been finished. In Edinburgh it was remarked that the character of the Wanderer (or pedlar) in Wordsworth's *Excursion* bore a striking resemblance to

James Hogg (see Lockhart, *Peter's Letters to his Kinsfolk*, I, 140-42).

(p. 99) Blucher, restorer of the thrones of kings: Field-Marshall Blucher commanded the Prussian army, defeated Napoleon, and entered Paris in 1814. He was instrumental in restoring the Bourbon monarchy in France.

(p. 102) It was the parlour-bell: the original reads, 'parlour-be'.

(p. 105) The lines unto the Daisy: Robert Burns's poem, 'To a Mountain-Daisy, On turning one down, with the Plough', was very popular during the nineteenth century. Hogg ridicules Southey by implying that the Laureate would only be capable of appreciating one of Burns's most tame and sentimental pieces.

COULD THIS ILL WARLD HAVE BEEN CONTRIV'D is reproduced photographically from George Thomson's *Select Collection of Original Scottish Airs* (Edinburgh, 1818), with music by Beethoven. It was reprinted by Beethoven, together with a German translation, in his *Schottische Lieder* (opus 108; Berlin, 1820). Beethoven's accompaniment is loosely based on the Scots tune of 'Mischievous Woman'. An early version of Hogg's lyrics had appeared in his *Spy* of 8 December 1810, under the title 'Scotch Song'.

No. 1 of THE BORDER GARLAND *Containing Nine New Songs, by James Hogg; The Music Partly Old, Partly Composed by himself and Friends, and Arranged with Symphonies and Accompaniments for the Piano-Forte* (Edinburgh, n.d.). This selection (reduced in size by one half) is reproduced photographically from a copy held at the National Library of Scotland.

Some controversy surrounds the dating of *The Border Garland*. Two separate editions, undated and identical except for their size, were published in Edinburgh. Hogg is reported to have said in his later years that 'The Border Garland was first published in 1813 by myself in a small Octavo Edition' (letter to Robert Purdie, cited in Purdie's letter to the firm of Lonsdale and Mills, 14 June 1830, NLS MS 2521, f 147). However, the earliest mention of this book appears to be an advertisement in the May 1819 number of *Blackwood's Magazine*.

(p. 110) 'I'll No Wake Wi' Annie': 'I composed this pastoral ballad, as well as the air to which it is sung, whilst sailing one lovely day on St Mary's Loch' (*Songs, by the Ettrick Shepherd*, p. 224).

(p. 114) 'The Poor Man': the 'Air, by a friend of the Editor', is apparently by James Hogg himself. In *Songs, by the Ettrick Shepherd*, he claims that 'The air of this song is my own, and is to be found in The Border Garland' (p. 63).

(p. 116) 'The Lark': more commonly known as 'The Skylark', and often reprinted under that later title.

(p. 118) 'The Laird o' Lamington': the laird has endeared himself by displaying neither vices nor virtues, with the exception of conviviality over 'Toddy jugs an' caups o' ale'.

HALBERT OF LYNE has never been reprinted since its appearance in Hogg's *Winter Evening Tales*. An early version of this poem had appeared as the 'Introductory Tale' in R. P. Gillies's *Illustrations of a Poetical Character* (1816); a copy of Gillies's book, now in the British Library, is inscribed to 'Mrs Grant, Princes Street', 'with the author's most respectful Compliments', and has the following words in the same handwriting, immediately beneath the title of the 'Introductory Tale': 'supplied by a friend of the Author'. Robert Gillies remained a life-long friend of James Hogg.

(p. 120) Horatio: Hogg uses this name to address the fashionable men of Edinburgh. It might suggest either Hamlet's friend Horatio, or the Roman satirist Horace.

(p. 121) To seize my little book: the original reads 'boook'. 'My little book' is the translation of a famous phrase from Horace, who is quoted and mentioned by name in several other pieces of Hogg's *Winter Evening Tales.*

(p. 122) by the clock | Of old Saint Giles: the square beside St Giles Cathedral, near the High Street in Edinburgh, was a favourite haunt of lawyers.

(p. 125) Of Boston, and Ralph Erskine: Thomas Boston and Erskine were eighteenth-century Scottish preachers whose influential books argued that 'good works' were insufficient to ensure salvation.

THE LAMENT OF FLORA MACDONALD was published on its own, but no copies of the first edition have survived. Both this and the following song are reproduced photographically from a copy of Thomson's *Select Melodies of Scotland* (London, 1822) held at the National Library of Scotland. Hogg's lyrics to the 'Lament' were 'composed to an air handed me by the late lamented Neil Gow, junior', a well-known Edinburgh fiddler;

> He said it was an ancient Skye air, but afterwards told me it was his own. When I first heard the song sung by Mr Morison, I never was so agreeably astonished,—I could hardly believe my senses that I had made so good a song without knowing it. (*Songs, by the Ettrick Shepherd*, p. 11)

The words and the melody-line also appeared in Hogg's second volume of *Jacobite Relics* (1821), where he records that 'the original of these verses' was 'a translation from the Gaelic, but so rude that [Gow] could not publish them. ... On which I versified them anew, and made them a great deal better without altering one sentiment' (p. 369).

(p. 130) Farewell to the lad I shall ne'er see again: following the defeat of the Jacobites at Culloden in 1746, Flora Macdonald helped her friend Bonny Prince Charlie escape to the Isle of Skye in a small boat. In the song Flora looks across the water towards Skye, and acknowledges the final defeat of Charles Stuart and the Jacobites.

THE HIGHLAND WATCH was probably written in 1815 or 1816, but was not published until 1818, when it appeared with music by Beethoven in Thomson's *Select Collection.* Beethoven also published his score, together with Hogg's first verse and a German translation, in his book of *Schottische Lieder* (Berlin, 1820). The present edition reproduces the more photogenic version of Thomson's *Select Melodies of Scotland.* Beethoven had been contracted by Thomson to compose accompaniments for several Scottish poems. Earlier letters from the composer complain about Thomson's habit of not letting him see the lyrics, but on the 15th of February, 1817, Beethoven wrote to 'Mon cher amis' 'Monsieur George Thomson, Edinbourgh', expressing enthusiasm for the task and thanking the editor for letting him see the *Poesies anglaises bien interessantes* (National Library of Scotland, MS 594, f 366).

GOOD NIGHT AN' JOY BE WI' YOU A' appears at the end of R. A.

Smith's six-volume *Scottish Minstrel* (Edinburgh, 1821-1824).
(p. 134) If e'er I led your steps astray: the poet is hoping that people have been dancing to his previous songs in the *Scottish Minstrel*.

WHEN THE KYE COMES HAME
First published as 'The Sweetest Thing the Best Thing' in Hogg's novel *The Three Perils of Man* (London, 1822), and then revised as 'When the Kye Come Hame', with music, in *Blackwood's Magazine*, May 1823. I have used the *Blackwood's* version, but in each stanza have altered 'come' to 'comes', on the grounds of a note by Hogg when the lyrics were published in *Songs, by the Ettrick Shepherd*:

> In the title and chorus of this favourite pastoral song, I choose rather to violate a rule in grammar, than a Scottish phrase so common, that when it is altered into the proper way, every shepherd and shepherd's sweetheart account it nonsense. I was once singing it at a wedding with great glee the latter way, ("when the kye come hame,") when a tailor, scratching his head, said, "It was a terrible affectit way that!" I stood corrected, and have never sung it so again. (p. 51)

NEW CHRISTMAS CAROL was first published in *Blackwood's Magazine*, December 1824, and was often reprinted under its later title, 'The March of Intellect'. The accompaniment is 'Fy let us a' to the Wedding' adapted from *The Scots Musical Museum*. In the lyrics the poet implies his reservations about modern inventions such as the stock market, steam engines, insurance companies, long pants, phrenology and other sciences, and dandyism.
(p. 137) To fill the auld moon wi' whale blubber: During the stock market boom of 1824-25, it began to be widely feared that the trend towards investing in faraway places 'would deprive Britain of money that she would need in wet seasons to purchase foreign food'; indeed, as Hogg seems to predict, the economic panic of December 1825, and the ensuing massive depression, were apparently the result of 'two simultaneous booms—in foreign investment and in foreign trade—[which] caused an external drain' of money in Britain (Boyd Hilton, *Corn, Cash, Commerce: The Economic Policies of the Tory Governments 1815-1830* (Oxford, 1977), pp. 205, 202). James Hogg distrusted the investors, bankers, industrialists, and fashionable people of his day, and consistently tried to preserve the more communitarian values which he equated with Scotland's past.

THE ANTI-BURGHER IN LOVE
Transcribed from the manuscript (Turnbull Library MS Papers 42, Item 17) dated 'Altrive Lake March 8th 1825'. A very different version appeared as 'The Elder in Love' in *Fraser's Magazine*, March 1832.
(p. 138) In God's true Anti-burgher meetinghouse: The 'most formidable enemies of the Kirk', according to Hogg's friend Lockhart,

> are those who have dissented from her on very trivial grounds, and are not, indeed, very easy to be distinguished from her in any way adapted to the comprehension of the uninitiated stranger. Such are the Burghers and

217

the Anti-Burghers, both of whom separated themselves from the Established Church, in consequence of their adopting different views, concerning the lawfulness of a certain oath required to be taken by the burgesses of a few towns in Scotland. (*Peter's Letters to his Kinsfolk*, III, 98-99)

(p. 139) there came a youth | Forth from the Border: With this implied self-portrait, James Hogg tries to distance himself from both the puritanical Gabriel, and the snobbish, cold-hearted Sir John, each of whom responds inadequately to the nature of art and metaphor. The dramatic ironies of this piece should be seen in relation to the widening gap between rich and poor, which was taking place at the time; Hogg's good friend Robert Gillies tells us that 1825 and 1826 were 'painful and dreary', 'both in London and Edinburgh',

> to all but *the rich*, who, instead of being annoyed by the changes, derived only the additional amusement of bolting and barring their gates, and raising their voices, against almost hourly applications for aid, which lent a piquancy and zest to their own welfare and comforts, otherwise unattainable. (*Recollections of Sir Water Scott, Bart.* (London, 1837), p. 257)

(p. 139) Lovely or not to something heavenly: there is no punctuation at the end of this line in the manuscript.

IF E'ER I AM THINE first appeared in R. A. Smith's collection of songs set to Irish tunes, entitled *The Irish Minstrel; A Selection from the Vocal Melodies of Ireland, Ancient and Modern, Arranged for the Piano Forte* (Edinburgh, 1825).

THE GREAT MUCKLE VILLAGE OF BALMAQUHAPPLE appeared, without music, in the 'Noctes Ambrosianae' (*Blackwood's Magazine*, June 1826. Hogg's poems and songs were frequently incorporated in the semi-fictional comic serial called 'Noctes Ambrosianae', an account of celebrations at Ambrose's Tavern, Edinburgh, in which 'The Shepherd' plays a leading role. The music for 'Balmaquhapple' is 'Soldier Laddie' adapted from Thomson's *Caledonian Muse* (London, c. 1790).
(p. 144) There's Cappie: the original reads 'There Cappie'.

SELECT AND RARE SCOTTISH MELODIES: *The Poetry by the Celebrated Ettrick Shepherd; The Symphonies and Accompaniments Composed and the Whole Adapted and arranged by Henry R. Bishop* (London, 1829). Both 'The Ladies' Evening Song' and 'I Downa Laugh, I Downa Sing' are reproduced photographically from a copy at the British Library. Bishop was a fashionable (but not overly talented) London composer now mainly remembered for his song 'Home Sweet Home'. According to James Hogg, the 'Ladies' Evening Song' was 'written long ago, for the singing of a young lady in a house where we drank very deep, rather too deep for me' (*Songs, by the Ettrick Shepherd*, p. 108). It should be stressed that the words of both songs were written prior to the music.

THE p AND THE q; OR, THE ADVENTURES OF JOCK M'PHERSON Reprinted from *Blackwood's Magazine*, October 1829. The manuscript has not survived, and the printed poem was apparently edited by D. M. Moir, who thought that

> Hoggs P. and Q. is written with much energy and spirit and has more real humour in it, than almost any thing I have ever seen of the Shepherds—but abounds in woeful abominations. These I have taken out with a pencil in the best way I could, although they are so constitutionally engrained in it, as to be ineradicable. This poem I would recommend you to insert—it is a curious affair, and worthy of the authors extraordinary powers. (Letter to William Blackwood, August 1829 (NLS MS 4025, f 202))

(p. 155) Barrow, and Parry, and Franklin: John Barrow was ambassador to China in 1792, and governor of the Cape of Good Hope in 1797; Sir John Franklin and Sir William Edward Parry made several attempts to find the Northwest Passage to China (1818 to 1827), and explored parts of northern Canada. All three men published accounts of their voyages (unlike Jock M'Pherson).

(p. 155) Hall's: educated at the High School in Edinburgh, Basil Hall travelled widely as a British naval officer, and published numerous accounts of his adventures, which included an interview with Napoleon at St Helena.

ST. MARY OF THE LOWS

Reprinted from Shoberl's London annual *Forget Me Not* (1829), where it first appeared. The poem was republished (with changes and without the last stanza) in Hogg's *A Queer Book* (Edinburgh and London, 1832).

(p. 157): The poet wanders through the ruins of St Mary's Churchyard, overlooking his beloved St Mary's Loch. In his 'Statistics of Selkirkshire' Hogg says that 'The only lakes in [Ettrick] are St Mary's Loch and the Loch of the Lowes, lying both close together, and famed for the angler's sport and the stillness and pastoral beauty of the surrounding country' (p. 185). The ruined graves include those of ancient warriors, Border thieves, Covenanters, the minister Walter Grieve (whose son John was one of Hogg's best friends), and an unnamed young woman.

THE MINSTREL BOY

Never reprinted since its first appearance in Thomas Pringle's Christmas annual *Friendship's Offering*, in 1829. The poet looks back to his early days as a cowherd and shepherd, and recalls the beginning of his interest in poetry. Dated 'Mount Benger, June 14, 1828'.

On 28 May Pringle had written to Hogg to explain that an earlier poem ('this strange wild ballad') which Hogg had sent him was 'unappropriate' 'for these "douce" & delicate publications the annuals'. In 'elegant publications of this description', said Pringle, the poet should 'admit not a single expression which would call up a blush in the Cheek of the most delicate female if reading aloud to a mixt Company'. Pringle then requested the Shepherd to

> give me a few lines or stanzas under the title of 'The Minstrel Boy'—for the illustration of one of our plates. It is a boy of perhaps 7 or 8 years of age with a shepherd's pipe in his hand & a highland bonnet & plaid lying

beside him—lying in the midst of a scene of wild magnificence—woods, hills and waterfalls. ... [G]ive me some of the glorious romance of your own boyhood when the spirit of poetry & romance first began to pour over you the visions of fairyland and which afterwards found expression in the immortal 'Kilmeny', & others of your loftiest lays. (Letter, NLS MS 2245, ff 122-23)

Although the resulting poem suffers from the respectability and sentimentality of the London annuals, it nevertheless gives insight into Hogg's development as a poet, as well as a glimpse of his childhood.

The second POETIC MIRROR

'A New Poetic Mirror, By the Ettrick Shepherd' ran in the *Edinburgh Literary Journal*, beginning with 'No.I.—Mr. W[illiam] W[ordsworth]: Ode to a Highland Bee' (5 September 1829), and 'No. II.—Mr. T[homas] M[oore], By the Ettrick Shepherd' (24 October 1829). 'Andrew the Packman: After the manner of Wordsworth, By the Ettrick Shepherd' (20 March 1830) is clearly part of the series, though not identified as such. The series ended under the title 'Poetic Mirror', with 'An Imitation from Catullus, By the late James Park, Esq' (5 November 1831), and an editor's note explaining that Park's verses 'have been transmitted to us through the medium of our friend the Ettrick Shepherd'. Earlier in that year three anonymous parodies appeared under the aegis of 'The Poetic Mirror': these are 'Campbell' and 'Crabbe' (May 28th), and 'A Common Lot: *Montgomery*' (4 June 1831). Immediately above 'A Common Lot' on the page is another poem, 'The Flower o' Glendale, By the Ettrick Shepherd', so that in effect 'A Common Lot' may be said to have been published under Hogg's name. A friend of the Shepherd tells us that at this time Hogg 'wanted some home-thrusts / At certain poets', but wished to avoid signing his name to them (see David Tweedie, 'Lines for the Eye of Mr. James Hogg, Sometimes Termed the Ettrick Shepherd', *Edinburgh Literary Journal*, 10 April 1830).
(p. 167): 'A Common Lot' is closely based on James Montgomery's 40-line poem 'The Common Lot', in which a poor man represents the human condition. Montgomery's poem begins,

> Once in the flight of ages past,
> There lived a man:—and WHO was HE?
> —Mortal! howe'er thy lot be cast,
> That Man resembled Thee.

> Unknown the region of his birth,
> The land in which he died unknown:
> His name hath perish'd from the earth;
> This truth survives alone:—

> That joy and grief, and hope and fear,
> Alternate triumph'd in his breast:
> His bliss and woe,—a smile, a tear!
> —Oblivion hides the rest.

A GRAND NEW BLACKING SONG from an untitled manuscript (Turnbull

220

Library MS Papers 42, Item 35). The title is taken from the *Edinburgh Literary Journal*, where the poem appeared (with slight alterations and with added punctuation) on 15 May 1830. No one has yet composed music for this song.

Hogg's manuscripts are scantly punctuated, and it is clear that he expected editors to add commas, semi-colons, and periods. I have wanted to avoid the over-punctuation of nineteenth-century editions, however, and have not made any changes to this piece, with the exception of a full stop added in the tenth, eighteenth, and fourth-last lines.

(p. 169): *Warren* and *Kyle* were familiar trade-names for boot polish.

(p. 169) Complete perfection o' the art: the antics of the animals in response to this mirror of 'art' might be compared with the 'peaceful ring' formed by the animals around Kilmeny.

(p. 169) The sly redoubted Robin Warren: I have not been able to find any explanation for this reference.

(p. 169) At Hunder an' twall the Canongate: perhaps a store or private residence in the Canongate, Edinburgh.

THE FIRST SERMON is transcribed from Hogg's untitled manuscript (Turnbull Library MS Papers 42, Item 31). The poem appeared with a much-revised ending in *Blackwood's*, June 1830.

More extensive editing was required in two places in this poem, where extra lines added by Hogg have caused confusion. In order to produce a readable text, I have taken the liberty of omitting three lines from each of the two passages. The manuscript is very puzzling, and does not seem to make sense; in the following transcription from the manuscript, I have used italics to represent the lines which Hogg added afterwards:

(p. 170): The heart's devotion. Unto whom? *Ask not*
   It is unfair; Suppose it to high heaven
Unfair to ask? Unto the comely dames
   Or to the comely maids gazing entranced
Around the gallery. Glad was I at last
   Or to the gorgeous idol self-conceit
To hear the soft and graceful long AY-MAIN!

(p. 171):   *All within*
The loss of reccollection and of mind the
   Became a blank a chaos of confusion
The agony within. He seized his hat
   Producing naht but agony of soul
And stooping floundering plaitting at the knees
   His long lip quivered and his shaking hand
Made his escape. But O how I admired
   Of the trim beaver scarcely could make seizure
The Scottish audience There was neither laugh

In the *Blackwood's* text these lines have been even more radically altered.

For other departures from the manuscript in the present edition, the originals of altered lines are as follows:

Of all things sacred many men have seen

I never Eyes close shut one cheek turned up (p. 170)

And some from Joseph Addison John Logan
Blair William Shakespeare Young's Night Thoughts (p. 171)

(p. 170) For Combe or Dr Spurziem to dissect: The eminent Johann Spurzheim, father of phrenology, had lectured in Edinburgh in 1816. His follower Dr George Combe founded both the Phrenological Society, and the *Phrenological Journal*, in Edinburgh during the 1820's. After criminals were executed, their heads were often given to the Edinburgh phrenologists for study. Another skull which excited great interest was that of the natural genius James Hogg: 'As for the Ettrick Shepherd, I am told that when Spurzheim was here, he never had his paws off him' ([Lockhart], *Peter's Letters to his Kinsfolk* II, 341).

(p. 171) Twas all made up of scraps: The scraps include excerpts from the eighteenth-century essays of Joseph Addison and Samuel Johnson, from Edward Young's long poem *Night Thoughts* (1742-45), and from more recent works by four Edinburgh divines: John Logan's *Elements of the Philosophy of History* (1781), Hugh Blair's *Sermons* (1777-1801), Thomas Gillespie's *The Seasons Contemplated in the Spirit of the Gospel* (1822), and Andrew Thomson's lectures and essays (1816-31).

THE LASS O' CARLISLE
An Excellent New Song, By the Ettrick Shepherd. *Fraser's Magazine*, July 1830.No one has yet composed music for this 'song'.

THE CUTTING O' MY HAIR
Blackwood's Magazine, August 1830.
(p. 173) Frae Royal Wull that wears the crown: King William IV was sixty-four when he came to the throne in June 1830.
(p. 173) Thro' Teviot, Ettrick, Tweed, and Yarrow: districts in the Borders, named for the rivers that flow through them.
(p. 173) On Boswell's Green: St Boswell's is a village near Dryburgh Abbey, in the Borders.

LINES FOR THE EYE OF THE BEAUTIFUL MISS E. B.
By the Ettrick Shepherd. Never reprinted since its first appearance in *Fraser's Magazine*, August 1830.

A BARD'S ADDRESS TO HIS YOUNGEST DAUGHTER
Different versions appeared in *Friendship's Offering* (1830), and in Hogg's *Queer Book* two years later. The present version is from Hogg's manuscript (Turnbull Library MS Papers 42, Item 62), with quotation marks and question marks added where necessary. For other changes, the original lines are as follows:
Thou hast that eye was mine erewhile (p. 176)
Then who can say thou happy creature (p. 177)
How dar'st thou frown thou freakish fay (p. 177)
Well hope is all thou art unproved (p. 178)
The bard's and nature's best beloved (p. 178)
Harriet Sidney Hogg was born in 1828. A letter from James to his wife, who had taken the baby to Edinburgh for medical treatment, expresses concern over

a deformed foot: 'How is my poor Harriet and what are they doing with her I can hardly think of my darling being put into steel boots like the ancient Covenanters' (letter to Margaret Hogg, 24 August 1828, printed in Norah Parr's *James Hogg at Home* (Dollar, 1980), pp. 54-56).

(p. 177) Thy very name: Harriet was named after the Duchess of Buccleuch, who had arranged for Hogg to receive the rent-free possession of Altrive Farm, shortly before her death in 1814.

A TRUE STORY OF A GLASGOW TAILOR

By the Ettrick Shepherd. Now printed for the first time, from Hogg's undated manuscript (Turnbull Library MS Papers 42, Item 30). Letters or words in square brackets indicate places where the edge of the manuscript has been worn away. No punctuation has been added to this poem, so that it appears just as Hogg left it. Correspondence between the author and William Blackwood indicates that this poem was rejected by *Blackwood's Magazine* in February, 1831.

(p. 180) Irvine, Ayr, and *Clyde* are rivers in the south-west of Scotland.

THE DOMINIE appeared in the *Edinburgh Literary Journal,* 26 March 1831. The present version is based on the second of two surviving manuscripts (Turnbull Library MS Papers 42, Item 26). On the manuscript Hogg has added what appears to be a second, alternative version of the first eight lines:

> A Dominie? What think you of the term? A Dominie!
> Is't not equivocal with something in't
> Of doubtful point or is't a word at all?
> Tis not in Walker nor in Dr Johnston
> And yet no term's more common. It must be
> Some verb of that old language spoke in Rome
> That language modelled by curst termination
> The bore of youth and pride of sycophants

Since neither of the alternative openings has been crossed out, I have preferred the first version, on the grounds that it shows greater energy and immediacy. The 1831 solution of printing both verses consecutively as one, makes for a lethargic, redundant beginning which almost certainly would have displeased James Hogg. 'The Dominie' has never been reprinted until now.

(p. 186) old Ismael: Ishmael, the son of Abraham by an Arab woman, was an outcast, one 'whose hand is against every man, and every man's hand against him' (Genesis 16).

(p. 187) Of Eschylus, and even of Zoroaster: Aeschylus, often regarded as the founder of Greek tragedy, is famous for his *Prometheus Bound* and *Agamemnon.* His predecessor Zoroaster, a Persian prophet, taught that people are free agents in whom the two spirits of good and evil battle for supremacy.

DISAGREEABLES

By the Ettrick Shepherd. Never reprinted since its first appearance in *Fraser's Magazine,* June 1831.

(p. 188) Agur: In his sermon on moderation, Agur the son of Jakeh says, 'For

three things the earth is disquieted, and for four which it cannot bear' (Proverbs 30).

(p. 188) AN OLD BLUE-STOCKING MAID: The Edinburgh blue-stockings were generally more respectable, devout, and prim, than the blues of England. 'The Edinburgh ladies, it is said, are all rather blue', declares Reverend M'Dow in Susan Ferrier's 1831 novel, *Destiny* (chapter 59). In 1814 Hogg had presented his manuscript 'Pilgrims of the Sun' to an Edinburgh publisher, who then 'sent out your MS among his blue-stockings for their verdict. They ... condemned the poem as extravagant nonsense' (' a friend', quoted in Hogg's 'Memoir of the Author's Life', p. 35). However, on his visit to London Hogg 'met with most of the literary ladies, and ... liked them better than the blue-stockings of Edinburgh' (*Lay Sermons*, p. 87).

(p. 189) When he thinks of days he shall never more see: This and the three following lines are from the printed version of 'Connel of Dee'.

THE SUMMER MIDNIGHT

Signed 'ETTRICK SHEPHERD', this piece has never been reprinted since its first appearance in *The Sheffield Iris*, 26 July 1831. Hogg's poems often came out in *The Iris*, but usually after a prior publication in *Blackwood's*. 'Summer Midnight' shows the poet attempting a more restrained, respectable, and English style. Another favourite writer in *The Iris* was its former editor James Montgomery.

THE MONITORS

Recited by The Shepherd in 'Noctes Ambrosianae', *Blackwood's Magazine*, November 1831.

(p. 193) Hainault scythe: a large scythe from the Flemish area of Hainault.

(p. 194) A little hame: 'We understand that his Grace the Duke of Buccleuch,with that munificence for which he is so peculiarly distinguished, has given orders to build a cottage this spring for the Bard, on the pastoral farm given him by his Grace, situate on the classic banks of the Yarrow' ('The Ettrick Shepherd', *Edinburgh Weekly Journal*, 4 March 1818). Looking out one evening from the window of his house, the poet contemplates his past and tries to foresee the future.

(p. 194) Bring ben the siller bowl: 'James Frank, Esq. of Bughtrigg, has presented the Ettrick Shepherd with an elegant and massy silver punch bowl, which contains upwards of eight pints. The devices and motto are said to be admirable' (*Edinburgh Weekly Journal*, 28 February 1816).

(p. 194) To the Young Shepherd, ... An' the young ladies o' the Lake: the author proposes a toast to his son Jamie and his daughters Jessie, Margaret, Harriet, and Mary.

A BOY'S SONG

By the Ettrick Shepherd. First published in the annual *Remembrance* (London, 1831), but now printed in its entirety from a manuscript at Stirling University

Library. A first version of the sixth verse (which has not been crossed out) is as follows:

> Why the men love women so well
> Poor little Johnie* never could tell
> But why the women like men to see
> That's the wonder of all to me
>   * Or any name

MY EMMA MY DARLING is here printed from Hogg's manuscript (NLS MS 4805, f 46) which he prepared for his 1831 *Songs*. The music is the melody-line from a previous printing of this song in the London annual *Musical Bijou* (1829). Several posthumous editions print 'human race' instead of 'human face'.

THIS WARLD'S AN UNCO BONNY PLACE
By the Ettrick Shepherd. Transcribed from a manuscript (T2078) held at the Bodleian Library, Oxford. The stanzas are numbered in the manuscript. This poem has previously been published only once, in *Fraser's Magazine* in London, October 1832. I have followed *Fraser's* in supplying the word 'lovely' in the third-last verse.

Various groups of people are caricatured in the first half of this piece, just as Hogg elsewhere makes fun of the English, the Irish, and even the Scots. James Hogg was never a racist (as his 'Pilgrims of the Sun' proves), and it should be noted that the poet is expressing his wish 'that all may happy happy be / Of every climate every race'.

THE CHICKENS IN THE CORN
By the Ettrick Shepherd. Now reprinted for the first time from *Fraser's Magazine*, September 1835.

TO MISS M. A. C——E
By the Ettrick Shepherd. From an undated manuscript letter, to Mr. S. C. Hall, held at the Beinecke Library, Yale University. A different version of these lines was published in James Hogg's epic poem *Queen Hynde*. Miss M. A. C. would be Mary Anne, the daughter of Hogg's publisher James Cochrane, whom he met on his trip to London in 1832.

LOVE CAME TO THE DOOR O' MY HEART has never been reprinted since it first appeared in Peter McLeod's *Original Scottish Melodies* (Edinburgh, c. 1835).

The following is a list of Scots, English, and other words which may be unfamiliar to some readers. For more information, readers should consult *The Scottish National Dictionary*.

abeigh, at a distance
aboon, aboun, above
aince, once
air, early
airel, a pipe made from weeds; a wind instrument
airy, showy; confident; conceited
Albyn, Albion; England
amain, in haste; vehemently
amarynth, an imaginary, eternal flower
an, if
anathema, an accursed thing
ance, once
anent, concerning
aneuch, enough
Anti-burgher, a member of a splinter group from the Secession Church in Scotland
apothegm, a pithy maxim
arles, money paid as an earnest; deserts; punishment
as, how
atour, attour, around; above
auld, old
auricular, told privately
ay, aye, yes; still; always
ayont, beyond; later than

back-water, the back-flow from a mill-lade which hinders the revolution of a mill-wheel; tears
bagnio, a brothel
bairn, a child
baith, both
baldrick, a belt for holding weapons
bannock, a thick flat cake made from oatmeal
barrow, a hill; a grave-mound
bauld, bold; fiery-tempered
beaver, a hat made from beaver skins
beb, to drink immoderately
bedeman, bedesman, an almsman; a recipient of charity; a clergyman
bedight, to adorn
beik, to bask
beldame, a witch; an elderly woman
bele-fire, a funeral-pyre; a large fire
bell, the top (of a hill); a blossom

ben, in; into the parlour
benshee, a spirit whose wail bodes death
bensil, a blow; an exposed area
besprent, scattered
bier, a stand on which a coffin is placed
big, to build
birk, a birch
birl, to spin; to spend
bit, small
bittern, a long-legged marsh bird
bizz, to splutter; to hiss like water on hot metal; to steam; to fuss
blacking, black-making, polishing boots or shoes; boot polish
bland, mild; polite; gentle
blatter, to rattle; to beat
blithsome, jolly; cheerful; happiness
bloustin, bragging
blow, to divulge; to boast
bluart, the blue corn-flower
Blue-stocking, an intellectual woman, usually one given to Radical or Whiggish political theorising
bob, a dance; the best-looking youth
bodle, a small coin
bomb, boom, boomb, to buzz; a noise made by a flying insect
boon, above; high; congenial; jolly
boonmost, highest
bootless, unavailing; ineffective
bosky, drunken; wild
bothy, a small, primitive dwelling made with stones or clay, and used by shepherds in remote areas
boud, had to
boun', to prepare; to do
bouncer, a lively person
bourack, bowrak, a hut; a heap of stones
bourn, goal; limit; a stream
bracken, brake, ferns; a mass of ferns
brae, a hill; a river-bank
brainzel, to break forth violently; to rave
braw, handsome; gaily dressed

bree, the brow; liquor

breechin, the strap passed round the breech of a shaft horse to let it push backwards

breek-knee, knee-breeches

brent, lofty; quite

brock a badger

brog, a shoe

broom, a yellow-flowering shrub found on sandy banks

brose, a dish of oatmeal with hot water or milk

brume-cowe, a broom

bught, a sheep- or cattle-fold

buller, to gurgle; to splash

burgonet, a military helmet

byre, a cowhouse

byson, the wild ox

cairn, a pile of stones; a ruined building; a high hill

Caledonia, Scotland

callan, callant, a stripling; a lad

canny, artful; gentle; agreeable

cantrip, a witch's trick; a spell

canty, pleasant; cheerful; lively

carkin', anxious

carl, carle, a man; an old man; a clown

cash-burdened, backed by ready money

cauldrife, chilly; indifferent

cerement, grave-clothes

chirk, a grating sound

chirl, to chirp; to sing mournfully

claes, clothes

claught, to clutch forcibly

claymore, a two-edged broadsword

cloots, hooves; feet; the devil

clotters, clods

club, to wear one's hair in a tight club-shaped knot, in the eighteenth-century fashion for gentlemen

cobble, coble, a tangle; a confusion; a pond for cattle or sheep to drink from

cobler, a cobbler

cog, cogie, a wooden vessel for drinking

compeer, an equal; a comrade

coost, to cast; to set aside

cope, a vault

corby-craw, a raven; a carrion-crow

coronel, a wreath

correi, a circular hollow on a hillside

corse, a corpse

coupit, tumbled; emptied

couryng, cowering

cow, to cut; to clip

crabbed, crabbit, sour; disagreeable

craig, the neck

crap, crept

crouse, lively; cheerful; keen

cruik-shell, a hook for hanging a pot over a fire

cygnet, a young swan

dadd, to strike, thrash

daffing, sport; idleness; folly

damask, red; linen ornamented with raised woven patterns

dandy, a fashionable, elegant person

dang, to knock; to beat

darn, to hide; to loiter

dean, a wooded valley

deave, to deafen; to bother

decking, ornamentation

dee, to die

deil, devil

den, a ravine

di'el, devil

dike-head, the top of a wall

dirl, to thrill; to tingle

Dominie, a schoolmaster; a teacher

Donald Gun, a nickname for a rifle

dool, grief

douce, gentle, sedate; respectable

douffe, dull; gloomy

dought, could

douk, to duck; to plunge

douse, gentle; sober; to strike

down, laid down; knocked down

downa, cannot; am unwilling to

dowy, mournful; dismal

draff, grain

drauck, to drench

dree, to endure

dreep, to drop slowly

driche, dreary

drouth, a thirst

drumble, mud

dud, a rag; a piece of clothing; a hare

dun, brown; dark

dyke, a wall of stone or turf

ee, e'e, the eye

een, eyes

eident, steady; attentive; steadily

eiry, fearful; uncanny

eithly, easily

eke, also

eld, old age

eldrich, eldritch, unearthly; ghostly; painful

elect, chosen

ell, a wooden measuring-stick, slightly longer than a yard, used by tailors

ely, to disappear

emmet, an ant

eneuch, enew, enough

erlich, uncanny

ern, an eagle

erst, in the first place; formerly

everilk, every single

ewe-bught, a place for milking ewes

exemplum, a brief interlude, often found in satirical poems, in which the author's moral purpose is expressed more directly through his depiction of an exemplary person

eyne, eyes

eynie, to presume; to think fit to

eynied, jealous

eynit, breathed; whispered; eyed

eyrie, a nest

faem, foam

fain, eager; affectionate; willingly

fane, a temple

fank, to entangle; to catch

farren, fashioned

fash, to trouble; to vex

fay, a fairy

fealty, smartly; neatly

feechtin', fighting

fer, far

fere, a dwarf; a friend

ferlies, wonders

ferren, wise

flack the breechin, to strike one's breeches in exasperation

flageolot, a small wind instrument

flauchtis, flies

fleech, to flatter; to fawn

flirds, vain finery

flisky, frolicsome; skittish

flood, a body of water

flounce, an ornamental border sewn onto the hem of a dress

flurr, to scatter; to spray

flyting, an exchange of abuse; a noisy, ranting quarrel; a scolding

footy, obscene; low

fou, full; drunk

frae, from

franeth, from beneath

fur, furrow

furze, an evergreen bush

gaed, went

gaik, to gawk

gairies, whims

game, a trick; pluck; courage

gang, to go

gar, garris, gart, to make; to cause

garret, an attic

gear, goods; clothing

geck, to mock; to gaze

ged, a pike

gelid, icy; ice-cold

gie, to give

gillour, wealth

gin, if

girn, to grin; to complain; a smile

glancin', reflecting; showy; flashy

gledge, to look slyly at

gleid, a spark; a flame

glisk, a flash

glitt, to seep; to ooze

gloaming, the evening twilight

gloffe, fright

gloffis, fears

gor-cock, a moor-cock

goud, gowd, gold

gove, to move awkwardly; to stare

gowan, a daisy; a buttercup

gowl, hollow; anything large and empty; to growl

grace, virtue; good qualities

gramercy, God have mercy

greet, to weep

grew, a greyhound

groat, a four-penny coin; a small sum

gude, guid, good; God

guerdon, reward

gurly, surly, deceitful

gushet, a pocket; a gill

haffets, haffats, haffits, locks of hair hanging from the temples

haggy, rough; broken; wild

hale, whole

haply, perhaps

hark, a secret wish or desire; a whisper

harper, a harpist

heather-lowe, a fire among the heather; red-flowering heather

herke, to urge; to listen

228

herpe, a harp
hight, named
hind, a farm-servant; a skilled farm-worker; a female deer
hindberry, a raspberry
hirplin', limping
hizzie, a housewife; a hussy
hoffats, locks of hair on the temples
holm, an evergreen oak shrub; holly
holt, a wooded hill
hoolet, an owl
houf, a haunt
hough, the leg; the thigh
howe, a hollow
howk, to dig out

ilk, ilka, each; every
inexpressible, trousers; breeches
ingle, a fire; a flame; a hearth
ingle cheek, a fireside
inurn, to place in a burial urn

jad, an old, worn-out horse
Jennies, country maidens
jilflirt, a senseless, giddy girl
Jockies, country fellows
Jock Robson, any lively fellow; Jack Robinson
joint-stock, capital divided into shares; a mutual fund
joup, a skirt
Juggernaut, a Hindu God, annually carried in procession on a rolling platform, under which believers could throw themselves, if they wished

kale, a kind of cabbage
kemb, comb
kend, knew
kerlyng, an old woman
kippling strings, ribbons or strings used to tie the hair
kirk, church
kirn, a celebration at the end of harvest; a kernel; a churn
kirtle, a gown; a dress
kist, a chest; a box
kye, cattle
kythe, to show; to appear
kythless, simple; unshowy; unknown

laibies, flaps
laigh, low
lair, a bed; a resting-place
lambent, softly radiant

lammie, a young lamb
lane, alone; by himself; by herself
lan'd, (?) touched the ground; stood still
laverock, a lark
law, a hill; a conical hill
lay, a poem; a song
lea, a meadow; grassy
leal, loyal
lee, very
leech, a doctor
leet-night, chosen night
leifu', lawful; modest; lonely; sad
leile, honest
leish, a rope; liberty
leman, a lover
leme, a gleam
len, to rest; to sit down
leveret, a young hare
levin, lightning; fire
lift, the sky
limmer, a rascal; a prostitute
limpat, a kind of mollusc found on ocean rocks
link, to walk arm-in-arm; grassland near the sea-shore; the winding of a river
linn, a waterfall; a pool of water at the base of a waterfall
linnet, a common brown song-bird
lintel, a horizontal stone or timber placed over a doorway or window
lint-swingling, separating the flax or hemp from the stalk by beating it
linty, a linnet; a common brown song-bird
lippie, a bumper; a half-gallon
lith, an arm or leg .
lithe, gentle; mild; pleasant; active
littand, causing to blush; staining
littit, coloured; dyed
loan, lone, a common; a paddock
loon, a rascal; a peasant; a lazy, stupid person; a lad
loup, to leap
lowe, a flame; a blaze
lowner, more gently
lucken gowan, a globe-flower; a buttercup
lufe, the palm
lug, the ear
lum, a chimney-top
lykewake, lyke-wake, a watch kept over a corpse prior to burial

maike, a mate; an image; a resemblance

mailin, a purse; a farm; the rent for a farm

maist, most

mang, among

marled, streaked; spotted

marrow, pickled meat; a lover

matin, a morning prayer or song

maun, must

mavis, a thrush

meed, a reward; a portion

meet, suitable

memento mori, a reminder of death

merk, dark

merl, merle, a blackbird

met, may

mickle, great; much; proud

mien, a person's 'air' or bearing

mill-hopper, an inverted cone through which grain is passed prior to milling

minnie, mother; a dam

mirk, dark; obscure; gloom; night

misleered, ill-bred

Monitor, guardian; augur; sign

moon-fern, a moonwort (a kind of plant)

mooted, moulted

muckle, muckil, large; great

mudwort, a mole

muir, a moor

musty, hair powder

naht, nought; nothing

nicher, to neigh; to whinny

noop, a round projection

novator, an innovation; an invention

nurice, to nurse

oleaginious, fatty; greasy; oily

or, before

ordinal, a prayer; a song

ostler, a stableman

ower, over

pang, strong

pannier, a basket

paste, confections, rich foods

pat, put

pawky, shrewd; sly; tricky

pearily, tiny

pech, to pant; to puff; to cough

peel, a pool; anything disagreeable

pen, a hill

peruke, a wig

phrenology, a science, once very popular in Edinburgh, in which a person's abilities and disposition were estimated by measuring the contours of his or her skull

pibroch, a musical theme and series of variations for the bagpipe; music for the Highland bagpipe

pile, a stalk

plack, a small copper coin

plastic, giving form; formative; creative; causing the growth of natural forms

plisky, a prank; a predicament

plover, a long-legged wading bird

poll, to cut off the head; to show the head

poortith, poverty

post, with haste

pow, powe, the head; head of hair

prinklin', a twinkling

proleptical, anticipatory

propine, a gift

pule, to whine

pumps, expensive evening shoes, usually worn for dancing

pyat, a magpie

qu-, used for 'w-' in imitating medieval Scots in 'The Witch of Fife'

quadrille, a kind of square dance

quean, an impudent hussy

quha, who

quhan, quhen, when

quhare, where

quhat, what

quhill, till

quhite, white

quire, choir

raik, to roam; a journey

rail, a fat, dull-coloured wading bird

rake, a man of fashion; an immoral, dissolute man

rampit, romped; stamped in fury; spoke violently

ram-race, a headlong rush

rathly, early; quickly

rave, to roar; to roam

reave, to steal; to deprive; to roam

Red-coats, English soldiers; Hano-verian soldiers

redd, to clear, to rid
reek, to smoke; to smell
rheum, a watery secretion
rill, a small stream
rimy, covered with hoar-frost; foggy; hazy
rood, cross; crucifix
room, a farm; a piece of land
routh, *rowth*, abundance
rug, to pull; to tear

Saducee, an unbeliever
sair, sore; sorely; greatly
saturnine, heavy; gloomy
sauf's, save us
saur, a smell
Sawney, a nickname for a Scottish peasant
scaithe, *scathe*, injury; loss
scart, to scratch
schaw, a grove; a flat piece of ground; a small piece of wood
scho, she
scotched, disabled; wounded
se, so
segs, weeds
sellible, pleasant, happy
sere, to sear; withering; withered
sesquialter, augmented by half
sey, to try
seymar, a scarf; a loose upper garment
shallop, a light open boat
shaw, a grove
sheen, a gleam; a sparkle; splendour
shillfa', a kind of finch
shoon, shoes
sic, *siccan*, such
Silesian, someone from eastern Prussia; a good soldier
siller, silver; pocket-money; money
sinsyne, ago; since then
skaddaw, *skaddow*, a shadow
skaith, injury; loss
skeel, knowledge; experience; medical skill
skelp, to strike
skirl, to scream
skull, a wicker basket
skyre, to scare; to startle; to be shy
sleek, to smoothe, to walk slyly
smiddy, a blacksmith's workshop
smoor, to smother
snell, sharp; fierce
snib, a button
Snip, a nickname for a tailor

snood, a ribbon for tying hair
solan, a gannet; a kind of seabird
soup, to sweep
souse, to fall
spatterdash, cloth or other legging worn to protect stockings from rain or mud
speal, a thin shaving; a game
speel, *speil*, to climb; to sport
speer, *speir*, to ask
spur, to kick; to sprawl
standish, an inkstand; a stand
stapple, a major article of commerce
stark, potent
steaming, travelling by steam; inventing commercial uses for steam-engines; bustling; indulging in fantastic daydreams
steek, a stitch
sternie, a star
stiddy, an anvil
stot, a young bull or ox
stound, an ache; a thrill
stour, dust
strath, a valley containing a river
strathspey, a slow Highland reel
streamer, a comet; the Northern Lights
streekit, stretched
street-raker, a vagabond
sturt, trouble, strife
subscribing, investing
swale, a swelling wave
sward, a sod; a peat
swarth, darkened
swaw, to make waves; to roll
swink, to work hard
syde, wide; long
syndit, rinsed
syne, since; to throw off

tap, the top; the head
tarn, a small mountain lake
Tartarian, infernal; hellish
tawny, dark-complexioned
theek, to thatch
thrapple, the windpipe
thraw, to throw
thraward, stubborn; ill-tempered
til, *till*, to; that; until
timbrel, a tambourine
tine, to lose; to kindle
tinkler, a gipsy; a vagabond
tither, the other
tod, a fox

231

tout, to sing; to trumpet
tove, to fly back
towe, a string; a thread
train, followers; servants
trapan, to trick; to seduce
trimmer, a scold; a virago; anything of high quality
trow, to feel certain
tryste, a promised meeting; an engagement to marry
tup, a ram
tuzzle, to hug roughly

uncanny, awkward; mysterious
unchancy, unlucky; ill-fated
unco, strange; uncanny; uncommonly
unhousseled, out-of-doors; unburied
unmeled, not meddled with

vaunty, merry; proud
viands, food; meat

wad, would; to marry; a pledge; an engagement
wadds, various games of forfeit; the game of 'Scots and English'
wae, woe
waik, a company of musicians; a watch or night-watch; vigilance; a ward or district to watch over
wain, to convey; a waggon
wake, a celebration or lamentation, usually held at night; to keep watch over a corpse before it is buried; to guard the sheep at night
wan, won; went
warren, a piece of ground where rabbits live
wassail, a festive occasion
water, a river or lake, as in 'Ettrick Water', 'Douglas Water', etc.
waur, to defeat; worse
waurst-faurd, least favoured
wawl, to gaze wildly
wean, a young child
weel, to boast
weir, war
wemyng, women
wene, a dwelling; a child; to boast; to think
westlin, western
whalp, whelp

Whig, a Presbyterian adherent of the Scottish National Covenant of 1638; a follower of the political party which supported the Revolution of 1688 and the Reform Bill of 1832
whiles, sometimes
whilk, which
whillilu, any popular song; a melancholy song
whilly-whaup, a curlew; a kind of wading bird
whud, a whisk; a lie; a hasty flight
wight, a person
'wilder, to bewilder; to delight with scenes of wildness
wile, to choose; a choice number
winna, will not
wist, wished, knew
wizzard, grassy; covered with dried grass and weeds
wold, a moor
won, to dwell
wont, to be accustomed
wot, to know
wraith, a ghost; an apparition of a living person
wreath, a snowdrift
wycht, a wight; a person
wysit, guided; enticed

ycleped, called
yeaning, new-born
yerk, a sharp blow
yett, a gate
yirk, to seize; to jerk
yirth, the earth
yorlin, a bunting; a kind of small bird
yout, to roar
yudith, youth

zephir, the west wind; a breeze

232